Unreasonably Yours

CHARLOTTE JEAN

First paperback edition July 2025

Cover design by Tara O'Brien

Edited by Ashley Bosch

ISBN 979-8-9993763-0-5 (paperback)

ISBN 979-8-9993763-1-2 (ebook)

www.charlottejeanauthor.com

 Created with Vellum

For my chosen sister Kelsey, who has—without question—read this book more than me.

Trigger and content warnings are on the next page. If you'd prefer to not see them, skip ahead.

Trigger + Content Warnings

Please be aware, this is not intended to be a comprehensive list, but rather a resource to help you make an informed decision about the content you'd like to consume.

- Sexually explicit scenes
- Mild BDSM/kink
- Military service (off page)
- Combat PTSD
- Suicide of named character
- References to past domestic abuse

CHAPTER 1

Toni

"NICER THAN I THOUGHT IT WOULD BE," BEN SAYS as he pushes my last three boxes of records off the dolly.

"What were you expecting?" I plop down on the still plastic-wrapped sofa.

My new landlords were nice enough to let the delivery folks in this morning. Sure, they only had to come downstairs and unlock the door, but I would've been screwed if they hadn't because my brother and I were still several hours outside of Boston.

He looks around, his eyes scanning over the cast-iron radiators and original pocket doors—all the little details that stuck out to me when Sophie showed me the pictures her cousin sent over.

"It's dated," she warned me, as if the building's hundred year-old charm would be a deal breaker. If anything, the details and imperfections made it appeal to me more. It was everything the millennial gray condo I shared with David for the last three years wasn't—interesting, inviting, inspiring, even.

A few months and a few thousand miles separated from David, and I could now see the similarities between that condo

1

and our relationship, or maybe just the condo and David himself. They were practical, good investments, at least moderately reliable, and neither felt like home.

"Something more... college-y?" He grabs a couple bottles of water from the bag of gas station spoils from our two thousand-mile journey, tossing one at me. "Isn't your friend's cousin in school?"

"I wouldn't say she's a friend." I owed Sophie one for this hookup, but we'd been coworkers—or whatever you called a person you saw a few times a week at a co-working space. "But her cousin's in a PhD program. At MIT. Not exactly the ragers-on-the-weekend crowd."

He nods, making a circuit of the cozy one-bedroom.

I take a long drink, pulling my shirt away from my skin. While June in Massachusetts was blissfully cool compared to Houston's already ninety-plus and humid temperatures, I still broke a sweat lugging in the scattered pieces of my life.

"Sure you'll be ok without AC?"

I shrug. "I'll just get a couple of window units."

"Not the first time, I guess."

None of my childhood homes had something as wonderful as central AC, or if they did, the units gave up the ghost long before I came along.

Ben sighs, sitting on the stack of flat-packed furniture pieces across from me. It was a sigh I'd heard several times over the last couple of days.

"Don't."

"I didn't say anything." He holds his free hand up.

"But you were going to."

Silence lingers for a few fleeting moments before he loses his fight for self-control. "It's just so far, Toni."

"That's the point." If there had been a sublease in Antarctica, I would have taken it. The farther from David, the better.

"And if something goes wrong?"

Why would that matter? Things had gone wrong in other places I'd landed over the years. In Austin there was a break-in, I gained a stalker in Atlanta, and my car flooded in New Orleans. All shitty situations and I hadn't needed him for any of them. I wouldn't have needed him for the Houston disaster had most of my so-called friends not taken David's side.

Only you'd be mad at someone wanting to marry you, Toni. Their admonishments still sting months later.

Even without them, I could have made the move on my own. Sure, it would have taken more money and logistical effort on my end, but had Ben not been able to help, I would have figured it out. I've been figuring things out alone since I was seventeen.

"I'll handle it," I say with a bit more bite than intended. It wasn't his fault. None of it was. He didn't owe his younger half-sister his time or his worry, and I should be grateful he offered up what he did. I force myself to give at least a half-hearted smile to smooth over any rough edges. "It's what I'm good at."

"Right." He nods. For a moment, it feels like he might say more, maybe crack open one of the many pieces of baggage between us. But no, in true Southern fashion, he pivots the conversation to food. "Let's figure out a place to eat and get the truck back. My flight's too early tomorrow to bother with that, and I don't want you to have to mess with it."

Given that we sit surrounded by my literal baggage, I'm honestly grateful. He and I could tackle all that after I deal with my current mess. "Sounds good."

✧

AFTER MORE THAN A MONTH, MY CURRENT MESS HAS, in fact, not been tackled.

In my defense, it wasn't as if anyone was likely to drop in

on me without notice. I could count on one hand the number of people who knew where I was, and of them, only my brother could pick Somerville, Massachusetts out on a map. That was one of the big pros of coming here.

Somerville is giving me six months away from the smoldering wreckage of my personal and romantic life back in Texas. Six months to become a new version of Toni. One who has her shit together. A Toni who moves with purpose, instead of blowing into whatever port would have her, wreaking havoc along the way.

Less hurricane, more . . . something I'd figure out in the next five months.

It was a sound plan. Even if right now, it felt more like it would be six months of me lying on my floor listening to Taylor Swift records on repeat, surrounded by unpacked boxes and unassembled furniture.

Pathetic.

The only way the current image I cut could be sadder was adding red wine and working at 1:00 am.

My phone vibrates against my chest, pulling me out of one spiral to, most likely, fling me into another. Without a doubt, it's a client who's convinced one of their marketing dashboards is malfunctioning when, in reality, they just don't know how to use it. I'd been lucky they'd all stuck with me when I went on sabbatical for a month to move, but the onslaught of emails upon my return had been actual hell.

Reluctantly, I look at the notification.

Not a client, but a new submission to my contact form. I consider ignoring it. But while my client roster was nearly full, packing up one's life and heading across the country was an expensive endeavor, even with my brother's help saving me from having to shell out for movers. Capitalism stops for no man, and especially not for a woman in crisis.

Groaning, I force myself to sit up and open the email on

my phone. Getting up to go to the couch where my laptop awaited was asking far too much of me at this moment.

> *Toni,*
>
> *Since you've blocked me everywhere else, this is the only way I can think of to get through to you.*
>
> *I know you said you need space. I want to give you that, but I just found out that you've moved? To Boston, of all places?*
>
> *I'm going to be honest, disappearing across the country without a word to me or any of our friends feels chaotic, even for you. Again, I want to give you the space you say you need, but this worries me. It just feels ridiculous to leave everything, and for what? Are you just going to be Hurricane Toni forever?*
>
> *I want to fix this, Toni. I want to fix US. I thought that's what this year was about. Taking space to learn and giving us a chance to come back and be better together. But instead, you go 2,000 miles away? Without a word? It just seems so selfish not to consider the impact of your choices given the situation you've put us in.*
>
> *All I'm asking is that you step back, stop being so unreasonable, and consider your choices.*
>
> *Yours always,*
>
> *- David*

My blood roars in my ears, drowning out the music. My hands shake. My chest tightens.

I read the words again. And again. One more time.

Each time, I hope maybe they'll transmute, become, if not softer, at least something that stings less. But no. They stay the same, smarting against all my frayed edges, all the places where friendships, security, and any ideas of a future had once been.

A thrum of razor-edged tension rakes through my body,

pulling me to my feet, driving me to pace. I weave circuitous paths around boxes and piles of art supplies and clothing. The word *unreasonable* is burning a black hole into my mind, threatening to suck me into an even darker headspace than the one I was sitting in just moments ago.

Maybe there was some truth to his words. Perhaps I was unreasonable. Maybe—

The image of him down on one knee at our friend's annual Christmas party barrels into me. His expectant expression, the hush of everyone around us, a solitaire diamond glittering in that classic blue box so many dream of.

It's easy to remember that moment—the calm before the storm. But it's harder to force myself to remember how his expectant expression melted into something just shy of fury as my lack of response dragged on for too long. The way the anticipatory silence switched to shocked murmurs. His mouth formed the words, "Don't embarrass me," even as mine formed, "I can't."

I didn't put us in that situation. He did. From day one, I told him I wasn't interested in marriage or kids. For the next three years, he tried to convince me otherwise, so sure I'd change my mind.

I didn't.

I wouldn't.

And that wasn't unreasonable.

I had to remember that. I was allowed not to want that life.

Just like I was allowed to wonder who the hell had told him where I was.

There was Sophie, of course, but she only knew of David as my partner first and then my ex. I couldn't imagine that she'd give him any information. My brother would sooner put David at the bottom of a swamp than speak to him.

Still pacing around my apartment, I send off a few texts,

hoping no one will respond with, "Why yes! I did tell your ex exactly where you're living now."

I glance at the time, just after three in the afternoon. Most folks were an hour behind and likely working, which meant if they did respond, it wouldn't be for at least an hour when people fell into the late afternoon slump and reached for the double dopamine hit of their phone and caffeine.

The second part of that sounded pretty fucking good.

And it would have been great if there were more than half a scoop at the bottom of my coffee bag.

Excellent.

CHAPTER 2

Toni

In theory, I could put on real people clothes and go to the store, get a five dollar bag of coffee and other groceries I desperately need. Or I could put on real clothes and go get a seven dollar oat milk latte from that coffee shop I've been meaning to visit. Both involve getting dressed. Only one sounds moderately appealing, and it is not the more frugal choice.

Besides, I could get some work done, and given that I haven't left this apartment in a concerning number of days, the coffee shop option forces me to be moderately social. It feels like the universe is saying, "Girl, please go outside."

Who am I to deny the universe?

My choices seem to be affirmed by the pleasant summer day awaiting me. The late July sun is warm against my exposed shoulders, but compared to the heat I was used to, this was nothing. It strikes me that I might actually enjoy the warmer months for the first time in my life.

When I pull on the door to the coffee shop fifteen minutes later, none of the typical fat girl summer gripes—like chub rub —plague me, and I've barely broken a sweat. Perhaps these are consolation prizes from the universe, considering I almost dislocate my shoulder pulling on a locked door with full force.

Behind the counter, a barista, clearly deep into their closing duties—judging by the dim lights inside and the hours on the door indicating in bold font they close at three o'clock—looks up at me.

I grimace and mouth, "Sorry." The last thing I want them to think is that I'm one of those assholes who has no qualms demanding someone reopen just to make them their triple shot iced latte with oat milk. I've worked far too many service jobs in my time to be that person, even if a caffeine headache is already forming behind my eyes.

My quick internet search for alternatives comes up painfully short; most places are already closed or are about to be. I consider telling the universe to soundly go fuck herself. If all she was going to serve me was more bullshit today, I would rather have had mediocre store-bought cold brew delivered and not bothered to put on real pants, er, shorts. Whatever.

The bell behind me jingles. "If you're hurting for it, the bar across the street uses our beans. It's a chill place, too," the barista says, body leaning halfway out the door.

"You're an actual angel." A simple thank you just didn't quite have the gravity I needed to express my gratitude.

They give me a wide smile, pushing a shock of bleach blond hair from their face. "I do what I can. You should come by sometime when we're actually open, though!"

"I definitely will."

With a wave, they disappear into a cloud of espresso fumes.

✧

I MUST HAVE SEEN TWO SONS WHEN BEN AND I walked around looking for a place to eat all those weeks ago.

The weathered green paint and gold lettered sign were hard to miss, but if I did, it didn't leave a lasting impression. Now, it sits across the street like a beacon of caffeinated hope.

While the outside isn't flashy, the wooden booths tucked into the two bay windows look inviting. One is already filled with a group of young men in crimson tees or rugby shirts. Decades of flyers wallpaper the vestibule around empty coat racks, colorful pages announcing everything from cover bands to school fundraisers to pet sitters. I bet if you were to take the time to peel them off, you'd reveal a history of neighborhood happenings worthy of an archive.

Inside, the space is well-worn but lacks the stale beer, sticky floor smell of a questionable dive. Dark wood walls hold pictures of patrons and flyers for bands I don't recognize, but someone thought were worth a frame. In the far corner, a small stage sits ready for a band to take to the mic at any moment. A gaggle of white-haired men and one older butch are gathered at the end of the shining bar top. They all look to be as much a part of the place as the tin tiles on the ceiling.

It's the kind of place I'd enjoy fading into the background of, spending a few hours people-watching and sketching on a weekend night.

"Grab a seat wherever!" A masculine voice calls out from somewhere, thick Boston accent softening the 'er' to an 'ah.'

The barstools look surprisingly fat-friendly: old, wide, and with a back, not the wannabe chic metal ones that bite into your thighs. I take a spot at the end of the bar opposite the older set, keeping the college guys to my back.

While I wait for the bartender, I begin unloading my laptop and notebooks. Just because I wasn't at a coffee shop didn't mean I couldn't knock out at least a few work-related tasks. Future me would be grateful.

My laptop is slowly dragging itself to consciousness when the same voice that greeted me asks, "What can I get ya?"

I look up and my brain short-circuits.

True, I've been in hiding for the last few months. The thought of pursuing anything casual or otherwise with any gender has caused even my rockstar gag reflex to act up. So it is possible that my reaction is partially due to a lack of exposure. Still, no part of me expected the owner of that voice to be one of the best-looking human beings I'd seen outside a thirst trap video in a very long time.

It takes a solid second for me to realize I'm quite literally gawking.

"Hmm," I hedge, testing my vocal cords. "This may be a little weird, but the barista across the street said y'all carry their coffee?"

"We do." He reaches beneath the bar, producing a standard coffee mug. It looks like a damn tea cup in his large, tattooed, be-ringed hand.

Those hands would look good- *Jesus, Toni. Not like you haven't encountered an insufferably attractive human in the wild. Get it together.*

"I'd love a cup."

"Irish or virgin?"

"Virgin, for now," I say, immediately regretting the choice of words.

The corner of his lips quirk, or maybe I just imagine they do. "You got it."

He turns his back, and I almost disintegrate. The black T-shirt does nothing to diminish the width of his shoulders, and those jeans, fitted but not overly tight, are a sin against all things right and decent in this world.

"Cream?" He sets the steaming mug before me.

"Nah, black is fine."

"Try it first."

I cock a brow. Maybe I'd be lucky and he'd out himself as one of those guys who think women can't handle things like black coffee, whiskey, or driving a stick shift. Admittedly, I was not a whiskey drinker and generally preferred the ease of an automatic, but still. "Trust me, I'll be good."

He crosses offensively muscled arms on his chest and nods at the mug. Was he intending to wait for me to taste it? I meet his eyes, spite overriding lust for a blissful moment.

I take a sip and fail to hide my shock.

It was excellent coffee, honestly better drip than I'd had at most coffee shops, but it was so strong it could knock anyone on their ass.

He barely holds back a laugh as I glare at him. "Don't feel bad, you're not the first."

"But let me guess, you drink it straight daily." I don't try to soften the note of snark in my tone.

"Absolutely not. More of a tea guy." Excellent. A flaw. He shakes a small pitcher of cream at me.

"Yes, please." He adds a splash, enough to take the edge off. I take a more cautious sip to find that it's perfect. "Thanks."

"You're welcome."

I give him the appropriate close-lipped smile and turn my eyes to my laptop. I need something to focus on immediately, before my self-control gives way. The last thing I needed to do was something foolish like chatting up the hot bartender walking distance from my front door.

"Password is sláinte," he says.

I look back up at him, trying to parse out what he just said to me and failing. "Sorry?"

"Wi-Fi? The password."

"Yeah, I made that connection, it was the other part." I attempt to echo the word back to him, "Sloan chair?"

Amusement crinkles the corners of his light-colored eyes. Were they green? Hazel? They could have been magenta, it wouldn't matter because I don't need to be staring at them like an idiot.

"Sláinte," he repeats, spelling it out. "Basically, cheers in Irish."

"Noted." I enter it and immediately wish I hadn't. David's email sits at the top of my inbox like a giant 'fuck you' to my state of mind. "Thanks again."

"I assume you're not from here."

All too happy to take any bit of distraction from the reminder of David, I bite. "Does everyone just know the Irish word for cheers?"

"In Boston?"

"Technically, we're in Somerville," I say.

"I'll give it to you that usually is a worthy distinction, just not in this situation." He leans against the back of the bar, pulling a silver pendant from under his shirt and letting it fall against his chest.

"Fine," I concede. "You're right, I'm not from here." I don't offer any more information and pretend to turn my attention back to the screen.

"Not even gonna give me a hint?"

I grin at my screen before sliding my eyes back to him. "I'm pretty sure I already did."

He seems to actually contemplate that for a moment. "I got nothin'."

"The y'all earlier didn't give me away?"

"So somewhere southern?"

"Texas," I clarify. He grimaces. "Ouch."

"Sorry. Just . . . not my scene, ya know?"

I nod. "I know too well."

"You here for school?"

"God, no." I scoff. "You couldn't pay me to go back to school. Well, you probably could. But I just needed a change of scenery."

"Big change."

"Big need."

He looks like he's about to say more when someone else walks in. "Well, welcome. Let me know if you need anything."

A few carnal needs flash through my mind, but I keep them to myself. "I will."

With David's email moved to its own folder to rot, it falls into the shadows of my mind. I spend the next hour being impressively productive. As an added bonus, I only shame-spiral a tiny bit over tasks I could have finished days ago because they took approximately zero time.

The universe couldn't let me get in a whole hour of productivity, though.

A vaguely man-shaped strip of crimson takes up residence in my periphery. At first, I write it off as him trying to get the bartender's attention. Then he's possessed by the spirit of assholery that seems to plague all men whose frontal lobes aren't fully developed. It's the only explanation for him sliding up this close to me at a practically empty bar top.

Some people have keenly developed flight responses; they feel the tingling of a situation and immediately seek ways to remove themselves from it. Me? I'm pretty sure I was born with a malfunctioning flight system.

Fight though?

But I wasn't in my early twenties anymore. I no longer threw the first proverbial punch. Even if I had to grind my teeth to keep from asking this Ivy League fuck if he doused himself in stale beer and Axe daily or if he'd done it just for me.

Maybe if I kept my mouth shut, he'd go away.

I was definitely out of practice being around humanity.

"What're you doing?" His voice is making my fight system go into overdrive.

"Working," I say with every ounce of dismissive energy I can muster.

"Who works at a bar?" Ivy leans in to peek at my screen.

"Do you mind?" I ask, tilting my screen away.

He ignores my tone. "What do you do?"

"Work."

"Oh, come on . . ." Frustration at my dismissal finally begins to color his tone "You gotta give me more than that."

"Do I?" I'm still not bothering to give him so much as a sidelong glance.

"It's only polite when someone shows interest."

Now I turn to him, letting my lips pull back into a smile that's more threat than invitation. "See, I didn't invite your interest. And you're not worth the effort it takes for me to be polite." Satisfaction warms my blood at the surprise reddening his cheeks. "If you'll excuse me, I'm busy."

"Excuse you?" Ivy huffs.

"Oh, I'm sorry. Maybe I wasn't clear enough. Fuck. Off."

With the kind of audacity only afforded to WASP-y white boys, he reaches over and closes my laptop, leaving his hand in place. "Here's a thought. How about you stop being such an ungrateful bitch and—"

The rest of his words stick in his throat as a long, tattooed fingers wrap around his wrist, flinging his hand into his face. "Hey!" Ivy blusters, thrown slightly off balance by the unexpected action.

"The fuck do you think you're doing, man?"

"I was just trying to be nice to—"

"In case you're too stupid to take a hint, she's not interested. When that happens, you fuck off. You don't touch shit that doesn't belong to you like a toddler."

Ivy puffs out his chest and tilts his chin a little too high in what I can only assume is an attempt to look intimidating. All it does, however, is make him look even more like a little boy throwing a tantrum, especially compared to the man behind the bar. "I was doing her a favor by—"

"A favor?" Cold laughter bubbles up almost reflexively. Men like Ivy can stand a lot, but being laughed at? That will almost always cause them to snap. And after the day, month, year I've had, I'm perfectly prepared to trade blows with a petulant twenty-something. "Oh, honey, bless your heart." A touch of my long-faded East Texas accent shows through, not unlike how predators flash a bit of color before attacking. "Tell you what, do us both a favor and scurry on back to your little friends before you make more of a scene."

"Fuck you!" Ivy blurts. He stumbles over his words, feebly reaching for something to sling back at me. After a few attempts, he arrives exactly where I knew he would. "Wasn't like I was actually interested in some fat bitch—"

"Get out," the bartender says without an ounce of emotion.

I'm used to deflecting men like Ivy. Ever since I hit puberty, they've made a habit of hurling their fragile egos at me, assuming, incorrectly, that my fat body will provide a soft landing. When they inevitably find themselves shattered, they always try to salvage the wreckage by attempting to bring me down.

What I am not used to is men intervening on my behalf.

"What?" The word drips with all of Ivy's blue-blooded indignation.

"You heard me."

If that man looked at me the way he was looking at Ivy, I'd be fleeing. Shocking no one, despite the prestigious university blazoned on his sweatshirt, Ivy is not bright enough to realize he's outclassed.

"Bro, come on! You know I was just—"

The bartender lays both palms flat on the polished wood, leaning his broad frame over just enough to make Ivy visibly uncomfortable. "I have no issue physically removing you from my bar. But I promise you it's in your best interest to leave on your own." Ivy gives the man a wary once-over, as if he thought this was a fight he had any chance of winning. "So I'm gonna say this one more time: you and your little friends need to get the fuck out of my bar."

No one in the building breathes.

"One," the bartender growls.

That's all it takes.

In a flurry of grumbles and expletives, the boys filter out while the white-haired group at the other end of the bar claps and whoops.

"Yeah, yeah. How about you all mind your fuckin' business?" he yells over to them, shaking his head. "Sorry about all that," he says, fixing me with a concerned look.

"Not on you." I sigh, sliding my laptop into my bag. "How much for the coffee?" I catch a glimpse of Ivy's half-full beer next to me as the bartender whisks it away. "And the jackass' beer?"

"We don't let jackasses like that have open tabs. There's always a fifty-fifty chance they'll ditch or do some stupid shit." His eyes slide to the window before answering the first half of my question. "Coffee is on the house. And, not to tell you what to do, you seem like a woman who can handle herself, but maybe hang out a few minutes before leaving. To be safe. Or I could—"

"No, I'm good without an escort." I toss a look over my shoulder. "After the day I've had, I actually wouldn't mind breaking his nose."

He chuckles softly. "Ya know, I bet he wouldn't be the first." I give him a noncommittal nod. "But probably not worth catching a charge. People like him, their daddy can do worse that put you in jail and you're too pretty to deal with all that."

I'm beyond grateful that he has the courtesy to turn away, giving me a moment to pick my jaw off the floor.

"Tequila or whiskey?" He asks, back still to me.

The question elicits nothing more than the equivalent of a dial-up tone in my skull. "What?"

He turns back to me, two bottles in his hands. "Tequila," he shakes the clear liquid, "or whiskey?" He sloshes the amber next.

I should say neither. Lie. Claim that I've never touched a drink in my life. Not a drop. Teetotaler. Yes. In fact, this is the first bar I've ever been in, kind sir. Thank you for your chivalry. I will see myself out.

Any of those, no matter how absurd, would be the reasonable choice.

Fuck that.

"Tequila."

"Knew it."

"Well, now I want to change my mind just to wipe that smug look off your face."

"Too late." He pours us each a shot.

"No lime?"

"Trust me, this is so smooth you don't need it." He raises his glass, "To turning a shitty day around."

"And knights in black t-shirts."

He smiles broadly. "Sláinte."

As promised, the tequila requires no accompaniment. It settles warm in my core, sending tingles through my tense muscles.

He sets his glass down and extends one of those beautiful hands to me. "Cillian."

I take it, unable to ignore the way it dwarfs my own or the calluses on his fingers and palms. "Toni."

"Short for?" He holds our shake.

"Antoinette."

"Antoinette," he echoes. Maybe it's the tequila, but I like how my full name sounds on his tongue. "Despite the circumstances, glad to meet you."

"Ey, Cilli!" One of the old men call. "Stop flirting. We're thirsty over 'ere!"

Cillian rolls his eyes, a good-natured smile on his lips. "Fuck off, Andy." He shakes his head. "I better go before they start crying like a bunch of babies." He sends the last word loudly in their direction. In response, they start sniffling.

We both laugh.

"Christ." He tucks a loose, silver-threaded, dark curl behind his ear. "Can I get you anything?"

"More coffee?"

"You got it." Cillian refills my mug and, once more, adds the perfect amount of cream before tending to the others.

I set up my laptop again with the best intentions of knocking a few more things off my to-do list. But the adage about hell and intentions proves all too true.

I blame the tequila.

And the charming man who served it to me.

How was I supposed to focus on something besides his easy manner with the other patrons? How he'd stepped up for me? How incredible his ass looked in those jeans? His friendly greeting to the tall, gorgeous blonde who walked behind the bar?

I can't help but wonder if this is the kind of place that only hires hot people, because . . . damn.

Focus. Toni.

I've barely gotten through the opener of an email when Cillian pauses in front of me. That's all the invitation I need to shift my focus from the screen back to the man.

"Uh . . ." he absently tightens the hair piled on top of his head "Please feel free to tell me to go fuck myself but my evening shift just got in and once my cook is here, I'm free for the rest of the night . . ." He trails off a bit before rushing into his question. "Any chance I could get you dinner? Or drinks. I know it's kinda early," he clears his throat, "for dinner."

My thoughts shift from their usual, but manageable, ADHD-fueled chaotic hum to a full-on cacophony. It isn't the asking that sends my brain off the rails. It's how nervous he seems—bashful in an endearing way that catches me off guard.

Or maybe I'm imagining things.

I need to stall. "I think we already had a drink."

"So . . . dinner?" A crooked smile softens his features.

"Didn't you say your cook is coming in?" I manage to ask while my mind screams: *Yes. No. Maybe. Fuck!*

"As much as I love this place, I'd prefer to go anywhere but here."

A young, lanky guy slides behind the bar and begins gathering glassware. "One second, sorry." Cillian steps aside to speak to him in hushed tones while I silently thank him for buying me a little time to sort myself out.

No is the obvious and correct answer here.

Sure, he could just be a nice guy offering to turn my shitty day around, nothing more. But he did call me pretty, and he did give me both free coffee and tequila, and I would let him rail me on this bar top in front of god and everyone.

So. The answer was simple: *No. Thank you, Cillian, you're so nice to offer, but I'm an absolute hurricane of a person, so it's best if—*

"Verdict?"

"Dinner sounds great."

CHAPTER 3

"Fuck." I drag the word out on a breath as I lean against the office door.

"Oh no." My eyes shoot open, meeting my cousin's already panicked expression from her place seated at the desk. I'd been too distracted by my own stupidity to notice she'd come back here. Had I known, I would have kept my mouth shut.

Ginelle sets her mascara down, letting out a dramatic sigh. "Cillian, if it's already that bad, you're gonna have to accept my resignation because I cannot—"

"No." I wave my hands in the air, trying to clear her concern like smoke. "No, everything is . . . It's fine." I collapse onto the sagging couch, my bad leg begging me for a bit of reprieve.

"Obviously. So fine. You seem completely normal." She retrieves her abandoned mascara.

"Who's the cute redhead you were talkin' to?" My heart stills in my chest. Was I that obvious? "Haven't seen her before." I wasn't obvious, Ginelle is just forever nosy.

Everything is fine. Relief only manages to send my pulse

back to the frenetic pace it was at. "She just moved here. Where's your brother?"

I almost feel bad asking. As the only girl in a family of six, she hated being responsible for any of them, especially the oldest. Knowing it will redirect her from anything Toni-related soothes my guilt. Keeping any and all members of my family away from some innocent woman was the best choice —and I do actually need to know where the fuck Joey is.

If he didn't show though . . . I wonder if Toni is the type to be offended by a perfectly reasonable raincheck request. I mean, 'My cook isn't here so I gotta step in,' doesn't sound like bullshit and it wouldn't be a lie. Then I could actually plan where we were going instead of running off at the mouth.

Dinner. What the fuck is wrong with me?

"As shocking and cliche as this always is, I am in fact not my brother's keeper. I don't know where he is. Did you call?"

"Nah. I just thought I'd wait the hour until you got here to ask purely for the pleasure of pissing you off." She rolls her eyes at me. "Of course I called. And texted. And left a voicemail."

She shrugs. "This is what you get for letting him do what-ever the fuck he wants."

"I don't let him do whatever the fuck he wants."

"Bullshit." She closes her mirror with a harsh snap. "If any of the rest of us showed up an hour late, once, you'd have our asses."

"Can't exactly run a bar without bartenders." I glance at my phone. Still nothing. "The food is a bonus."

"Whatever. You're too fucking easy on him."

I want to argue with her, explain for the hundredth time that I'm not easy on him, I just have a little extra grace. Func-tioning as a person is hard enough, trying to do it with the baggage combat brings? It was too much sometimes. I under-stood that far too well.

"Too easy on who?" Joey asks as he flings open the back door.

"You, who the fuck else?" Ginelle gets to her feet, shoving her makeup back into her bag.

"What crawled up your ass?"

"What craw—You're an hour late and you're not even gonna apologize," she accuses, spinning on him.

Joey raises his hands as if fending off a blow, "I just got in the fuckin' door." He looks over at me, "I am sorry. Traffic."

"Right. And traffic, what? Ate ya phone?" Ginelle crosses her arms over her chest, waiting for his answer.

"If you must know, the screen broke." He pulls an apron off a hook on the wall. "Took it to a repair shop to get fixed. It's part of why I was late."

Ginelle turns away, shaking her head and checking herself in the ancient floor-length mirror. "Always an excuse," she mutters.

"You fucking asked. I answered. How is that—"

"Kids," I say loud enough to fill the room. "Kindly cut it the fuck out." I sigh and lean forward, resting my elbows on my knees. "Joey, just go get the kitchen going, and please don't be late again. Ginelle, Shane's been out there on his own while you two've been bickering so—"

"Something's up with you." Joey cuts me off.

"Nothing's up with me." I counter.

"No, he's right. You came in here all, 'Fu-uh-uh-ck,'" She dramatically reenacts my earlier entry against the door for her brother.

"I wasn't that fuckin' bad," I grumble.

"Pretty close," she perches on the arm of the couch beside me.

"So what's up?" Joey asks. Both of them stare at me expectantly.

"Is it the cute redhead at the bar?" Ginelle asks in a loud whisper.

"I gotta see this." Joey manages to get his big head just outside the door before I can extricate myself from the sand trap of a couch.

I grab him by the collar of his white tee, pulling him back inside and slamming the door shut a little too loudly for my liking.

He laughs as he regains his balance. "Definitely about the redhead."

"Weren't the two of you just fighting? How the fuck are you suddenly on the same side?"

Ginelle slides down the arm to lounge in my vacated spot. "See, when you have more than one sibling, you learn to put your allegiances wherever best suits your needs at the time." Joey nods as if she'd just imparted some sage wisdom.

"Remind me to thank Michael for not being insane," I say. I remain by the door, not trusting either of my cousins.

Ginelle sighs, pulling her phone from her pocket. "Tell us what's up or I'll just text Lucy and she'll tell me."

"Oh, so you two are talking again?" I ask.

"We're always talking," she says dismissively. At least she has the decency to deliver the lie without looking me in the eyes. My cousin's off-and-on-again relationship with one of my best friends was a mess worthy of a B-plot on a prestige lesbian drama.

I pull her phone from her hands. "Hey!" She jumps up to try and grab it. Ginelle may be pushing six feet, but I still have a few inches on her, so I easily keep it out of reach.

"You are not going to ask Lucy shit because Lucy doesn't know shit, and she doesn't need to." I move to hand the phone back, only to pull it away once more. "Neither does Oliver."

"What you're saying is there is something to know," Joey says.

"This is why family businesses fail." Pushing past them both, I walk over to the desk, pull out my keys and wallet, and shove them into my pockets.

My cousins remain close to the door, both practically salivating as they wait for me to give them a morsel of anything.

I rest my hands on the buttery soft wood of the old desk, my shoulders sagging. "Fine." I am absolutely going to regret this. Not right now. But eventually, one or both of them will make sure I regret telling them anything. I just know it. "Yes, it's the cute redhead at the bar."

"I fucking knew it!" Ginelle pumps her fist in the air. "She's so cute and so your type, also I love her—"

"Let the man finish." Joey nudges his little sister's shoulder.

"Sorry."

"Anyway," I straighten and rub a hand down my face, "my mouth may have gotten ahead of my brain, and I asked her if she wanted to grab dinner."

We all stare at one another for a few breaths. "And she said . . ." Joey hedges.

"Yes. Why else would I be like this?"

Ginelle squeals while Joey says, "I'm missing the problem here."

I throw my hands up, letting them fall just a bit to cradle the back of my head. "I don't know. I . . ." I turn my eyes to the ceiling, huffing a loud breath. "I don't know where to go or what she likes or what to say or . . . I just . . . I don't know." I shrug, letting my arms hang limp at my sides.

"Proud of you for taking a swing, man." Joey ties his apron, sated with this little bit of personal drama. "But I'm useless here. Gin, you take over. I gotta get the grill going."

When the door shuts behind him, Ginelle turns a warm smile on me. "This is a good thing."

"Don't do that shit."

"What?"

"That whole condescending, good-for-you thing. I hate it." I didn't need coddling or to be told the most mediocre shit was a great feat.

"I'm not being condescending, you ass. It's just," she leans back against the door, "it's been a while since Kevin, and it's good to see you putting yourself back out there. It's hard after a nasty breakup. For anybody."

Much to my surprise, I didn't react to hearing my ex's name. Which, I suppose, shouldn't be shocking since it has been almost three years, but when someone you considered spending your life with decides you're just not worth the effort anymore, that shit lingers.

"What do I do, then?"

Ginelle grins. "First off, and I know this is going to sound crazy, you can just ask her what she likes."

"Fuck you," I say with a smile.

"Or better yet, ask what she doesn't like. Usually, that's a shorter list. But if you want something close, The Barrel is a good option, just down the block, nice-adjacent without being over the top." She thinks for a second. "Or Masala, you know Mr. Joshi will hook you up."

"Yeah, not sure overloading on potato naan is the right call here." Though it is amazing, and he does give my family a little extra every time.

She shrugs, "So as long as she doesn't hate a good truffle fry—and if she does, she's a monster and you should run—just go to The Barrel."

I nod, releasing a sigh as I force my muscles to relax.

Ginelle walks over and cups my face in her hands. "Don't overthink this. Just have a good time."

"Thanks. Seriously."

"You know I always got your back." She playfully punches me in the chest.

Before she heads out the door, I call, "And do not tell Lucy or Oliver."

"Yeah, yeah." She waves me off without a second glance.

I massage the bridge of my nose, accepting that I'd be fielding a barrage of questions from my best friends tomorrow morning at the very latest.

◇

"YOU KNOW, WHEN YOU SAID THIS PLACE WAS called The Barrel, I had my doubts." Toni looks around at the warm wood paneling and brass accents while I try not to stare. The ambient amber light filling the space makes the woman across from me look more radiant than anyone has a right to. "But it's cute."

"Cute as in, 'Wow, this is the worst, but I don't want to hurt this strange man's feelings,' or—"

"Cute as in it's actually cute," Toni says.

I lean across the table a bit, lowering my voice to a conspiratorial whisper. "If it was the other, this was my cousin's suggestion, so I won't be offended."

"Dinner was your cousin's suggestion, huh?" She takes a shallow sip of her cocktail. "If you happen to be referring to the tall blonde, she could tap in, and I wouldn't be mad."

I place a hand over my heart. "If I were a less evolved man, that might hurt."

"But you're above that sorta thing."

"Exactly." I wonder if she knows how powerful the dimple on her right cheek, that pops up with every little smirk, is. "But I refuse to give Ginelle credit for the whole idea. Dinner? All me. I just didn't quite have the logistics locked down."

"And she generously volunteered to help?"

"Enthusiastically."

"Invested in your social life, is she?"

I snort into my whiskey. "Invested is a nice way to put it." Toni cocks her head questioning. "That side of my family is very Italian, very Catholic, and very nosy. If meddling were an Olympic sport, they'd all be gold."

"You and your cousin just happen to work at the same bar, or . . . ?" Toni asks.

"It's my family's place. For better or worse, it usually means a lot of family running things."

"Do you like it?"

I can't help the wistful smile. "Much to my inner teenager's dismay, I love it." I'd gone to extreme lengths to avoid ending up right where I was now. Funny how things work.

"Our teenage selves didn't have fully developed frontal lobes, it's ok for them to be a little let down sometimes."

While teenage Cillian may be disappointed about our career path, he would not be let down by the woman across from us. "What about you? Would teenage Toni be ok with her choice of career?"

Toni doesn't answer immediately, taking her time to consider. She levels her dark eyes on me. "Do you want the honest answer or the easy one?"

Something about the way she asks sends a thrill through me. Most folks weren't willing to be so forward, especially not with someone they just met. "Honest. Always."

She nods. "Teenage me wouldn't care about the career. She'd just be shocked we made it to thirty-three."

It's the kind of answer that gives the smallest glimpse at her inner workings, a nod to the origins of the grit I'd seen in her earlier.

"On behalf of both our teenage selves, we're all glad you did."

"I'm glad, too," she pauses, "even on days when various body parts decide to randomly malfunction."

I chuckle. "I'd say it gets better, but I try not to lie." My body hurts more days than it doesn't, though that has more to do with spending almost eight years of my life being shot at and blown up for no good reason than my thirty-seven years. Even so, I was still happy to be here, something I couldn't always say. "It is still worth it, though."

"Noted," Toni says, a smile lifting her round cheeks.

"What would the easy answer have been?" I ask.

She swishes her cocktail in her mouth before swallowing. "She'd have no idea what the hell a marketing consultant does, so I think the confusion would outweigh any disappointment."

"Huh." The sound slips out before I can stop it.

"What?"

"I just—" I take in her cropped tank, the collection of metal in her ears, and the large peony tattoos covering her shoulders and sneaking down her arms. "I wouldn't have pegged you for the corporate type."

"And what would you have pegged me for?"

"A creative. Visual art of some kind." It's fast, but I know I don't imagine the flicker of pain in her eyes or the subtle way she seems to fold in on herself. Just as fast as it appeared, that easy self-assurance slips back over her.

"Sorry to disappoint."

I scoff. "I doubt you've ever been within a hundred miles of disappointing."

"Oof. I'm either a master of deception, or you're not great at reading people." She finishes her cocktail. "Bad trait for a bartender."

"Manager, thank you very much." Our appetizers arrive, shifting our focus for a bit.

I pivot us back, enjoying excavating small pieces of this woman far more than the cheese tray we'd ordered. "What would you know about being a good bartender anyway?"

"Had to get through college somehow, and OnlyFans

didn't exist yet." She pops a grape into her mouth, clearly savoring it. "You'd be hard pressed to find a service job I haven't done."

"Stripping not your thing?" I ask and immediately regret it. Toni just huffs a laugh.

"Too niche a market."

"You'd be surprised." Be it the woman or the whiskey, something had completely removed the filter between my brain and my mouth.

"I really wouldn't. Loyal fanbase." Toni settles back into her chair a bit, shoulders squaring, that dimple making another appearance as she pins me with a stare I'd almost call challenging. "Just not always the majority."

I can practically taste the stupidity on my tongue. I want to tell her I'd make sure she'd never spare a thought about the majority again because if she let me between those perfect thighs, I'd—

The entrées arriving save me from myself.

Our dinner chat is much safer. Though I notice her efforts to keep the focus on me, pivoting away from anything that gives her a chance to show too much of herself.

By the time the server is clearing our plates, she knows that my dad is mostly retired, leaving the bar running to me and my older brother, Michael. She knows Michael handles the books for the bar, while I handle the day-to-day, and that three of our cousins work for us. I tell her about Lucy and Oliver, my two best friends who are practically family. That my parents still live in the house I grew up in, and that they are, in fact, still blissfully in love.

As for her? She has an older brother, ten years her senior, but she pushes us away from that with a comment about her drink. I know she grew up in Texas, but as to where exactly, we manage not to get into it. I observe that she loves an espresso martini and leans salty over sweet. Beyond that, she remains a mystery.

The moment she takes a bite of the cheesecake we agreed to share, I ask a question that's been burning in the back of my brain for hours now. "At the bar, you said you needed a big change. Why?"

Toni's eyes widen a bit, and she chews a little longer than necessary. I don't do anything to break the silence. Just let it hang.

Please, give me something real. Let me see you. I beg silently, keeping my foolish mouth busy with the creamy sweetness of the dessert.

She licks her bottom lip. It makes me want to bargain, tell her she doesn't have to answer anything as long as she lets me know what that mouth tastes like.

Before I can give in to my lesser self, she answers. "I had been with someone for a while. We broke up. And . . ." She trails off, but I don't dare interrupt. "And the opportunity to get away from it all presented itself, so I took it."

"Recently?"

She shrugs. "End of last year. I don't know if seven-ish months ago is recent."

"When the hurt is big enough, it is." I know all too well how long it can take to heal from a breakup, especially a bad one. "How'd Somerville, of all places, become your getaway?" I love my hometown, but it tends to get overshadowed by its more prestigious neighbors, Boston and Cambridge.

This earns me a tiny smile, and even that is enough to set my gut fluttering. "A woman I knew from the co-working space I used had a cousin who needed someone to take over her lease. Figured two thousand miles was enough distance between me and my problems."

"And you'd never been here?"

"Never even set foot in New England," she admits.

I don't try to hide my surprise. It's one thing to move to a place you're at least a little familiar with, another entirely to dive headlong into the unknown. "That's bold."

"One way to put it," she says with a sardonic laugh.

"How would you put it?"

"I don't know." Her focus slips to somewhere in the middle distance, her teeth catching her bottom lip. "I've heard variations on reckless. Crazy. Unreasonable." She spits the last word like it leaves a bad taste in her mouth.

"Most brazen decisions are a little of all those things." Her expression softens. "But that's what other people have said. I don't care about them. I want to know how you view it."

Toni opens her mouth only to snap it shut. She lets out a deep sigh. "Necessary."

I nod, lifting my glass. "To necessary changes."

"To brazen ones." She hesitates before touching her glass to mine. "Sláinte?"

I couldn't stop the smile that question summoned if my life depended on it. "Sláinte."

CHAPTER 4

Toni

"WHY'D YOU ASK ME TO DINNER?" THE WORDS FLY from my lips before Cillian can swallow his whiskey.

His visible surprise makes me want to pull the words back, throw cash on the table, thank him for a nice evening, and run. At least if I did that, I'd be in control of ending this situation. Detonating it all before it goes too far.

As if sensing my latent flight response activating, Cillian's fingers slide from where his hand rested on the table to tangle loosely with mine.

"Honestly?" he asks, almost an echo of my earlier question.

"Always." Truth, even if it stung, was better than convoluted lies or half measures.

He looks down to where our hands touch, tightening his grip ever so slightly. When he raises his gaze, I barely breathe. "I asked because you're not the kind of woman who comes around often."

"Are you trying to tell me there's a shortage of abrasive redheads in Boston?" I ask, desperate to downplay the way his answer is making my heart crawl up my throat.

He laughs. "Definitely not." This man has to know his smile feels like staring into the sun, dangerous and far too inviting. "But ones who're charming, beautiful . . ." his calloused fingertips brush the back of my hand, and I pray he doesn't notice the shiver that crawls through me in response, "and fully willing to throw hands with some rich prick? I don't claim to be a smart man, but even I'm not stupid enough to let someone like that slip by."

"Well . . ." It's the only word I can muster through my surprise.

His eyes narrow, reading me far too easily. "You expected a shitty answer."

"No," I say far too quickly for it to be anything but a lie.

"Yes, you did." He pulls his hand back until just our fingertips touch. My stomach drops, and I fight the urge to reach for him. "If you wanted an out, you don't need—"

"I don't." I blurt. "I—" *Am a disaster human and I don't know how to do this anymore and you're gorgeous and kind and I think I'm beginning to understand Icarus way more than I'm comfortable with and*—"I have a tendency to run from anything that has even the whiff of being too good about it."

Honest. Not quite the full chaos in my skull, but still far more honest than I'd intended. I catch my bottom lip in my teeth, physically keeping myself from digging the hole deeper.

Cillian's expression softens. I bite harder. "We have that in common." He reaches across the table, his thumb gently freeing my lip.

It's a small thing. A quick, intimate gesture. It shouldn't matter. Yet I feel undone.

With the immaculate timing gifted to all service industry professionals, our server interrupts the moment. "Anything else for you guys?"

I should be grateful, but I'm not.

Pulling willpower from a reserve I didn't know I had, I

shake my head and manage to extricate my hand completely from Cillian's.

"I'll take the check," Cillian says, eyes pinning me in place. He looks at the server to thank him, giving me a moment to finally pull in a shaky breath.

"I can pa—"

He cuts me off, "I asked you to dinner, so I'm paying. If you ask next time, you're welcome to get the check then."

Next time. There wouldn't be a next time. That fact doesn't stop the flutter in my gut at imagining what a next time could be.

Once outside, my stomach drops. I don't want this to end. It needs to. It has to.

Right?

"Can I give you a ride?" Cillian asks.

The hedonistic devil on my shoulder screams, *God, yes, please. Your face seems like an excellent option.* I'd like to say there's an opposing response, but my better angels gave up on me years ago.

He positions himself at a friendly distance, hands in his pockets. Close enough that I could reach out and touch the broad expanse of his chest, but far enough not to crowd me.

"I don't . . ." *Live far.* That's what I had every intention of saying. Instead, I blurt, "I don't want to go home."

Pretty had rarely made me stupid, and when it did, a man had not been the cause. Yet here I am, experiencing a full loss of every ounce of sense I possess.

What the hell is wrong with me?

But dammit if he doesn't look pleasantly surprised.

"We could get another drink?" he suggests.

"Do you want that?" Another drink doesn't sound bad. More than anything, I just don't want to say goodbye. Not yet.

"No." He shakes his head, huffing a little laugh.

I take a step toward him. "What do you want?"

He sucks in a breath, studying me. Being the focus of his attention sets my nerves on edge with delicious anticipation.

Cillian's fingers slide between mine, his palm warm. "I wanna pull you around the corner and kiss you breathless."

Fuck it.

"So why are we still standing here?" His surprise quickly melts into a wolfish grin, curling his full lips and crinkling the skin at the corners of his eyes in a way that makes me weak.

Judging by the speed at which we round that corner, both of us are committed to outpacing any doubts we may have.

Cillian presses me gently into the brick, his body shielding me from view of the small parking lot. Cupping my jaw tenderly, his thumb traces my bottom lip.

My heart slams against my ribs.

The warmth from his body against mine, the slight whiff of cologne—something peppery and warm with just a touch of floral—rising off him, the weight of his attention. All of him. All of this. It's deliciously overwhelming.

His lips brush mine. A question. An invitation. Giving me space to change my mind.

"Kiss me," I whisper.

That was all he needed. His hand cradles the back of my skull, protecting my head from the wall behind me, and then—

The world falls away.

When his mouth drags down my neck and he presses a muscular thigh between my legs, I gasp, unable to care who might hear. My body takes the invitation to grind against him, all of me screaming for more.

Cillian pulls back, holding my head in place with a gentle grip on my hair as I try to chase his kiss. The heat between my legs thrums. He shifts, his knee providing the perfect place to press my need against. And I do, with more than a little shameless abandon.

"Greedy," he says in a low voice, green eyes burning through dark lashes. I nod, biting my lip to keep from making a noise as he presses his knee up once more. My own knees threaten to buckle, but he moves his hands to my ribs, holding me steady.

I reach for the front of his jeans, stroking the hard length of him through the denim. He presses into my touch, resting his forehead on mine.

"Where?" He asks, voice rough with need.

"Take me home." An alarm sounds in my head because I'd rather die than bring this man into my apartment. "Your home. Or we can—"

"Mine's good." He lowers his mouth to mine again, kissing me until I'm considering how bad it would be to let him fuck me right here. Breaking the kiss, he rests his palms on the wall flanking either side of my head. He drags in a deep breath, "Just need a second."

An admittedly self-satisfied laugh slips from my lips.

"Don't be so smug," he teases. His hand shoots down, cupping my very, very wet pussy. "Pretty sure you've soaked through your shorts, doll." Before he pulls back, I grip his wrist, holding him in place. It feels too good, all of it.

He chuckles. "Impatient, too." His fingers press against the dampness just enough to turn my spine to liquid.

In a flash, he has my wrist pinned against the wall. "But you're gonna have to wait." He kisses my shocked expression gently. "Come on."

I take his offered hand as we walk to where he parked behind Two Sons.

"125 Monument Ln, Charlestown," Cillian says as he opens the passenger door for me.

"What?" I look up at him, brain still stuck in a lusty haze.

"My address. I'm a stranger and I'm taking you home, I assume you're telling someone where you're going, and if not, you should."

Yeah. I should.

"Such a good idea," I say.

"I have my moments."

I pull my phone from my bag, planning to go through the motions to at least make him think I was being remotely responsible with my personal safety and not flinging myself into the sun.

As though the universe is scolding me for my reckless choices, the first notification is from the only person I would even consider texting at a time like this.

BELLE

What?! Fuck no. But you tell me who did and I'll put sugar in their gas tank.

I knew there was no way she'd been the one to tell David where I'd gone, but I wanted to be sure to cover all bases.

Isabelle Terry is the only person I still speak to from my hometown, and my best friend. Even though we went to the same schools for years, we didn't run in the same circles—she was the 4-H type while I leaned more toward black lipstick and drama club—but when we both started working at the diner in town, we immediately clicked.

No matter how our paths led us in different directions, we never lost touch; we always effortlessly picked up right where we left off. At least until her husband was diagnosed with cancer a few years ago. From that point forward, there hadn't been any need to pick up because we never left off.

He'd been gone a little over a year now, and leaving her behind was the single hangup I had when the opportunity to move here arose. Sure, while I was crashing with my brother in New Orleans, I wasn't exactly down the road from Dripping

Springs, Texas, but a few hundred miles was different than a couple thousand.

> I KNEW you didn't, but still . . . And once I find out who did I won't stop you from vandalism.

> Hard pivot: I promise to tell you EVERYTHING later, but tldr: I met a gorgeous man at a bar and I'm going home with him and I know it's stupid but I need a little stupid. And I need someone to know, so if I end up a statistic, I can be avenged.

"All good?" Cillian asks, starting the car.
"Mhm." I nod.

BELLE

> So. Many. Questions. But yes, give me the details, and if you die, my mom will find him.

We're pretty sure Belle's mom was a PI in another life.

BELLE

> And share your location with me.

I give her all the info I know and share my location.

Now this was only slightly stupid.

Cillian's hand rests on my thigh, giving it an appreciative squeeze. His fingers tease, running up, stopping just short of where my thighs meet, the touch causing my breath to quicken and making me shift in the seat.

After ten minutes of torture, I finally break, "You're mean."

At the light, he turns to me, the red wash of taillights making his wicked grin even more intoxicating. "I could be." He grips my chin, pulling me toward him to deliver a chaste kiss. "If you'd like." I swallow hard, trying not to vomit out just how much I'd like that in excruciating detail.

The light changes.

✧

EVEN THOUGH IT FEELS LIKE HOURS, IN REALITY, IT only takes about five more minutes to pull into his driveway.

"Are you some kind of trust fund kid?" I ask, taking in the detached townhome before me.

Admittedly, as someone who has unironically uttered the statement "that's a nice double-wide" more than a few times in my life, my opinions on architecture aren't the most refined. A fact my ex absolutely loved to point out. However, with at least three stories, a charming red brick driveway, ivy growing up the side, and a lovely, well-maintained brick patio surrounded by flowers, the place is inarguably stunning.

"My dad ran a bar and my mom's a school counselor, so. . ." He slips an arm around my waist, settling my back against the car. "No."

I press my hand to his chest, temporarily pausing his kiss. "Ok. Are we about to meet your six roommates then? Because, while I'm sure they're lovely people, if so, I will get us a hotel."

He cocks a brow. "No. Just us."

I look around him to get another peek at the facade. "The only other option is the mob or a rich spouse, because there is no way you live here alone. No offense."

Cillian laughs, that rich sound once more turning my insides molten. "You know, not everyone in Boston is in the mob, right?"

"A wife, then?" I ask, grinning up at him. "I'm down to be a third, I just want to be sure all sides are consenting."

"No sugar mommy or daddy. Just me."

"Look, no millennial without a wealthy family or a nefarious side hustle lives like this on their own."

"It's my uncle's house. He and his husband moved to Florida a couple of years ago, and he didn't want to sell." Finding the answer sufficient, I nod and let him lean in to kiss me.

"Now, do you need to see the deed or?" he asks, taking a step back, leaving me breathing heavily against the car.

"Maybe later," I concede.

I was kidding, but when we walk into the kitchen, I realize I may actually want to know everything about this house. Old wooden beams run along the ceiling while a brick fireplace and oven take up an entire wall. All original. All dreamy.

We don't pause at the first-floor living room, but I take note of the deep sectional, tastefully scattered with blankets and pillows, and the uncluttered coffee table. In fact, as he leads me up to the fourth-floor primary suite, it's clear everything is uncluttered. Lived in, yes. But overall, incredibly clean.

Shame sends a twinge through my gut. My own apartment was a rat's nest in comparison.

Thankfully, the bedroom manages to distract me. Not because it reveals all the mess the rest of the house lacks, but because one wall of the attic room has been replaced with a massive floor-to-ceiling window.

"Oh," I breathe. Little lights twinkle down the hill from the house, and to the left, a sliver of Boston proper glows against the night sky.

"Best part of the house," Cillian says. He wraps his arms around my middle, pulling my back to his chest. I shiver with pleasure as his lips graze my ear and move down my neck.

He releases me to settle on the well-worn loveseat facing the window. "Come here," he says, extending a hand to guide me onto his lap. I straddle him, happy to find the furniture doesn't let out even the barest hint of protest.

Between the room's warm light and the glow of the city behind me, I'm able to study him more closely than before.

Too pretty.

My palms itch to pull the sketch pad from my bag. Beg him to play Rose to my Jack. Instead, I try to memorize his features: green eyes framed by dark lashes, thick brows, full mouth, freckles scattered across strong cheekbones, and a short, well-groomed beard. Even the few things that could be accused of being flaws—like his nose, strong and broad but clearly broken at least once, or the flashes of white through his dark beard and hair—only make him more appealing.

I pull the elastic from his hair, running my fingers through the shoulder-length waves. He practically purrs with satisfaction as my nails graze his scalp. When his eyes slide shut, I pull him into a kiss.

Rough hands travel up my bare thighs to the exposed skin at my midriff. He tosses my top aside, leaving my breasts exposed.

Silently, I thank past me for embracing one of the few perks of being a card-carrying member of the 'Small Tits Fat Ass Club' and skipping the bra today.

Cillian looks just as grateful, smiling as he trails his mouth down my neck to my chest.

My head falls back, and my hips grind against him as he teases each of my nipples with his tongue.

He takes his time, his mouth and hands mapping my upper body until I'm practically whimpering with want. "Bed?"

I just nod. *Finally.*

Before I can move, he places my arms around his neck, takes hold of my ass, and stands.

I shriek, clinging onto him like my life depends on it.

A laugh vibrates through his chest. "I've got you, doll," he says against my hair.

"I hope so," I squeak.

He sets me down on the edge of his bed, the duvet cool and soft beneath my hands. He lifts my chin to look at him. "You ok?"

"Yeah," I say with a nervous laugh. "I. . . that has never happened to me."

"Glad to be your first." He winks. I roll my eyes and playfully push his head away.

His laugh distracts me from his hands. They grab my hips, pulling me to the very edge of the mattress, and I suddenly fall to my elbows. He unbuttons my shorts, tugging them off along with my underwear in a fluid motion.

Cillian takes me in and I let him, savoring his slow appreciative gaze. "Gorgeous," he says.

He goes to his knees, slipping my sneakers off, kissing my ankles, my calves, my knees, all the while keeping his eyes on mine.

With every inch closer to my center, my anticipation ratchets up.

His lips trail the inside of my thighs, the delicious scratch of his beard sending gooseflesh across my body. He nips the lower edge of my belly. "Let me taste you," he says, breath hot against my skin.

I nod. My *yes* hardly audible, even to my own ears.

Cillian wraps an arm around one thigh, fingers teasing before opening me to him. His tongue dips down, moving up slowly to circle my clit, but not quite making contact.

I whimper, need threatening to burn me alive.

His laugh puffs against me, and my hips buck. His free hand presses me down with swift, solid force. "Patience," he chides.

"Not a virtue of mine," I manage. "Please," I sigh. If he asked, I'd happily beg at this stage and probably enjoy it.

The tip of his tongue flits across my clit and my breath catches.

As a less-than-chaste fat girl, I've had my share of disappointing head. Not for lack of trying by my partners, but sometimes they simply don't know how to properly please a body like mine from jump.

This man was not going on that list.

He draws me close to the edge, pulling me back, building and building my pleasure. The moment this divine torture becomes too much, he slides a finger inside me, then another, stretching me slowly, fingers finding my G-spot with ease.

"Cillian," I rasp. A tremor thrums through me, my whole body beginning to feel staticky and weightless. "Cillian," more a cry now. "I-I'm—"

Stars explode across my vision.

He lifts his head, slowly pulling his fingers from me. Moisture glistens on his dark beard, and a satisfied smile rests on his face.

Shaky but determined, I sit up, grabbing his t-shirt and dragging him to me. I want to taste myself on his beautiful mouth, want to burn this moment into my memory.

When we finally pause to breathe, I slide my hands beneath his shirt. Beneath the ink on his left side, the skin is bumpy with a latticework of scar tissue. I don't linger, moving my hands to feel the muscles of his back. I lightly drag my nails down his spine. He shivers.

"It seems unfair that I'm the only one without my clothes on," I say into the shell of his ear, playfully tugging on the piercing in his lobe with my teeth.

He grabs my chin, kissing me fiercely. "Guess I should fix that."

Clothed, Cillian was enough to make me more than a little stupid—as my present state made painfully clear—but naked?

I try to tell myself not to openly stare. Surprising no one, I fail, drinking him in.

He's built like a power lifter or rugby player—not sculpted but solid. Every inch of him, from his broad chest to those thighs, screams strength. No wonder the man had carried me to the bed without fuss.

The silver pendant I noticed earlier sparkles against the dark hair curling on his chest and trailing down his abdomen. My gaze follows that path to his cock, hanging hard and so thick I almost moan at the thought of how damn good he'll feel.

I want to trace the tattoos across his chest and down his legs with my tongue. I want to tell him he's beautiful. Instead, I just watch as he reaches into his nightstand, rips the condom open with his teeth, and rolls it down the length of his cock.

Cillian kisses me, slow and deep, as he pushes me onto the mattress.

I scoot back as he does, taking advantage of the swath of soft space offered by the king-size bed.

His cock twitches against my pussy.

My body rises to meet him. I had been patient enough.

He teases before sliding halfway into me. I gasp, the ache excruciating and wonderful.

"Want all of me, doll?" His nose brushes against mine.

"Yes," the word comes out like a plea. Cillian pulls my thigh up onto his hip and slams into me.

I cry out in pleasure, back arching, opening myself to him as much as possible.

So good. So—I come around him, hands fisted in the duvet, body shaking.

He doesn't stop. "That's it, Toni," his voice is low. "Gonna give me another, doll? Go on." His lips hover above mine, green eyes burning. "Show me how good this cock feels."

"Fuck!" I cry. Cillian swallows the rest of my sounds with his kiss.

The muscles of his back tense. "Toni," he breathes, brows knitting. "Oh god." He tucks his face into my neck, his own orgasm pulsing through him.

He lifts his head, pressing a kiss to my forehead. "You ok?"

I huff a laugh. "I'm great." No lie in sight. Every muscle in my body is warm and relaxed, my head comfortably hazy.

He nods and gets up to dispose of the condom. When he returns to the bed, he pulls me to his chest, covering us both with a light blanket. I don't resist, settling comfortably against his right side.

My fingers trace the wing of a large black bird, its body covering much of his left shoulder, carefully avoiding a puckered circular scar above his heart. Cillian absently strokes my temple, the motion matching our steady breathing, and begins to lull me too close to sleep.

I force myself to sit up. God, the sleepy, satisfied look on his face makes me want to kiss him. "Bathroom?" I ask.

"Through that door." He gestures to the left of the large window. "You're welcome to anything in there," he says as I make my way across the room.

I dry my hands on a neatly folded hand towel.

Everything is so perfect. The bathroom accoutrements on the shelf behind me, the spotless etched glass of the large standing shower, and the mirror over the sink. Even the towels are crisp and white, complementing the very 1980s shade of teal tiles covering most of the room.

Ordered. Settled. *Not for you.* I tell the woman in the mirror, her cheeks still rosy with pleasure. *Don't bring your chaos here.*

It shouldn't make me ache. It should be easy to accept that this has to be one and done.

But good things are hard to let go of, and while I don't know this man, something about Cillian seems . . . good.

I shake my head, square my shoulders. That goodness is even more of a reason to exit his life expeditiously.

When I step out of the bathroom, I find Cillian leaning against the foot of the bed. A dark robe in a floral pattern covers his shoulders, hanging open, stopping at his mid-thigh. Something about the juxtaposition of his masculine frame and the feminine pattern makes my heart trill.

He looks up, gives me an easy smile, and offers a bottle of water.

"Nice robe," I say, accepting the drink.

"Thanks. I have one for you if you'd like." He gestures to a robe, cream with a peacock pattern, laid on the bed next to my own clothes. "But I have a feeling you won't be staying." I meet his eyes, my chest constricting. "You're welcome to."

"No." I shake my head, summoning all the determination I possess. "This was—You're—" I gesture to him, "wonderful. I just—I don't—"

"It's ok." He lightly presses a finger to my lips. "You don't have to explain." I swallow hard and nod, reaching for my shorts.

"Would you like a ride home?"

"I can call a car." It wasn't even past midnight, so there should still be plenty of drivers out. "Thank you, though . . . for everything."

"Nothing to thank me for." Running fingers through his mane, he huffs something like a laugh. "If anything, it should be me who's thankful." He pushes off the bed and grabs my bag from where I'd abandoned it earlier. "It's, uh, been a minute."

I raise a brow at that. "If that's you out of practice, I doubt I could handle you in peak form." I pull my phone out, my fingers protesting my attempts to open the ride app. Still, I manage to make the appropriate selections.

The sound of his laugh made me want to cancel it, crawl into that bed, and fall asleep surrounded by this man. It was also a reminder that I needed to get the hell out of this gorgeous house and back to my cave before I made any more unreasonably selfish choices today.

His broad palm rests on my waist. "I have no doubt you'd handle me just fine."

Move back, Toni. Step away. Don't— I step into the warmth of his touch, letting his arms circle my torso and pull me closer. "I guess we'll never know."

I imagine there's disappointment behind his half smile.

"Never is a long time."

"Trust me." I trace the silver pendant, noticing the name St. Cecilia etched around the figure of a woman. "You don't want to be stuck too close to a hurricane for too long. They tend to make a mess of things."

His protest shows on his face before it reaches his lips, but my phone vibrates, announcing my driver's imminent arrival.

"I'll walk you down," he says, tying his robe.

Rather than lead me to the kitchen, Cillian takes me to the front door. The small foyer, much like the other snippets I'd seen of the home, was tidy and curated, with a shoe rack, an entry table, and a few pieces of art I fight myself not to study.

At the door, he turns to me with a sigh. I don't pull away when he reaches to cup my cheek, instead letting myself lean into his touch, aching for just a little more of him.

He kisses me. Slowly. Intentionally. Both of us memorizing what the other feels like, tastes like, something to reflect on when we're alone in the dark.

My phone vibrates in my pocket. This fantasy is over.

Breaking the kiss, he presses his lips to my forehead, drawing in a deep breath. "I'm glad I got to meet you, Toni."

"Me, too." My voice sounds too small.

"If you need anything, you know where to find me."

I nod. "Goodnight, Cillian." Goodbye feels too final.

"Goodnight."

CHAPTER 5
Cillian

"Hold the fuck on," Lucy cuts me off. "A beautiful woman," she holds up one well-manicured hand, ticking each point off one by one, "walks into your bar. She's entirely your type."

"I don't have a type," I protest.

"Yes, you do," Lucy and Oliver say in such perfect unison it's almost creepy.

"Don't interrupt me, it's rude." Lucy continues, "You take her to dinner. You take her home." The last word she says loudly enough to make me wince. "Supposedly, have a great time."

"That feels like an attack," I grumble into my whiskey.

"And," she says, ignoring me, "you don't get her number, her socials, anything?"

"Correct." I keep my tone as neutral as possible. If I can bore Lucy, her notoriously short attention span will save me.

She stares at me slack jawed. "This might be the most insane thing you've ever done."

"Most feels hyperbolic," Oliver says.

"No. It's not. And I'm including the fucking Marines."

She shakes her head, popping a fry in her mouth. "That's how insane this is to me."

"I'm gonna kill Gin." I toss the rest of my drink back.

Oliver laughs. "In her defense, you're the one who told us you took . . . what's her—"

"Toni," Lucy fills in the blank.

"Toni, home."

"And if Ginelle kept her mouth shut, like I asked her to, I wouldn't have had to tell either of you anything."

"You don't tell anyone anything, Cilli." Lucy grins. "That's why I have to coax information from your cousin." She waggles her fingers suggestively.

I grimace. "Please, I've got enough fucked up images in my head. I don't need to add that to it."

Oliver gestures to me with a fry. "Ok, but if you had a good time—"

"Are you really on her side here?" I cut him off.

"I'm on her side when she's right."

"And I am usually right." We both give her the look that statement deserves. "What?"

"Dani?" I ask.

Oliver points in agreement. "Meredith?"

"Stevie?" I add.

"New York?" Oliver and I say at the same time.

"Bringing up New York is transphobic." She huffs dramatically, crossing her arms over her chest. Oliver and I laugh at her faux offense.

"Answer the question," Oliver says once we've caught our breath.

"Like I said before Lucy started this inquisition, she didn't want anything beyond one night, so it didn't make much sense to trade information."

"And what about what you want?" Lucy asks, her tone suddenly serious.

I shrug. "What about it?"

"I'm assuming you communicated your preference to her?"

"Nothing to communicate."

Lucy's eyes narrow. "Bullshit."

"What is it I want, Lu? Tell me, since you seem to know so well."

"I don't know. But I do know it's usually good form to at least try to figure it out for yourself and communicate with the other person."

"No offense, but should you be handing out relationship advice you clearly aren't capable of taking yourself?" I see the jab land and almost regret it.

"Oh, fuck you," she snaps.

"Spicy," I mock.

"At least I'm out here trying to take my own advice and not stewing in my own misery alone all the damn time."

"Stewing—"

"Ok," Oliver interjects, "no fighting before a show."

I often wonder if Oliver listed refereeing our spats on his resume when he decided to become a teacher. I'd die for Lucy, and she'd do the same for me, but we've had some earth-shattering fights in our time.

"Sorry," I sigh, meaning it.

"Me, too." She reaches across the table, taking my hand.

"It's not like you were wrong." I let my head thud against the booth cushion behind me.

"I wouldn't say you stew. Maybe marinate a bit here and there," Oliver says. I give him a look.

"We'll table our discussion of your love life." Lucy squeezes my hand before letting it go. "For now."

Our collective focus pivots to the set list for the night. Not that it was going to change much. I hadn't been able to make many rehearsals—or much of anything else—recently, ironically too tied up with running the bar to focus on entertainment for the bar.

"In all seriousness," Oliver levels one of his signature concerned looks at me. "You good? You've been sparse lately, even by your own standards."

The usual apology was always perched on my tongue, ready and waiting. Sorry for not being around, sorry for making them worry, sorry there were reasons they had to worry in the first place. It sat right next to the reassurances that I was ok, just a bit overworked, a little tired, that I'd do better.

A mass of red hair by the entry to the restaurant catches my eye and steals my ability to process any thoughts outside of her name:

Toni.

Toni with her curls piled on top of her head and her curves looking far too good in a leopard print satin slip dress and a leather harness.

Toni.

Walking toward us.

I immediately sink into the booth, cursing—not for the first time—my conspicuously large frame.

"Cilli—" Oliver begins.

"Shh!" I cut him off, shielding my face with my hand.

"Hey, Cillian . . ." Lucy trails off, the worry in her voice slapping some reason back into my skull.

Unfortunately, my best friends weren't strangers to me hiding from some invisible threat. In those instances I was usually reacting to ghosts of my own shit decisions, not a stunning redhead.

Shame burns hot in my veins. Unwelcome as it is, I latch onto it, let it remind me of the core reason I have no business getting any closer to Toni—or anyone, for that matter.

You're too much, Cillian. This is all too much. Kevin's voice echoes in my head.

I did not need this, any of this, right now.

"Sorry," I say on an exhale. "I'm good. Just . . ." I gesture to Toni, making her way to the restaurant's bar.

"No fucking way!" Lucy says too loudly.

"Could you chill?" I beg. I try to sink deeper into the booth, wishing it would open up and swallow me into another timeline where this isn't happening to me.

"Chill?" Lucy turns a shocked expression on me. "Kismet is happening right before my eyes, and you're telling me to chill?"

"Looks like she's waiting on someone," Oliver observes, leaning his chair back on two legs.

"See, not kismet. We just picked a stupid, trendy place to have dinner."

Lucy returns her focus to Toni in the most conspicuous manner possible. "Waiting for someone who clearly isn't here."

"Lucy!" I hiss.

She waves me off. "Relax. Her back is to us."

Emboldened by that, I peek my head above the booth just enough to catch a glimpse. From my angle, I can see the barest hint of her profile, her phone next to her on the bar, and her focus on a little sketchbook.

A touch of satisfaction loosens my shoulders. I knew I wasn't wrong when I clocked her for an artistic type.

"I adore that dress," Lucy says. My attention quickly snaps back to the problem at hand.

"Ok, enough." I reach across the table and grab Lucy's chin to physically remove her focus from Toni.

She shoos me off.

Oliver looks at his phone. "She's either early or whoever she's meeting is late."

"How could you possibly know that?" I ask.

"It's just after eight. So if they were meeting at eight thirty, she's wicked early, and if not-" he shrugs.

"It doesn't matter, can we go?"

"No!" Lucy turns her attention back to me. "I don't want to just hang out at the bar because you or all of us will inevitably be sucked into working and we are supposed to be having a fun night."

I groan.

"Drama queen," Oliver scolds.

"I think I'll go say hi," Lucy announces.

I latch onto her wrist, moving so fast the force of it shakes the table. "I will give you a hundred dollars right now if you don't." I was pretty sure I had that in my wallet anyway.

"I'm offended you assume I can be bought."

"And all my tips from tonight."

"I bet you could get him up to three hundred plus tips," Oliver says, smugly popping a piece of chicken in his mouth.

"Lucy, please," I beg.

She pats my cheek. "Those puppy eyes don't work on me. Besides, this has nothing to do with you." She plucks my hand from her wrist. "She's new in town and has clearly been stood up. I'm going to be a good neighbor and find out where she got that dress."

With a wink, she saunters off to ruin my night.

"I'm leaving," I announce the moment Lucy taps Toni on the shoulder.

"You are not." Oliver stands, blocking my path to freedom.

"Just meet me at the bar." I try to push past him, but he lays a hand on my chest, pushing me back. "Oli—"

Plenty of folks would look at the two of us and place their bets on me in a fight. I'm a couple inches taller and, thanks more to genetics than true effort on my part, built like a brick shithouse. But they'd be wrong. Oliver Rosado is all lean muscle and intention. Cards down, I'd pick him over me easy, especially when he's got that look on his face.

"Sit. Down," he says, the teacher voice almost working on me.

"I can't do this." I sound desperate. I know I do. I can't be bothered to care as senseless panic claws at my chest.

His expression softens. "You don't have to do anything. Just be open to the possibility that something good could happen here. That's all."

"I am open. It's just—"

"You're not."

Frustration makes tension hum through my muscles. Maybe I'm not as open as he and everyone else seem to think I should be. But what kind of person leaves the doors to a haunted house wide open for any unsuspecting beautiful stranger to wander in?

He sighs. "I'm not saying ride off into the sunset with the woman. I'm just asking you to not run from something just because it might—" he holds up a hand to silence me, "might, have a whiff of potential."

"Who says this has potential?"

"If it doesn't, why do you look like a fuckin' deer in headlights?"

I open my mouth to protest, but no words make it past the lump in my throat.

"Stay. And if nothing good comes of it, I'll let you get a few solid hits on me in the ring."

Before I can say anything, Lucy returns with a plus one.

"You already know Cillian," Lucy gestures to me.

Toni meets my eyes, and all the air leaves the room. "Small world," she says in greeting.

Stunning. Simply stunning. The low neck of her dress exposes her chest, the shadow of her collar bones, the curve of her shoulders, the peonies tumbling down her arms. My mind is flooded with memories of how her skin feels under my fingers and how much I want to see that deep crimson lipstick smeared across her face.

"Yeah." My tongue feels too big for my mouth.

"Going somewhere?" Lucy asks the two of us.

"No," I shake my head both for emphasis and in a useless attempt to clear my thoughts. "Just getting more drinks."

"We already did that," Lucy says.

"I'm Oliver." He holds out a hand to Toni.

She takes it, smiling warmly. "Toni."

Oliver returns to his seat, but I seem unable to move.

"You wanna sit so Toni can join us, or are you just gonna stand there?" Lucy asks.

I glare at her even though I'm grateful the question makes my body take action. Sliding back into the booth, I press myself as far into the corner as possible to avoid crowding Toni.

"I am so sorry," I whisper to her when she sits.

"Don't be." Her perfume teases my nose, I want to lean closer, pick out the notes, ask her what she likes about the scent. "Unless this is weird and—"

"No!" I say a bit too fast, so grateful for the server distracting the others with our drink order. "Not at all. I just don't want you to think I sent my friend over to harass you."

"I made it clear this was a Lucy decision and not a Cillian one," Lucy interjects.

"It's rude to listen to other people's conversations," I say.

"First off, you're less than three feet from me. Secondly, she's my new friend." Lucy passes Toni her cocktail. "Your gin and tonic, love. And Cillian, the usual."

"Maybe I wanted something else," I say, accepting the whiskey.

"You didn't," Lucy says dismissively, passing Oliver his

scotch. "Despite making a mean drink, the man almost always gets Jameson. Neat. So reliably Irish."

"I'm telling Dad you're besmirching our people."

Lucy laughs. "Not your people, just you." She winks. "Besides, Mickey could never be mad at me."

"You know she's right," Oliver says.

I couldn't argue. My parents had always viewed my best friends as bonus kids, but when Lucy came out to them as trans, they tripped over themselves with delight at finally having a daughter. I wouldn't have it any other way. The only issue was that now they were likely to side with Lucy on most things.

Lucy presses a hand to her chest, beaming. "That's the second time you've said those words tonight, Oliver."

"What was the first?" Toni asks.

"Some nonsense," I say quickly. "What're we toasting?"

Lucy smiles at Toni. "To new friends."

"I'll drink to that." Toni meets Lucy's warmth without an ounce of hesitation.

"Sláinte!" Oliver raises his glass.

"Have y'all known each other a while?" Toni asks, casting a glance around the table.

"Only thirty years," Lucy answers.

"Thirty-one," Oliver corrects. "You two met in kindergarten, and I came in first, remember?"

"Aww, that's right." Lucy leans her head on Oliver's shoulder. "Then I had two idiots to protect."

"I take offense to that," Oliver says, pushing her off him.

"And if you're wondering what a glorious thing like me is doing protecting the likes of these two." Lucy leans conspiratorially toward Toni. "Just know it was far funnier when everyone thought I was just a scrawny twink and not a raging dyke."

Toni is not a person who laughs in half measures. It's rich

and boisterous. The kind of laugh that sends its ripples through the people around her, leaving traces of her joy in its wake. I have the ridiculous thought that if it were the last thing I ever heard, I'd go out happy.

"I feel like you're implying we're cowards," I say.

"Not cowards. Just gentle giants," Lucy clarifies.

"I wouldn't say I'm a giant," Oliver protests.

Lucy playfully squeezes his bicep, "Close enough."

"If they're gentle giants, what does that make you?" Toni asks Lucy.

"She's more of a feral cat," I say.

"Rude," Lucy says.

"But very true," Oliver agrees.

"You see the abuses I endure."

"It's ok-" Toni extends a hand to Lucy- "I happen to adore cats."

Lucy smirks. "How much do you like cats?" The implication is not subtle.

"Lucy," I chide.

"What? I'm just asking how much the lady likes cats."

Toni laughs. "I like cats, dogs, the occasional rabbit. I'm an equal opportunity . . . animal lover." Toni grimaces. "This metaphor has too many uncomfortable implications."

"No wonder you and Cillian hit it off. Like calls to like and all that." She turns to Oliver. "Still the only heterosexual. Sorry, buddy."

"Whatever shall I do?" Oliver sighs. He looks at Toni, "Cillian told us about that prick at the bar when you guys met, on behalf of my fellow heterosexuals, I do apologize."

Toni shrugs, "At least it's a good story."

"Oh, that's nothing," Lucy interjects. "You should hear the really colorful bar tales."

"Remember the incident with the guy who got his cock stuck in—"

"Let's not." I cut Oliver off with a laugh.

"Oh no." Toni turns to me, incredulous. "Beginning a story with 'cock stuck in' and not finishing is cruel and unusual." Her big brown eyes are expectant.

I sigh. "Some drunk moron during St. Patrick's Day went into the bathroom and tried, inexplicably, to put his dick in a beer bottle."

"Tried, but I'm assuming did not actually succeed?" I raise my brows. "No," she shakes her head.

"Yup." I nod, taking a sip of whiskey. "Managed to get enough in that it got stuck."

"Oh my god," Toni says with a horrified laugh. "And how did this come to your attention?"

"Someone complained about a man sobbing in the stall."

"I'd sob," Oliver says.

"You wouldn't stick your dick in a bottle," Lucy says.

"Fair."

"So I go in and sure enough this man is on the floor, pants down—"

"Cock partially in a bottle," Toni finishes.

"Cock in a bottle," I confirm. "Found his friends, and they insisted we not call the EMS, I assume to save his dignity."

"True friendship," Toni says.

I nod. "They tied a jacket around his waist and disappeared into the night."

"It haunts me that we'll never know what happened to ol' bottle cock," Oliver sighs.

"Any other harrowing tales?" Toni asks.

Lucy immediately launches into another story from the Two Sons' archives.

"Now every June we host a charity walk-off."

"Just a bunch of old men in heels, it's amazing," Oliver adds.

"And did that guy's knee ever heal?" Toni asks, choking back a laugh.

"No clue," I say. "My dad told him he'd break the other if he ever caught him in his bar again."

"And while Mickey is the nicest man alive, do not fuck with him," Lucy says. "Oh shit!" She looks at her phone. "We gotta go."

I glance at my watch. We should have headed over to the bar five minutes ago.

"Well, thank you for the drink and the quality entertainment," Toni says, scooting out.

"Uh, you're coming," Lucy says as if it's the most obvious thing.

"I am?"

"Of course you are." Oliver steps aside, allowing Lucy to hook her arm through Toni's.

Toni looks back at me, face colored with surprise and not a small amount of delight. I chuckle awkwardly and mouth, "Sorry," as Lucy whisks her out the door.

CHAPTER 6

Toni

"WHAT'RE YOUR OPINIONS ON DRUMMERS?" LUCY asks once we're outside.

"I don't know if I have one." Laughter colors my words, and my cheeks are genuinely starting to ache from smiling.

When my date didn't respond to my earlier text, I had to admit I was relieved. I'd rather spend the evening people watching and sketching while sipping on a gin cocktail than field the real-life version of his attempts at conversation. In no way did I expect I'd happily find myself on the arm of Cillian's best friend, letting her take me to a show.

"You will after tonight," Lucy declares.

"Whether or not that will be a good thing . . ." Oliver says, walking backward to better show off his cringe face.

Lucy slows our pace. "Cillian, will you take over escorting our guest? I need to shove a drumstick up Oliver's ass." Laughter pings off the walls of the buildings flanking the side street we'd turned down as Lucy brandishes a drumstick like a switchblade, slashing at Oliver.

"I am so sorry about them," Cillian says. Despite his words, a warm smile glows on his face.

"They're kind of delightful."

"Don't tell them that. They'll never let it go."

I recognize the small parking lot we enter as being the one behind Two Sons. Cillian's car even sits in the same place. It hits me that I actually have no idea where this show I'm being dragged off to is.

"Is the venue far?" I ask.

He looks confused for half a second. "Oh! No, it's . . . just the bar." He huffs an awkward half-laugh, running a hand through his hair.

"That's convenient," I say, kicking myself for how uncomfortable I sound. "To have a place to play whenever you want, that is."

He shrugs. "It's easier than playing other places, that's for sure. Which we do sometimes."

No one could be blamed for assuming we'd never spoken, much less had wildly fantastic sex a couple of weeks ago. Neither of us seems capable of making eye contact, our bodies tense, leaning away from one another.

This was a bad idea.

"I don't need to tag along," I say. My attempt at nonchalance falling flat. "If you'd rather I didn't, I totally—"

"No!" Cillian says so suddenly, it surprises me. "I mean, if you don't want—I know Lucy can be a bit of a steamroller and—"

A laugh bursts from my lips before I can stop it, the absolute absurdity of this exchange catching up with me. Cillian, rather than looking offended, joins in.

"Jesus Christ." He wipes a tear. "I'm sorry. I promise I'm capable of half-decent communication most days."

"Personally, I can't make those kinds of promises." I catch my breath.

"I'd like you to stay for the show. If you want."

I study him for a beat, trying to find any lie, any indication that he was just being nice. All I find is that the smoky black liner he wears makes his eyes even more beautiful.

"I do want."

"Good." He opens a metal door, and I realize Lucy and Oliver had already headed inside. "Temper your expectations, though. We're just a cover band."

"My only expectation is that Lucy will blow me away." I blow her a kiss as I walk in. She catches it, pressing her closed fist to her chest.

"Don't let him be humble," Oliver says. The two of them sit on a sagging old sofa against the far wall of, what I assume, is the bar's office. He leans his ear to the acoustic guitar in his hands, turning the knobs. "The man has perfect pitch."

"Had," Cillian corrects him. He pulls a chair from beside the desk for me.

Lucy scoffs. "Cillian, you got blown up and still have a better ear than most people."

"I'm sorry, what?" The question comes out before I consider the implications. Lucy looks apologetically at Cillian and regret stirs in my gut.

Cillian clears his throat. "It's fine Lu." He looks at me. "I was, um, in the military for a bit."

"For too long," Oliver says, not looking up from the guitar.

"Not gonna argue with that," Cillian says.

I hadn't dwelt on the scars I'd noticed when Cillian and I were together. They could have been from any number of things. However, military service hadn't even crossed my mind. He just didn't seem the type.

Which, in retrospect, was ridiculous. The only real 'type' I knew of was people who lacked generational wealth. Plenty of kids I grew up with wound up either in the military or married to someone in the service. Less out of patriotism and more out of sheer desperation. Given the choice to rot in a single-wide or be treated like cannon fodder, many chose the latter; at least that had benefits.

It just seemed like a path I only attributed to those who grew up without access to public transportation.

The door to the bar opens, filling the small space with a flood of noise, chasing out any discomforting silence.

"We got 'em warmed up for you kids!" An older man with a head full of salt and pepper hair and a softened Irish accent announces.

"Mickey!" Lucy cheers.

"Hello, sweet Lulu!" The two embrace. Oliver sets the guitar aside and accepts his own warm hug.

As a couple of other older gentlemen filter in, I stand and move to hover beside Cillian, unsure where I should be. It's not something I have to consider for long.

"And who is this?" Mickey asks, catching me in eyes that match his son's.

"Dad, this is Toni. She's a new friend, just moved," Cillian introduces me.

"Mickey O'Sullivan." He extends a warm handshake. "Pleasure to meet you." When most people say that, it feels hollow, just an empty platitude. When this man says it, you know he means it.

"Likewise."

He leans in, mischief tripping off his words. "Now, anything this one may do to bother you, don't go blamin' me. All the bad comes from the other side."

"I heard that!" A tall, bald man says. "Don't listen to a damn thing he says."

"I assume he's from the other side?" I ask.

Mickey taps his temple. "Smart girl." He looks up at his son. "What's she doing hanging out with you lot?"

"Thanks, Dad," Cillian snarks. Mickey just laughs, patting Cillian over his heart.

"Alright, you kids go get set up, don't want to leave people waiting," Mickey says.

"You not staying, Mick?" Oliver asks.

"Not this time. Promised my Kitty I'd be home at a reasonable hour." He turns back to me. "You tell my niece to take good care of you at the bar."

"Yes, sir," I say.

"Smart and respectful!" He declares. "Darling, you are too good for this lot."

"Hey!" Oliver and Lucy object in unison.

Mickey waves them off. "You know I love ya. Have a good show!"

"Bye, Dad," Cillian ushers his dad and the other men out.

$\diamond$

A SURPRISING PORTION OF THE CROWDED BAR cheers when the trio takes the stage.

"Wow," Cillian says, pulling his hair up into a messy knot. "That was fuckin' pathetic." The crowd laughs, some cheer even louder, while others hurl insults at the stage. "Better. Still shit, but better."

Instead of continuing the banter or even giving an introduction, they dive right into a cover of Dropkick Murphys "The Gang's All Here." An excellent choice, seeing as the entire place joins in.

Cillian beams at the crowd as the music fades. "Now that we've got your attention, here's how this works for those who've never been to one of our shows: We've got some songs we're gonna play and we'll play some requests."

"If you feel like it," someone in the crowd yells.

Cillian nods. "Exactly."

"And if you ask for 'Freebird,' you will not get your wish and you will be buying the band a round," Lucy says.

"Any questions?" Cillian doesn't wait for a response. "Good."

Oliver begins playing the opening notes of Coheed and Cambria's "Welcome Home" on his acoustic guitar, Cillian joins on bass, and Lucy falls in on the drums. It's a stripped-back rendition, but when Cillian begins to sing, it doesn't feel like it.

Clearly, he'd been holding back before.

I watch slack-jawed as he takes control of the entire room. It isn't just the way Cillian's voice flows, with seeming ease, from impressive heights to rumbling lows, but his entire presence. He fills every corner of the space with the force of his performance.

The room erupts with applause and cheers when they finish, while I remain gobsmacked.

"Wicked talented, isn't he?" Cillian's cousin Ginelle appears behind me at the bar, a knowing grin on her face.

I nod. "He should just be doing that. And only that. All the time."

"I know." She sighs, her hands making a drink with the skill of someone who could do it in her sleep. "He had a full ride to Berklee, ya know?"

"In California?" I ask, accepting the fresh gin and tonic she passes to me.

She shakes her head. "The music school in Boston. A bunch of famous musicians went there and shit."

I look back at the man on the stage, working the crowd like it was second nature. It's as if the clouds of doubt and self-consciousness leave him when he's behind that microphone, allowing the audience to enjoy the full force of his light.

"What happened?" I ask.

"Bad luck," she says as though it's an acceptable answer.

As the set progresses, I continue to be impressed and not just by Cillian. Lucy and Oliver were great at working the crowd as much as their respective instruments. Their arrangements of familiar songs were creative and refreshing, and it was clear they were all having an absolute blast.

"Sweet Caroline," a song I barely know but that the entire bar seems to—everyone singing so loudly I swear they hear us all the way in downtown Boston—closes the set.

By the final note, fueled by the high of a great show and possibly a smidge too much gin, I'm beyond ready to make a few ill-advised choices. No matter how irresponsible or unreasonable they may be.

CHAPTER 7
Cillian

SWEAT IS BEADING ON MY NECK, MY LEG IS STARTING to ache, and I feel fucking incredible.

Nothing—and I've dabbled with enough poor decisions in my life to have a large sample set to pull from—beats the feeling of playing music with my friends. All the noise in my skull goes quiet. I forget the ghosts, my guilt, and everything else.

I soak it in with one final deep breath.

"As always, tip your bartenders." I gesture to the bar, and they all take a bow. The crowd cheers in their direction. "And don't be an asshole. Goodnight!"

Toni slow claps as we make our way over to the bar. "Holy. Shit. Y'all." She emphasizes each word, and I notice a little twang sneaking into the edges. "That was amazing!"

"I know I am," Lucy tosses her long bob.

"Shots!" Ginelle announces, setting out shots for the four of us.

I raise a brow. "Just handing out shots?"

Ginelle rolls her eyes. "They're from Matt."

As if being summoned, Matt manifests, along with a whole group of people. Everyone is nice enough—mostly friends of Lucy and Oliver—but the press of bodies and the din of everyone trying to be heard begins to sap away the dopamine from being on stage.

I look down at Toni beside me, she's quiet but doesn't seem uncomfortable in the chaos.

"I'm gonna step out for a minute," I say close to her ear.

"Can I join?"

I nod, taking her hand in mine on reflex and lead her through the crowd. It's not until we're outside that I realize, but neither of us lets go immediately.

She let's out a large sigh. "That's better. I was struggling to hear myself think."

"You hid it well."

"I mean, I was fine. Everyone seems great. It all just becomes static after a bit." She makes a dismissive noise. "But that might just be me, or maybe that last shot."

"Not just you," I assure her.

She releases my hand suddenly, placing herself in front of me. "Why didn't you tell me you could sing like that?" She crosses her arms over her chest.

"Why didn't you tell me you draw?"

Her perfect mouth opens and closes, arms falling to her side. "How . . ." She shakes her head, blinking as if she could clear the surprise from her features. "Don't change the subject. You have an actual gift."

Old bitterness slithers through me. There was a time when anyone making comments like that would sour my mood for days, send me into a spiral of what-ifs and could-have-beens. Years of therapy had certainly helped temper that reaction, but this was a wound I'd likely never be rid of.

"Thank you," I manage. "It's just a hobby, though."

"Ginelle said you had a scholarship. To some prestigious music school?"

My cousin and I were going to have to have a talk about not telling other people's business. "Had. It didn't work out."

"Why not?"

"Could we change the subject?" I snap. Toni flinches back, so subtly I'm sure most wouldn't notice it. But as someone who started pushing six feet by the age of 14, I've had a lifetime of being aware of people's reactions to me.

"Sorry," she says.

I shake my head. "No. I am. I just—It's the first domino in a long line of shitty things. Things I'd rather—"

"You don't have to explain. We all have our skeletons."

Some of ours are literal. I think sourly.

"Oof." Toni huffs, letting herself lean heavily into the brick facade.

"You good?" I ask, reaching for her waist, stopping short of touching her.

"Mhm," she nods, eyes closed.

"That last shot?" I ask.

She smiles lazily, opening her eyes. "Might be."

"Want a ride home?"

"Nah." She shakes her head. "I live close. I can just walk."

"I can walk you," I offer.

"I'm good. You should go back in there." She gestures to the door with a bit too much force, testing her fragile balance. I close the distance between us, steadying her with my hands on her shoulders.

I chuckle. "I'm king of the Irish exit. No one in there expects me to be back." I run my thumb along the sliver of skin between the strap of her dress and harness. "Come on, let me get you home."

Toni grabs my hips, pulling me even closer. My hands travel from her shoulders to her back, holding her to me.

"Or maybe . . ." She traces my St. Cecilia pendant with one finger. "Your place?"

The mere suggestion practically makes my mouth water. "Not tonight, doll." I can't resist the urge to trace the edge of that adorable dimple that pops up with her exaggerated pout. "Don't think I don't want to."

"Then, what's the issue?"

I lower my face to hers, our noses brushing. "You are drunk." She steals a fleeting kiss, and we both laugh.

"Not that drunk."

"Drunk enough that even if I desperately want to know if this," I wrap my fingers around the leather strap running up her spine, giving the slightest tug backward-, "is just an accessory or an invitation, I'm not going to be finding out tonight."

She sighs. "I'm annoyed that I'm mad at you for being a decent man."

"I'm sure I'll do something indecent soon enough."

"Don't threaten me with a good time."

I laugh, releasing her. "So . . . am I driving you home or walking you?"

"Again, you don't—"

"Those are your two choices. The third option is me getting you a ride share. Pick."

She cocks one perfectly arched brow at me. "So bossy."

I am a decent man. At least I try to be. Sometimes. And sometimes, I fail.

My hand shoots out, grabbing the front of her harness. I pull her to me, swallowing her sound of surprise with a kiss that leaves us both panting.

"Pick one," I say. My voice sounds rough, the effort of holding back all the ways I'd love to boss her around weighing on my vocal cords.

"Walk," she says on a breath.

I nod, releasing her.

"So that sketchbook?" I ask as we turn off the square and onto a quieter residential street. She gives me a sideways glance. "What do you draw?"

"Just doodles," she keeps her attention on the sidewalk. "Something to keep my hands busy. Nothing special."

I pull her to a stop. "If you can look me in the face and say that, I'll believe you."

"What makes you think I'm lying?"

"People don't try to avoid talking about things that are 'nothing special.'"

"Like you and your mysterious scholarship domino?" She asks, a touch of venom in her tone. "Sorry," she blurts in practically the same breath. "That was shitty."

"I can drop it if—"

"No. I . . . I need to stop acting like it's nothing." She pulls a small sketchbook from her purse. "I never used to. But my ex convinced me it was frivolous and . . . Fuck him, ya know? Why would I keep listening to him—" Toni stops, drawing in a deep breath. "Anyway." She hands the sketchbook to me and starts strolling along the sidewalk.

I join her, flipping open the book, soaking in as much of the content as I can from the streetlights.

Instead of page after page of the same thing, Toni's sketchbook is a menagerie of color, style, and talent. One features swaths of abstract pastels with lines running across, another contains detailed drawings of buildings I don't recognize, and another is full-color renderings of hydrangeas in bloom. Even the ones that could be classified as doodles are literal works of art.

"Your ex is a fucking moron," I say. "You should be showing in galleries and shit."

I'm drawn up short as I turn to a more recent page. My

own face stares back, everything slightly out of focus save for the eyes. I'm flattered and admittedly a bit unnerved, not because she drew me—though I want to tell her she should focus her skills on more worthy subjects—but because of what she captured. The man on the page doesn't look sad per se, but there is a clear melancholy there, peeking out through his eyes. I feel exposed.

I close the book and hold it out to her.

She takes it, putting it back in her purse. "I did years ago. Used to do murals, too."

"Do you want to do that again?" She shrugs. "Lucy shows her metalwork sometimes. I'm sure she'd—"

"Thanks." Toni looks up at me with an expression too sad to be a smile. "I won't be here long enough to get something off the ground, but I appreciate the vote of confidence."

"Won't be here?" I ask, not liking any of the myriad implications brought on by that statement.

"That sounds so bleak." Toni laughs. "I'm almost two months into a six-month sublease."

"Ah." I try to push my disappointment down. "Where to next?"

We come up to a duplex, and Toni sits on the stoop. "Don't know." She leans back on her elbows, looking up at me. "I thought about New Orleans, certainly my brother's preference, but I hate the heat."

"What about your parents?" I ask, leaning against the brick railing.

Darkness flickers across her features. "They're... Well, technically, they're not dead... at least I don't think they are. We haven't spoken in over a decade."

"Damn." I shove my hands in my pockets, unsure of what to do with them.

"Eh. It's fine. I moved out when I was 17, so it's not like we've ever had much of what you'd call a relationship."

"That's so young," I say, like I didn't enlist at that age. Not that I had any right to do that so young, either.

"I'd been freelancing adulthood for a few years by then, so I just went professional, upgraded to legally emancipated teen, rather than girl who sometimes sleeps in her car. And trust me, it was better than the alternative."

She's smiling up at me, but I still want to gather her into my arms. I'd made so many dumb choices while being lucky enough to have a family in my corner. I didn't want to think where I'd be if I were on my own or how tiring and lonely that must've been.

"Why not just stay here?" The question slips past my better sense.

"I . . ." She pauses, sitting up, expression thoughtful. "I don't know. Coming here wasn't so much a plan, more an act of desperation." She looks away, sheepish. "To be honest, I haven't even gone into Boston yet. Hell, I've hardly left my apartment, which is something sober me wouldn't be owning up to."

I take a seat one step down from her, placing us nearly at eye level. "So what you're saying is you haven't been giving this place a chance."

"I guess."

"Bet I could make you stay." There goes my mouth again, writing checks I'm not entirely sure I can or should cash.

She smirks. "Oh? Gonna use your siren song on me?"

I bark a laugh. "Yes. Lure you into the depths of the Charles with the sweet sounds of construction and aggressive drivers."

"Not really selling it," she teases.

"Can't sell you on a lie." I rest my elbow on the step beside her. "But I can convince you to give Boston a real chance."

"This is Somerville," she points out, grinning.

"Ok, Miss Details. I bet I can convince you to stay in the greater Boston metropolitan area."

"And if you can't?"

"I'll personally help you move anywhere you want." She raises her brows at that. "The physical labor alone has to be worth at least a few hundred."

She weighs the merit of my proposal for a beat before standing to extend a hand to me. "Deal."

I give her hand a firm shake and pull her down onto my lap. It's a dumb choice, one a better version of me wouldn't make, but I just want to feel the weight of her against me. She lets out an adorable shriek that reminds me of how she clung to me when I carried her to bed.

"If seducing me is a part of your grand plan . . ."

"Nah." If only I had an actual plan. "Anything involving me should be squarely in the cons column."

"I don't know about that." She settles her arms around my neck.

I let her pull me into a kiss, her tongue teasing my mouth open, her teeth nipping at my bottom lip. I groan, pulling back.

"Sure you don't want to take me home?" she teases.

"We're already at your home." Not that it mattered. She might have sobered up a bit, but not enough that I felt good about taking her to bed. No matter how much my aching cock was begging me to make a different choice.

"No boys allowed." She boops my nose. It's so fucking cute I could scream.

"I want to." I savor the little shiver that runs through her as my fingers trace the back strap of her harness. "Just not tonight." I lean in, pressing a kiss to the crook of her neck. "But if you're no longer worried about hurricanes or whatever, I'd be glad to take you home some other night."

"Just at night?" Toni asks, voice rough with need.

I huff a laugh, just below her ear, watching the gooseflesh rise. "Woman, I'd have you in the middle of this street in broad daylight if you'd let me."

"Not typically an exhibitionist, but I'll try anything once." There is no way she doesn't feel the way the mere thought makes my cock twitch.

"Ok," she says with a sigh. "I will let you try to convince me to stick around. And we can just . . ."

"Not overthink it," I say it with the full confidence of someone talking entirely out of his ass. I always overthink everything. Except when making unreasonably reckless choices, like enlisting or letting myself get far too entangled in this beautiful woman.

But if I couldn't truly have her, maybe I could at least be something good in her life for a little while.

She nods, a gentle smile lifting her lips. "Not overthink it."

I can't resist pulling her mouth to mine one more time.

Eventually, with painful effort, we break apart. I make sure she's steady on her feet by her door before stepping back.

"So when should I expect the sales pitch to start?" she asks.

I smile, even though my brain feels like a hornet's nest. "Next week?"

"Looking forward to it." She kisses me on the cheek. "Goodnight, Cillian."

"Goodnight."

I'm at the bottom of the stoop when she calls out. "Oh, and Cillian."

I turn back to find her leaning against one of the porch's supporting pillars. "Yeah?"

She runs her fingers across the leather crisscrossing over her ribcage. "It's not just an accessory. And if you want, it can absolutely be an invitation."

My self-control had already been dangling by a very thin

thread. Now that I'm imagining everything that invitation might entail? Fuck.

"Good to know," I manage to say. "Now get inside and drink some water."

She smirks wickedly. "Yes, sir."

Maybe she was right to warn me about the dangers of hurricanes.

CHAPTER 8

Toni

I read Cillian's text for approximately the hundredth time in the last fifteen minutes.

CILLIAN

I know tomorrow is a Monday, but any chance you're free during the day?

When he said next week, I didn't think he meant Monday. An invite for Saturday or even Wednesday would have been enough time to come up with a solid excuse to let him down gently. Tell him I appreciated the gesture, but it was a bad idea. All of it.

But forty-eight hours after seeing him? The memory of his voice and his kiss and his . . . HIM-ness, still fresh?

Exasperated with the situation, myself, and the clothing pile on my bed that I'd been in a losing battle with for no less than eight days, I fling my phone away from me with a groan. Plopping on the edge of my mattress, I slide to the floor.

It's a short distance since my bed frame still sits unopened in the corner. My whole apartment looks like it belongs to a gay 20-year-old frat boy. Chaotic. Unkept. But hey, there's a pink couch.

My ass hits the floor and, of course, my phone chooses that moment to vibrate from somewhere within the mountain of clothes behind me.

"Excellent," I say to no one.

I manage to excavate my phone before Belle's video call goes to voicemail.

"Video calls require at least an hour's warning," I say, returning to my position on the floor.

She scoffs, leaning the phone on her counter as she pulls her long brown hair into a ponytail. "I've seen you trash can punch drunk. Sunday goblin mode is nothing." Her East Texas accent makes me oddly homesick for a place I hate, or maybe I just miss her. She squints at the screen. "Girl, is that the same laundry—"

"Please. I am suffering. Don't judge me."

She laughs. "Ok. Ok. Honestly, my recycling pile isn't much better."

Belle, at least, has a legitimate reason for being a mess. Watching your husband die over two years was a fucking horrible way to kick off your thirties. In comparison I have nothing to bitch about.

"So tell me what happened!" She insists.

"Nothing." I groan. "Just Hurricane Toni bullshit."

"Come on, I'm living vicariously through you here."

She still spent most of her time on the ranch she'd shared with her late husband. Fifteen acres about an hour outside of Austin at the foot of the Hill Country, a place they'd planned on turning into a rehab center for horses and people alike.

Now, there were no horses or people—just Belle.

"You could come visit me." I hate her being all alone out there.

"I will." A screen door slams before the familiar chorus of summer cicadas hums in the background. "Now talk."

I give her the details of what happened Friday. Being stood up, meeting Cillian's friends, the show... And of course, the wager he'd laid at my feet.

"He asked me where I was going next," I say. Sighing, I trudge to the kitchen for iced coffee. "Which drove home that I don't have any idea. I'm thirty-three. I'm supposed to have an idea. Right? A plan? Something?"

Belle laughs sardonically. "If I've learned a damn thing these last few years, it's that even if you do have a plan the universe is just as likely to set fire to it as not." She pauses. "Honestly, if anything, maybe not having a plan is best. Less shit to bog you down when it fails."

My heart aches for my friend. "If you feel bogged—"

She makes a buzzer sound. "We aren't talking about me."

"Fine." I return to my nest on the couch. "So, yeah. That's where I'm at. Hot-nice-man is too hot and too nice. I'm—"

"Also hot and nice."

"The former, sometimes. The latter, debatable. Especially if I willingly bring all my bullshit to this hot-nice-man's nice life."

"First off, 'hot-nice-man' cannot be his codename."

"Got better ideas?" I ask.

"Hmm," she strokes her chin. "Hung-and-handsome? Bearded-and-burly? All I've got is alliteration." I laugh, nearly choking on my coffee. "Or we can just call him his actual name."

"Ugh, and treat a man like a person? Fine." I joke.

Belle shrugs. "I feel like Cillian has earned that, seeing as he's got you all stressed by following through with what he said he'd do."

"I . . ." Damn her. "First off, I am not stressed."

"Says the woman who just claimed she was suffering. But continue."

I sigh, flipping the camera to sweep it around the troll cave that is my apartment. "This is the physical manifestation of what is going on in my skull and in my life. No one wants to deal with that. Especially someone who has clearly already sorted their shit out."

"You don't get to decide what he wants to deal with."

"Isabelle," I grumble. "You're supposed to tell me this is a bad idea."

"It is."

"Thank you."

"A bad idea to say no to him," she adds.

"I hate you."

She grins. "No, you don't."

I make an annoyed noise.

"Look, I'm not flying all the way to Boston just so you can blindly take me around. Let him try to sell you on the place if for no other reason than you can be a better tour guide for me."

"So what you're saying is, this is all about you?"

"Obviously." Silence hangs for a beat before we both laugh.

Another call notification pops up, this time from my sister-in-law, of all people. "Weird, Dianne is calling me."

"Find out what she needs. Keep me posted on what happens with Cillian?" She asks.

"I will."

I don't get a word out before one of my ten-year-old twin nephews' faces fill the screen. "Ant-Ant!" The nickname the boys had called me since they could talk brings a smile to my face, even if Parker's volume makes me worry for the phone's mic.

"Hey! What's up?" The video takes a Blair Witch-esque

turn, all muffled sound and shaky camera work, for a solid minute. "Y'all still there?"

"Fine!" Parker says. "We can both be in it." Parker and Asher, mirror images of my brother at their age, come into focus.

"Does your mom know you have her phone?" They exchange a conspiratorial look. "Thought so."

"We can use it for important stuff, and this is important," Asher reasons.

Parker nods in agreement.

I barely hold back a laugh. "Alright then. What important stuff do you need to talk to me about?"

What follows is an impassioned debate—one I take sole responsibility for—about who the best Star Trek captain is. Unsurprisingly, Asher, the more bookish of the boys, argues in favor of Picard while Parker is Team Kirk.

Once I knew I'd be moving to Somerville, I decided to save money and take up my brother's offer to stay with his family in New Orleans for a few months. To say the least, it had been an experience.

Not a bad one. I just didn't know how to do the whole family thing.

The last time I'd spent any significant time cohabitating with a blood relation, I'd been seventeen. While I wasn't nursing several bruised ribs and a fractured orbital bone this time, I felt just as shattered. Yet again, seeking some kind of shelter with the brother I hardly knew.

I hated it . . . for all of a week.

It was hard to be too miserable with two funny, sweet, loud swamp gremlins around. Sure, I'd seen them for holidays and a few long weekends here and there, but never enough time to really get to know them. But this time, I threw myself into full auntie mode, finding that I kind of loved it.

As an added bonus, hanging out with them made things a

little less awkward between Ben and me. We still struggled, but it felt less like we were well-acquainted strangers and a little more like we were brother and sister.

"Ok," I cut into their tirade. "You've both presented solid arguments. But you're wrong."

"Which one of us?" Asher asks.

"Both of you." They look flabbergasted. "You haven't even gotten to the best captain yet."

"Boys, have you seen your mama's phone?" I hear Ben's deep drawl call out.

"Busted," I taunt.

"Why're y'all botherin' your Ant-Ant?"

I laugh. "They're fine. We were just discussing who the superior Star Trek captain is."

"You've ruined my children." He takes the phone, my brother's face replacing the boy's. There was little denying the resemblance between us. For better or worse, the Devereaux blood ran strong. "Say bye to Ant-Ant and go help your mama with dinner, please."

"Bye Ant-Ant! Love you!"

"Love y'all, too!" I call back.

Ben waits until the thunder of their retreat fades before asking, "How are you?"

I shrug, a twinge of guilt at not checking in with him souring my stomach. "Not bad. Settling in."

"Given any thought to where you're going next?"

Why was everybody obsessed with asking me this fucking question?

"I haven't even unpacked all my boxes, Ben." Or practically any of them.

"No pressure. Just checkin'. Gotta know if I need to fly up in January."

"Well, if I move elsewhere, a . . . friend might be helping with that."

84

His eyes narrow. "What kind of friend?"

"A friend-friend."

"This friend wouldn't happen to be a guy?"

I sigh. "I'm just as likely to be shacking up with a woman if that's what you're getting at."

"What? No!" A red blush rises on my brother's full cheeks. "I just . . . I worry, alright?"

"Well, you don't need to. I can handle myself." Always had.

"Yeah. I know."

"I gotta go," I say.

"Right. Take care." *I love you* had never really been our style.

"You, too."

The silence feels heavy, but I resist the urge to put on a record to fill the void.

Why not just stay here? Why not at least try?

For most of my life, I'd had little bandwidth—or income —to do much more than follow the path of least resistance to my next zip code. And each place always felt off, like wearing shoes that don't quite fit, but that your mom assures you you'll grow into. Except I never grew into any of them. Even so, I tried to make them fit—stuffed the toes with lovers and acquaintances and standing brunch dates, only to find my heels still bled from the blisters.

Maybe this could be different.

True, I hadn't picked Somerville off a list. An opportunity arose and I took it, but it wasn't the easiest choice I could have made. For once, I had the benefit of both time and resources, and I still chose this.

"Why not?" I say aloud.

I text Cillian back.

The joy of being self-employed is making my own schedule . . . for the most part. What've you got in mind?

CILLIAN

You'll see. Meet at the Davis Square station. 10:30?

I'll be there.

CHAPTER 9

Cillian

My palms are sweating. Actually fucking sweating.

I shoot a text to my group chat with Lucy and Oliver.

> Is this overkill?

I flick my lighter open and closed, pulling nicotine deep into my lungs while I wait for one of them to respond.

OLIVER
> Overkill? Why would it be overkill?

LUCY
> It isn't overkill. Stop overthinking this.

Their responses are on brand, as always. Oliver, introspective. Lucy, direct. Both are probably right.

I stamp out my cigarette and duck into the coffee shop.

In the fall, this place will have a line out the door. For now, the summer lull tempered the crowd to a comfortable level of busy.

"Hey!" Jac greets me with a wave. I return the gesture. "Usual?"

"That'd be great, thanks." I glance down at my phone.

TONI

I'm running a few minutes late because of who I am as a person. Sorry!

"You good?" Jac asks as they make my tea.

I huff. "Do I look bad?"

They chuckle. "Not bad. Nervous. But like, cute shelter dog who just wants a belly rub, nervous."

That pulls an unexpected laugh out of me. "I don't know if I should be offended."

"Everyone loves shelter dogs." They lean on the counter while my tea steeps. "What's up?"

I sigh. "I'm showing a new friend who just moved here around the city."

"Friend or *friend*," they emphasize the last word.

"Friend," I assure. "We have a bit of a bet going that I can get her to move here permanently."

"If you lose?"

"I have to help her move wherever she ends up going next. So it could be a very pricy loss."

"Would I know this friend?"

"You actually sent her over to the bar for coffee. Cute redhead. Plus size."

"Toni!" They exclaim with such enthusiasm that I almost take a step back. Clearly, Toni has been making an impression on more than just me.

"That's her. Actually . . . You wouldn't happen to know her coffee order, would you?"

Jac grins. "I would happen to. One sec." They step away, the espresso machine hissing and return with two cups in hand.

"Your usual. And one cold brew with a shot of espresso and a half pump of simple syrup."

My brows rise. "Seriously?"

They nod. "The woman does not fuck around with her caffeine." They hand over the drinks. "Or her tips. This is on the house."

"Jac—"

They push my card away. "Just get out of here and show her a good time. I could use another quality regular."

"I'll do my best!" I promise, flinging $10 at them and moving for the door before they can try to give it back to me.

"So sorry!" Toni huffs as she jogs up to me.

Sundresses should be illegal.

My caveman brain registers how fine this woman looks before I can form a coherent response. The black button-up dress flows over her curves, complementing rather than diminishing them. And that hemline...

I swallow hard.

"I—" She begins. Rather than let her explain unnecessarily, I cut her off by holding her coffee in front of her face. "If this is what I think it is, I might kiss you."

"What it is, is a drink with enough caffeine to level a bear."

"We all have our vices. At least mine makes me moderately functional." She takes a sip, lashes fluttering with satisfaction. "How did you know my order?"

"Courtesy of Jac," I confess.

"Remind me to kiss Jac next time I'm in there."

"Will do."

She looks at my drink. "What do you have?"

"Iced green tea with honey." She screws up her face like I'd said something vile. As cute as it is, I still protest, "It's good!"

"Keep telling yourself that. So . . . where are you taking me?"

"Are you opposed to being surprised?" As someone who

isn't a big fan of surprises, I can understand preferring to know.

"Not necessarily. I'm just impatient."

"I remember." I relish the way she blushes. "Anyway, we are about to take the Red Line, so . . ." I let my words drag off.

"That means absolutely nothing to me."

I lead us to the platform. "Our train system. It is functional, but she's an old girl. Your patience will be tested."

She shrugs. "Somewhat functional is better than nonexistent. I've never lived somewhere with even half-decent public transit."

"Seriously?" I ask.

"Yeah. The town I grew up in quite literally has one stoplight. And everywhere I've landed since has had mediocre options at best."

"I'm sure you at least got into less trouble in your one-stoplight town than we did here."

Toni scoffs. "In the sticks you've got very few choices for entertainment outside of illicit substances, fucking, and church." I muffle a laugh. "And you'd be surprised how often those three things intersected. We got into plenty of trouble."

To my absolute delight, Toni opens up. She tells me about her hometown, hitchhiking back roads with her friends, pasture parties, and the local boudin man. A different world from the one that made me.

Notably, she doesn't say much about her family. In fact, her parents or brother hardly make an appearance. Given what she'd said about her parents before, I assume they're off limits. But her brother had helped her move, so I'm a little surprised at his absence in her tales.

We're almost to our final stop when I ask, "Did your brother leave town after high school?" I knew he was significantly older than her, so it would make sense.

"Oh, no. He grew up with his mom in Louisiana. When I was really little, he came out for some holidays and summer weekends, but that stopped when I was about six."

"Why?"

She goes for a dismissive shrug, but I see the way her body tenses. "Nothing crazy. A painfully cliche white trash domestic unfolded, and he didn't have to come back."

Nothing crazy. I don't believe that, but I am also not going to push the topic. And we're at our stop anyway.

The public garden is in full summer glory. Everywhere you look, vibrant greens glow while flowers lend pops of color. On the pond, a few folks are even out in the swan boats. It's an image worthy of a postcard. Even I'm impressed.

"It's no Central Park," I say, leading us to the shoreline of the pond. "But it has its own charm."

"It's lovely," Toni says, soaking in everything. "Do you mind if I-" She pulls a sketch pad from her bag.

Satisfaction explodes in my chest. "Not at all. I figured this might be the kind of place you'd like to sketch." I take a set of pastels and pencils from my bag, offering them to her.

She looks from the tools to me and back. "Cillian . . ."

"I didn't know what you typically use, so I got some tips from Lucy. But I wasn't sure if you'd have anything with you, so just in case."

"They're perfect." Toni takes them, eyes wide. "Thank you. I won't keep us long, I just want to get a general—"

"We can stay as long as you want." I pull a pocket picnic blanket from my bag. As I lay it out, she doesn't move, just stares at me, almost confused.

I sit and gesture for her to join me.

"Won't you be bored?" She asks.

"Nope." I pull out my book, but she still doesn't move.

"Toni." I lower my voice a touch, hoping to gently

command her attention. "Sit down. Or walk around. What-ever you want to do. But you can't just stand there staring at me."

That breaks the spell. She settles beside me, her exposed thigh pressed against my pant leg.

I can't resist giving her thigh a squeeze as I lean over to whisper in her ear, "Good girl."

A bright laugh tumbles from her lips as another blush colors her round cheeks. "Oh, fuck you." She playfully pushes me away.

"Can dish it but not take it?" That, "Yes, Sir" she left me on the other night has been burning in my mind ever since.

"Oh," she purrs. "I'm very good at taking it."

"We'll see about that." I open my book and gesture to the view before I do anything too foolish.

Silence has always been my mother tongue. So much so that my parents worried something was wrong when I was a kid. Nothing was; I just never felt the need to fill the void like everyone else seemed to. It's a trait that hasn't historically served me well in the human connection department.

After a time, it becomes clear Toni is just as fluent in silence as I am. The quiet that falls between us isn't just comfortable, it's easy. So easy that before I know it, more than an hour has passed and my stomach is growling.

Toni's hand still moves across the page, stealing inspiration from the scene before her, transmuting it into something more enchanting than the reality could ever be.

"That's beautiful," I say.

I catch her half-smile. "It's just a sketch."

"Do you always take compliments so well?"

"What was it you called music? Just a hobby?"

I can't even be butt-hurt about that. "Touché."

She stretches, letting herself fall back onto the blanket, eyes on the blue summer sky above us. I can't look away.

"This was great. Thank you." In the sunlight, her eyes are almost auburn. Rich and warm and . . .

I clear my throat. "We're not done yet."

CHAPTER 10
Toni

WORDS FAIL ME AS I STARE UP AT THE ISABELLA Stewart Gardner Museum's pink stucco walls.

Striking is the only word for it. The way the foliage takes on a jewel-like quality, the play of shadow and light, all set against the unique architecture. It feels like something outside of time, a little magical bubble of inspiration.

This was right here, a train ride away, all these weeks.

I'm too happy to let guilt take root and ruin the beauty before me. But it's still there all the same. A small voice chastises me for not getting out and discovering this on my own.

"Not what you expected?" Cillian asks.

"Definitely not. Pink courtyard isn't the first thing that comes to mind when I hear 'we're going to a museum.'"

"Good." He passes me a brochure, I take it, but he doesn't let go. "Important question: Are you a museum sprinter or marathoner?"

"This feels like a question you should ask before buying the ticket."

"Too late for that. We're in this together. What's your approach?"

A part of me wants to deny him the answer just to see what he'll do. I've never considered myself a brat, but, God, something about him makes me weigh the merits of giving it a go.

My desire to see the rest of the museum proves to be stronger.

"Marathoner. Long distance." It's why I hated going to museums with other people. They always wanted to move too fast, annoyed by my desire to linger over one piece or visit an exhibit more than once.

David and I went to the MFA in Houston exactly one time. He spent the entire visit bored and grumpy, grumbling about not 'getting it', despite insisting he wanted to come with me. It was a miserable time all around.

"Thank god." Cillian releases his hold on the brochure. "Shall we?"

Over the next two hours, we wander the blissfully eccentric halls of the museum. Each room has a distinct theme, brimming with art and ephemera, with every detail, from the floors to the ceiling, carefully curated.

"This might be my new favorite place," I say, giving the courtyard one final study.

"In Boston?" Cillian asks.

"Anywhere."

"That has to be at least 500 points in my favor, right?"

I look up at him. "We never agreed on a point system."

"How else can we ensure a fair and unbiased outcome? I got a lot on the line here."

I lay a hand on his chest, my face a parody of sincerity. "Trust."

He covers my hand with his, narrowing his eyes. "I don't know. You seem shifty."

"Me?" I scratch at my nose with crossed fingers. "Never."

✧

CILLIAN'S HAND SETTLES ON THE SMALL OF MY BACK as we work through the crowd of late afternoon commuters. I can't tell if it's a gesture meant more for him or me, but regardless, I enjoy the warm pressure of his presence.

"What train are we taking?" I ask.

"Huh?" He tilts his head toward me, eyes not quite meeting mine. Instead, they scan the crowd with methodical precision. A muscle in his jaw ticks. Tension rolls off him like heat waves off concrete.

"Not a fan of crowds?"

"Sorry." With visible effort, he pulls his attention away from our surroundings. "I'm not . . . I just . . ." He trails off.

"Don't like crowds." I finish for him. "Nothing weird about that." He didn't have to spell it out for me to put the pieces together, and besides, people without his history had plenty of reasons to prefer not being trapped with the masses.

"Kinda depends on the crowd." He looks up as a train pulls in. "This is us." We luck out, snagging two seats near the back of the car with a bit of breathing room. The small win doesn't seem to do much to relax him.

"What would be an acceptable crowd?" I ask as the train starts moving.

"On a stage or behind a bar." Once again, I watch as his eyes scan every person in range. "Those are fine. Usually." He shifts beside me. "Places with clear and easy exits. Crowded train station underground? Not my favorite place to be."

"Do you have one? A favorite place that is?"

Maybe if I can get him talking about something positive, his mind will wander to those better places and distract him from the present circumstance.

"In the world or in Boston?"

"Both."

"Haven't been many places in the world, to be honest. At least not for pleasure." His fingers move in a rhythmic beat against my thigh. "I have a place in New Hampshire. Nothing fancy, just a shitty little cabin on a lake. But it's peaceful."

"No crowds," I gently tease.

"Nope—unless you count the wildlife," he chuckles. "As boring as it is, that is one of my favorite places to be."

"That's not boring. What about in Boston?" I ask. Some of the tension has left his shoulders.

Cillian doesn't answer immediately, looking at the display showing the stop. "Would you want to see it?"

"Now?" He nods. "Sure."

We get off at the next stop and walk up the pedestrian lane of a bridge spanning the Charles River.

"Here?" I ask, looking up at him, confused.

"Yup." He gestures to the view.

"Oh . . ."

Verdant green trees line a river dotted with the red and white sails of early afternoon boaters. Just beyond, in strong contrast, the city rises in brick and glass. There is texture, color, and life everywhere you look.

"You should see it at sunset," Cillian says. He rests his forearms on the railing, looking out.

I join him. "Why this place?"

"Honest answer or easy one?"

"Honest. Always."

He drags in a deep breath. "About nine years ago, I was . . ." He studies his palms as if they hold a script. "It was my fourth alive day—"

"Alive day?"

"It's a . . . military thing. The day you should've died but didn't." His gaze settles on the distant buildings. "I wasn't in a great place. Needed to clear my head, so I just started walking

97

—something that I wasn't sure I was gonna be able to do for a while there."

Before I can ask, he pats his left thigh, "Shattered femur. Wrecked the muscle, nerves, the works."

"Shit." Lucy mentioned he'd gotten 'blown up' the other night, and I'd noticed the way the skin there puckered under his tattoos. I just hadn't imagined the damage had been that bad.

He nods. "Yeah. By the time I got here, my leg wasn't having it. I was in so much pain, I had to stop. The bridge was undergoing refurbishment, so it was kind of a mess." He rubs the area, whether from habit or need, I can't tell.

Concern floods me. We'd done quite a bit of walking today, and that couldn't be kind on a bad leg. I blurt, "I don't mind getting a car back. We've done a lot of walking today, so—"

Cillian directs one of those disarming smiles at me. "You're sweet, but I'm good. It's . . . well it's still a massive pain in my ass, but I've learned how to deal with it." My disbelief must've shown on my face. "Promise." He reaches for my hand, and I let him pull me back against his chest, his chin resting on top of my head as we both take in the view.

"So you and the bridge were kindred spirits." I prompt him to continue.

His chest rumbles behind me with a soft laugh. "You could say that."

I relax into him.

"Something about the hum of traffic, the combination of the river and the city, and everything. It grounded me."

"I get that."

"Now, when I need to recenter, this is where I come."

"Thank you for sharing this with me," I say, so quietly I worry he might not hear me above the sound of the cars behind us.

"Thank you for asking."

CHAPTER 11
Cillian

I haven't even put my keys down on the kitchen table when my phone rings, 'LITTLE MICKEY'—my older brother's hated childhood nickname—in big letters flashes across the screen.

I almost don't answer. Michael calling me at 6 pm on my day off is not a good sign. Was it too much to ask the universe to let me ride the high of an excellent day for just a little longer?

"No," I say instead of hello.

"You have to." Michael's voice doesn't hold an ounce of humor.

"What happened?" Monday's weren't dead, but they rarely got rowdy.

He sighs heavily. "I had to send Joey home." My stomach drops. "Which means, either I can work the grill or you can, but I need another body."

My leg gives a throb of protest. "I'll take the grill." At least if it wasn't too busy, it would be easy enough to get off it here and there. "Let me unload my groceries."

"I'll fill you in when you get here."

✧

WE DON'T GET THE CHANCE TO TALK UNTIL I LOCK the doors at 11:15 pm.

"Go home, Sean," I tell our little cousin. He'd balk if he knew I still thought of him as little; the kid was 18 and almost my height.

"You sure?" he asks. The tub of clean glassware clinks in his skinny arms as he watches me limp my way over to a chair.

"Yeah." I swallow a groan as I sit. "Give Ginelle something to do tomorrow." Streaks of searing pain tear through my thigh as I prop my leg on another chair.

"I'm telling her you said that." He pulls his phone out to text her. "I am not getting yelled at for some stupid shit twice in twenty-four hours."

"If she's pissed she can take it up with me," Michael says. He pats Sean on his shoulder. "Good job tonight."

Sean lights up as Michael hands him his tips, the combination of cash and the approval of his older cousin—something I'm convinced we never quite grow out of—working their magic. "Thanks." He clears his throat, "Joey . . ."

"Keep that between us, yeah?" Michael asks.

"Yeah," Sean nods.

As soon as we hear the back door shut, Michael grabs a bottle of whiskey and two glasses.

"You wanna stay there or move to the couch?"

I press my fingers into the screaming muscle, silently begging for any break in the pain. My voice cracks, "If I get on that couch, I won't be getting off it."

Michael nods, taking the other chair and pouring us each a drink.

"Has it been bothering you?" He asks.

I shake my head, dragging in a wobbly breath. "Spent the day in the city." I keep the bitter, *And I didn't plan on being on it all night,* to myself. It would only make both of us feel like shit. Besides, it wasn't Michael's fault.

"Doing what?" He nudges my glass toward me.

"Showing a new friend around." I try to focus on the whiskey. The taste. The pleasant burn down my throat. Think about how good it felt to look out over the city with Toni in my arms. Anything else but the pain.

"This friend wouldn't happen to be a pretty redhead?" My focus shoots to Michael, a smirk plastered on his face. He chuckles into his glass, sounding so much like our dad it's almost eerie. "Dad mentioned meeting her. Had nothing but glowing things to say."

"Would it kill this family to mind their own fucking business?"

"Maybe. Too risky at this stage to try and find out, don't you think?"

I shrug, "I don't know, might be worth it."

"Nah. I'd rather my kid have all their family members around." Michael's wife Camille was just entering her second trimester. Come December or January, there would be a new little O'Sullivan in the world.

I never wanted to be a dad, but a cool uncle? That was a role I couldn't wait to fill.

"All? Let's try not to traumatize the next generation too much."

"Ok. Most." He sighs, "Speaking of . . . Joey."

"How bad?"

"Bad." Michael finishes his whiskey and pours us both a bit more. "Sweating liquor, jumpy, started yelling at Sean for no fuckin' reason. Threatened me."

"God dammit," I say under my breath.

"I know he's family, but . . . he's a liability. I really don't know if we can—"

"Would you say the same if it were me?" I snap.

"It's not you."

"It could be." My voice sounds tired, even to my own ears.

Michael looks at me for a long moment. "But it isn't. And you've fought damn hard to make sure it isn't."

"That doesn't make me any better than him. Just luckier."

"Lucky? Cillian, you think—" Michael runs a hand over his face as if he could erase his frustration. "Whatever. How the fuck are you gonna feel if he hurts himself, or hell, someone else back there because he's too drunk or too . . ."

"Too what?" I practically spit the question.

He takes a deep breath. "Look, I understand that—"

"You don't, though. You have no fucking idea." He couldn't. There was no way for him to understand how hard just existing could be, how getting through the most basic actions could feel like moving through wet sand, how fucking loud it could be in your skull. And I wouldn't want him to understand any of it, neither would Joey. I just need him and everyone else to be willing to cut the man some slack.

My brother looks at me not with pity—Michael never did and I loved him so much for that—but with sad acceptance. "You're right."

"He just needs someone to help keep him afloat. That's all. He'll find his stride again."

"Maybe." His tone shifts, determination hardening his features. "But Cillian, I won't let him pull you under."

Michael had kept me afloat more than a few times over the years. Hell, he was the sole reason I hadn't spent the last decade in a wooden box, written off as a statistic. I couldn't blame him for being a bit overprotective.

He continues, "And I won't let him put anyone else at risk either. One more night like tonight and I'm bringing in Dad to make the call." We ran things for the most part, but Dad was still the final call if we needed him to be.

"Fine." I throw back the rest of my whiskey.

We finish closing, and rather than follow Michael's tail-lights from the parking lot, I sit in my dark car. With the engine off, the most distinct sound is my breathing, the world outside muffled and far away.

Placing one hand on my stomach and the other on my chest, I close my eyes and breathe in deeply, focusing on the feeling of the air in my lungs and the movement of my body. I do the same on the exhale and repeat until the warm air in the car feels uncomfortable.

I can't say I feel better, but perhaps a bit more settled in my body. Given the pain in my thigh, I'm not sure if I appreciate that. I fish around my bag for my cigarettes. The irony of doing that after a breathing exercise isn't lost on me. But what had Toni said about vices and functioning? If the worst things I put in my body were nicotine and whiskey, I had improved greatly.

Before I find the familiar rectangular box, a rolled-up piece of paper teases my fingertips.

I unravel it, revealing a sketch of the view from the bridge, Toni's signature scribbled at the bottom. She must've done it on the quiet last leg of our ride back and slipped it in when I wasn't paying attention.

If I didn't know it was something she did quickly, I wouldn't believe it. All the life and texture were there in graphite. With just her pencil, she managed to capture the unnamable spark I felt in that place.

Looking at it, for just a moment, I feel grounded.

CHAPTER 12

Toni

ART SUPPLY STORES SHOULD BE REQUIRED TO POST warning signs on the door: *Contents may cause absolute loss of self-control. Enter at your own risk.*

I'd already deposited a stack of canvas and a travel easel at the counter, and my hand basket was dangerously heavy.

Over the past week, I'd burned through the scraps of paint and canvas I brought with me. To be fair, that didn't account for much. They were the dregs left over from my time with David.

A total restock was necessary. But did I really need the gold leaf?

I toss it in.

With each year I spent with David, I found myself creating less and less. Never replenishing things when I ran out, or him insisting I get rid of them. Reducing my footprint bit by bit to make space for . . . What? His rowing machine?

I also put copper leaf in my basket.

"Wow. Cheating on me, I see." Jac, the barista I'd become friendly with over the last few weeks, takes a long sip from an iced drink, the logo of a different local coffee shop matching the one in my hand.

"Didn't realize we were in a monogamous situation."

They laugh. "I would never! Not that I'm yucking anyone's yum."

"Of course."

"What'cha got going on here?" They peek into my basket.

I hold up my spoils, letting them paw through the contents. "A hefty credit card payment."

"Do you have a project you're working on or just in it for the vibes?" It's a fair question given there's a bit of everything shoved in there. Watercolors and oils and gouache and brushes and charcoal . . . and . . . and . . . and . . .

"Both? I've always gravitated to whatever felt right for a piece rather than sticking to one medium." One of the reasons I didn't major in visual arts. The other was that I didn't have a trust fund to fall back on.

They nod. "Can't wait to see where this ends up." They hold up the gold leaf. "I'm a slut for shiny things."

"Once I know, I'll update you."

"We rotate the art in the shop, ya know? You could show some of your stuff."

I fight a grin. "You sure about that? I could be terrible."

They give me a once-over. "I don't buy that."

"We'll see."

"If you stick around?" I don't try to hide my surprise. "Cillian gave me the skinny last week. It's why I sent him with a free coffee."

"To bribe me?"

"Whatever works."

An awkward laugh slips out. "Why would it matter to you if I stay?"

They shrug. "You seem cool."

"As a person hurtling toward her mid-thirties, who spent

last night listening to Taylor Swift and drinking box wine, I'm going to hold onto that compliment for dear life."

Jac bursts out laughing. "I'm only judging you a little for the T-Swift inclusion."

"What happened to not yucking yums?" I ask.

"I . . . Ok, but . . ."

I loudly slurp my coffee while they try to find the words.

"Fine. If you agree to put one piece up in the shop, I'll let it go," Jac relents.

"Deal." I needed to stop making these bargains.

"Jac!" A skinny guy in patchwork overalls and a frohawk calls from the door.

"Shit. Right. I need rhinestones."

"Fun!"

Jac bounces on the balls of their feet. "Actually, I'm performing at a drag show on Sunday. You should come! It's gonna be weird."

"I love weird."

They give me the info and sprint off. "See you Sunday!"

✧

AFTER THREE TRIPS TO UNLOAD MY CAR OF SUPPLIES and groceries, I'm hungry, sweaty, ready to collapse in front of the window unit for a while, and to my absolute surprise, happy. And excited. And inspired. I can't remember the last time this heady combination danced in my veins.

I turn on the AC, but rather than collapse, I fish out *Heartbreak Express* by Dolly Parton. It's an old vinyl—one I'm pretty sure I stole from my mom's collection when I moved out—but the rough state just adds texture to the sound.

As the record plays, the groceries get put away, and not just the refrigerator items either. Everything. The dishes that had been drying on the counter for a week find their place in the cabinets. I even pull a few more kitchen items—mostly coffee-related—from the boxes they'd been hiding in and find them homes.

By the time the whole album finishes, I have the kitchen of a fairly functional person.

Riding the wave, I grab a Loretta Lynn record next and move into the would-be dining room. When I saw the pictures of the apartment, I loved how this room got so much light. I could envision the built-in filled—not with china as intended —but with paint and supplies, the floor covered with a drop cloth, my newest work sitting by the window.

I move a few boxes to the edge of the room and lay out the drop cloth.

One of the paper bags of paints, brushes, and other goodies crinkles in my grip as I hesitate. There was a better, less chaotic way to do—

"Fuck that," I say to no one.

Who would see me? Who would judge me? What did it matter if I went about this in a way that worked for me? I was the only one here.

I dump everything out onto the drop cloth so I can see it all laid out.

It's fully dark outside when I stop and take in my little studio space. Sure, I was using a couple of boxes as tables, and I could benefit from a shelf or two, but overall, it wasn't bad.

Still a mess, David's voice echoed in my head, level, calm, and so condescending.

He wouldn't be wrong. But it was my mess. My life.

I pull out my phone and open my conversation with Cillian.

We'd only hung out once since he took me into the city a little over a week ago. I joined him, Lucy, Oliver, and some other friends for a beach day. It was an exceptional time, even if the water was frigid by my standards.

Beach access was absolutely going in the pros column for New England. Not something I'd been anticipating.

Even though we hadn't had much face-to-face time, we hadn't stopped talking.

Our text chain was a constant flow of random side conversations, suggestions for places I might like—he'd even recommended the local art supply store I'd been at earlier—and, admittedly, some spicier things. All were great, but the best part may be how he hadn't once gotten touchy when I didn't respond immediately. No passive-aggressive *hello*s or quips about something being *more important than him.*

It was my life. And I wanted to enjoy it. I muster up an ounce of courage and text Cillian.

> Got any plans Sunday night?

CHAPTER 13

Cillian

"THAT CAN GO HERE," LUCY POINTS BESIDE HER table.

"This is why I don't agree to these things." I set the box down with a huff. "You always turn me into a pack mule."

"Oh, please." She opens the plastic tub, directing me to start pulling carefully wrapped jewelry and small sculptures out. "You don't come because you've turned into a boring old man."

I rub the place over my heart. "Damn, already been shot in the chest once, Lu."

"Not funny." She pretends to adjust the intricate chest piece she wears over a leather bustier.

"Come on." I set the piece I was unwrapping down and try to pull her toward me.

She half-heartedly pushes me away. "Get off me!"

"Nope."

She rests her chin on my shoulder with a huff, giving in to the hug. "You know I don't find that shit funny." She was right, I did. Lucy hated my gallows humor.

"I know." I plant a kiss on her temple and hold her at arm's length. "Forgive me?"

She huffs a sigh. "I guess. But only if you help me pack up."

I was already planning on it. "Fair."

Several other vendors and performers stop by as we set up, awestruck by Lucy's work.

When one of them leaves, I ask, "Am I actually a boring old man?"

"Maybe Toni will make you fun again," she says.

"I'm being serious." I don't know why, maybe it's turning forty looming in a few years, but it's bothering me.

She plucks a small half-circle with silvery rays shooting from it off the table. "I mean, when was the last time you agreed to come to something like this with me? Even when I'm not vending."

I sigh. "Too long."

When Toni asked if I wanted to come tonight, I almost said no. I had very few nights off and—as Lucy made painfully clear—too often I chose to spend them at home alone rather than doing anything social. But I knew Lucy was vending and that she hadn't even asked me to come, assuming she already knew my answer. It felt like the powers that be were very clearly telling me to get out for once.

She nods. "I know the bar is demanding. But you've gotta make time for Cillian. Which can be boring and restful at times, but it should be fun, too, at least sometimes." She points the silver rays at me. "And before you say anything, I've had the same conversation with Oliver."

"I wasn't gonna say anything." I knew balancing his family's gym and his work as a teacher was a lot. Still, he showed up. "He's more together than any of us."

"Freak of nature, that boy," she says with nothing but love.

"We should get him a massage or something."

"Like he'd accept it. Come here."

I side-eye her. "Why?"

"You're lacking sparkle. This is a drag show. You need some flair." She gestures with the crescent in her hands.

"How am I lacking?" I waggle my fingers, showing off my rings and silver nails.

"Trust me. You need more WOW." She turns me around, pushing me to kneel. With skilled fingers, she pulls the tie from my hair, parting it and pulling half of it back up. She settles the half circle around the bun, attaching it with a hairpin.

She walks around me to inspect her work. "Perfect."

I stand and check the mirror on her table. The base of the hairpiece is almost invisible, making the silver rays appear as if they were each attached to my hair. Admittedly, it looks cool as fuck. A bit of flair, like she said, without being too much.

"Ok. You win. This is fucking sick." Lucy's lack of gloating over her victory strikes me as suspicious. I look up to see her transfixed on something—or rather someone— behind me.

"Bro," she says, wonder in her voice.

"What?" I follow her gaze.

Toni stands near the door, cheerfully chatting with a slender guy in an iridescent ensemble. He shakes his frohawk at her, fine glitter sparkling in the air, making her laugh with delight.

As if that laugh of hers isn't enough to make me stupid, she's chosen a look that might actually kill me. Black lace covers her from neck to ankle, a modest silhouette excepting the fact that the piece lacks any lining save for her black under-garments. She shifts, revealing a dangerous slit crawling up her thigh. The effect leaves an interested onlooker with the knowl-edge of exactly what they're missing out on.

"Jesus Christ," I huff, heat crawling up my neck.

"Remember what I said about forgiving you if you helped me pack up?" Lucy asks, still gawking.

"Yeah?"

"I take it back, so long as you take her home."

"You're a fuckin' saint, Lu."

"Don't give me too much credit," Facing me, she begins walking backward toward Toni. "If you fumble this, I'm shooting my shot." She winks.

Toni meets Lucy's enthusiastic embrace without hesitation.

"Did you make this?" She asks, holding Lucy at arm's length.

Lucy's chest piece really is an incredible work of art. The front is a metal sternum and ribcage, each bone connected to the whole with delicate links of handmade chain, while individual vertebrae hang down the back.

"Of course!" Lucy spins, giving Toni a 360 view.

"She does know it's unfair to suck up all the talent in the room, right?" Toni asks me.

"She knows. Just doesn't care."

"It's not my fault I'm incredible," Lucy says over her shoulder before turning her attention to a potential customer.

"Speaking of incredible." I indicate Toni's entire being. "How am I supposed to focus on the show?"

A slow grin makes her dimple pop, and my knees shake. "Maybe I don't want you to focus on the show."

Given half a chance, this woman might undo me.

I spend the rest of the night trying and failing to keep my hands to myself.

When we grab our drinks at the bar, they wander to Toni's waist, pulling her against me. At our table, they reach for the soft expanse of her thigh, giving a greedy squeeze here and there. When my arm makes its way across her shoulders, her hand finds mine, fingers tangling casually.

The only thing that could coax me to relinquish the connection for a moment is Jac choosing Toni for an impressive lap dance during their already fantastic performance. As they finish, they grace me with a knowing wink that seems to echo Lucy's earlier warning.

Don't fumble this.

When they return to the stage, I grab hold of the back of Toni's harness, pulling her against me gently.

"Jealous?" She whispers into my ear. The puff of breath makes me tingle all over.

"Nah." I let my lips graze her ear lobe, feeling more than a little smug at the way her body reacts. "Just making sure you remember who you're coming home with." I drag a finger across the soft curve of her jaw, letting my thumb barely graze her bottom lip. "If you want," I add.

Toni's eyes burn. "Oh, I want."

I steal a brief kiss. "Good."

CHAPTER 14
Toni

Despite the temptation, Cillian and I display an impressive amount of self-control throughout the evening. No one could call us chaste, but we do make it through the entire show without slinking off to a secluded corner of the venue. In fact, we even manage to linger long enough after the closing number to congratulate Jac on an incredible performance and greet an acceptable number of people.

This does mean that by the time we make it to Cillian's car, I am considering the merits of forgoing any extracurriculars in lieu of fucking in his backseat like teenagers. However, I remain strong. Not for any sensible reason like not wanting to get caught. No, my self-control is rooted solely in knowing—based on several blush-inducing text exchanges—Cillian would make the wait worth it.

The thought of what the evening may hold does little to keep my hips from lifting desperately when his fingers slide under the hem of my panties.

He chuckles, the low rumble sending a little shock up my spine. "Someone is eager."

Taking advantage of his focus on the road, I reach over,

feeling the hard outline of his own impatience. "I'm not the only one who's eager," I say. His cock pulses against my hand for a brief moment before he grabs my wrist in a firm grip, moving my hand to my lap, holding it there.

"I hope you enjoyed that. Because, to me, it seems like someone needs to learn how to keep her hands to herself." He kisses my knuckles. "Put your hands under your thighs until we get home." The command in his voice is so delicious, I want to glut myself on it.

The rest of the drive is torment. He continues to tease me, a kiss to my neck, fluttering touches to my thigh, tracing the shell of my ear with one finger. When we pull into his drive, I almost fling myself from the car, mad with the need of some kind of release.

As if reading my mind, he pulls the keys from the ignition and orders me to stay put.

"Anything you want to discuss before we go upstairs?" He asks as he opens my door.

"No," I say with full confidence. We'd gone over any necessary boundaries in our texts. He tilts his head a little, waiting. "No, sir," I amend.

"That's better," he hums, grinning with satisfaction. I take his offered hand and step out of the car. "I'll get your bag, and you keep your hands behind your back until I tell you otherwise. Understood?"

I nod, clasping my hands obediently behind my back.

"Words." The stern tone makes my pulse drop from behind my ribs to between my thighs.

"Yes, sir."

Cillian motions for me to lead the way to his attic-level room, and I feel his attention—and my calves—burning the whole way up.

At the foot of the bed, he takes hold of the back strap of my harness, drawing me to a stop. Holding me in place, he traces the high neck of my dress before loosely wrapping his fingers around my throat, tilting my head back onto his shoulder.

The contrast of his rough palm and the cool texture of his rings against my skin is delicious.

His lips barely graze my ear as he says, "Tell me your safe word, Toni."

I shiver. "Hurricane."

"Thank you." He kisses my temple.

I drink him in as he comes to stand before me.

Tall and broad, Cillian cuts an intimidating image without much effort on his part. But it's the way he softens his edges that I find irresistibly compelling. The loose fit of his sheer button-up, the smudge of black making the green of his eyes stand out even more, his silver manicure.

As he traces my bottom lip with his thumb, my tongue flits out, hungry for the salt of his skin. Taking that as an invitation, he slips it into my mouth. I tease the digit with my tongue, delighted at the way his nostrils flare as he tries to take a steadying breath.

With visible effort, he drags his eyes from the moisture he left on my lips to meet my eyes. "Take my rings off."

Without thinking, I reach out to do as he says.

Grinning wickedly, he grabs both my wrists. "Did I say you could use your hands, doll?"

My body tingles. "No, sir."

He guides my hands back to their previous location. The action brings him close enough that I can breathe in his scent this time, a piney, musky fragrance and a touch of tobacco from his cigarettes. My mouth waters.

"Now," he says, index finger brushing over my lips. "Take them off."

I wrap my lips around the first ring. He pulls away, holding his hand out to receive it. I let it fall into his palm. We repeat the process for all of his rings, the taste of salt and metal and desire coating my tongue.

"Very good." He slips the rings into his pocket as he pulls me in for a kiss.

We hadn't kissed like this since that night on my porch, the same night he'd placed his wager. It's the kind of kiss that overwhelms everything. I can't say I forgot how good it felt to kiss this man; I'd thought about it far too often for that to be true, but I had begun to wonder if I'd blown it out of proportion. After all, the first time I'd been painfully hard up after several months of self-imposed celibacy, and the next I'd been pleasantly drunk.

But no. I hadn't. If anything, I'd undersold it.

My body melts into his, the missive to keep my hands to myself lost. I take hold of his shirt, pulling the soft chiffon into a death grip.

Gently, he tugs my hands away, holding them against my thighs. "Guess I'm gonna have to do something about these hands, huh?" He asks, panting.

"Guess so." I wiggle my fingers.

His rumble of laughter makes gooseflesh rise over my whole body. "Alright, then."

Cillian repositions me a bit to make room for the chest he slides from under his bed. My eyes pop at the delightful collection of tricks and toys. A bevy of fun to be had, though, as I anticipated, there isn't a single impact tool present. Pain, he'd said, wasn't something he enjoyed dabbling in. Pleasure though-

He closes the chest, having found what he wanted, and pushes it back under the bed.

"Hold this." He presses a bell into my palm before binding my hands to the front of my harness with bondage tape. Each movement of his hands displays a practiced proficiency that makes comfort and excitement sing through my veins.

When he's satisfactorily dealt with the issue of my wandering hands, he grabs a thick fleece blanket from the foot of his bed, laying it on the floor before him. "Kneel."

It isn't just the effortlessness of the command that sends me to my knees so fast a better woman might be ashamed. I'd mentioned, cheekily but sincerely, that I felt slighted he'd gotten to taste me last time, but I hadn't had the pleasure. Clearly, he'd paid attention and intended to fix this imbalance.

"The bell?" I ask giving it a little ring.

Cillian looks down at me, a wolfish smile crinkling the corners of his eyes. "Your mouth will be too busy for your safe word, I'm afraid." He unbuckles his belt. "Eyes up here," he says, the sound of a repressed laugh coloring his words.

I blush furiously, realizing I'd fixated on his cock as he freed it from his pants. In my defense, it's a thing of beauty. I felt the echoes of him for damn near two days after the last time.

He takes my jaw in a firm but gentle grip, ensuring my eyes remain on his face. "If you need me to stop for any reason, you ring that bell. Understood?"

"Yes, sir."

"Good girl." His hand slides to cradle the back of my head. "Open for me." I do, tongue out and ready. "Keep your eyes on me." I nod.

Cillian slides his cock between my lips until he taps the back of my throat. I gag against him, but he holds me in place for a moment before pulling back halfway. His heavy lashes flutter with pleasure as smug satisfaction makes me smile despite the mouthful.

Our eyes meet, and he takes my mouth with abandon.

I love it. Love the feeling of being possessed by him, love the way there isn't room for anything else in my skull beyond keeping my eyes right where he wants them, no matter what.

Every growl and groan that falls from his beautiful mouth sends shivers across my shoulders and down my spine.

"You like this, baby doll?" He asks, voice breathy. "You like me using that pretty mouth?" Unable to answer with words, I moan with satisfaction. "Fuck," he huffs.

I feel a shudder run through him just before his fingers dig into my hair, pulling my head back suddenly.

As I catch my breath, he drops to one knee. With a tenderness that makes my chest ache, he cradles my face, using a small towel he'd had waiting on the edge of the bed to wipe the moisture from my chin and cheeks.

"You ok?" He asks, eyes moving from my mouth to my eyes.

I swallow. "Very ok."

"Good." He kisses me softly at first, but when I eagerly respond, he doesn't hold back.

Finally, he slides a hand between my thighs. I feel rather than see him smile with satisfaction when he finds me utterly soaked.

"All this," he presses three fingers against the wet fabric, "and I've hardly touched you."

Cillian grabs the back strap of my harness, forcing me to arch back and look up at him. "Do you want me to touch you?" Distracting me, his fingers tease as he kisses my neck. "Answer me, Toni." He catches my earlobe in his teeth. I suck in a breath. "Do you want me to touch you?"

"Yes," I answer. "Yes, sir. Please, sir."

He pulls my panties to the side. A low sound rises from my chest as he slides in one finger, then another. Slowly, he works me open for him, his eyes never leaving mine.

My breath quickens with his pace. A steady increase until he's fucking me with his fingers so forcefully the only thing keeping me upright is his hold on my harness.

His thumb grazes my swollen clit, his fingers pulsing against my front wall as he thrusts.

My muscles tense. My lungs burn.

"Cillian," I manage between gasping breaths, clenching down on him.

"Breathe," he instructs. "In." I do. "Out." I exhale a moan. "That's it. Come for me, baby doll."

I shudder, head falling back as I come.

"I think we can do better than that," he says softly into my ear.

"Cillian," I whimper, already feeling another orgasm building.

"Give it to me," he demands. And I do. "Another."

I shake my head. "I ca—I don't—"

"Yes, you can," he says gently. "Breathe." I drag in one shaky breath, and another, the expansion of my lungs seeming to make room for more pleasure in my body. "That's my girl."

"Cilli—I—" I just shake my head. Words failing.

I'm pure electricity—every nerve-ending singing. Every synapse is snapping for the dopamine, adrenaline, and serotonin he's flooding my body with.

It's incredible. It's invigorating. It is too fucking much.

I begin to pull back.

Cillian rests his forehead against mine. "Don't run away from me." The green of his irises is almost eclipsed by the black of his pupils. "I want you to let go, Toni. Trust that I've got you." I stop my retreat. "I've got you." Something in me gives way. All resistance fleeing. "Come."

I barely make a sound as I come entirely undone.

Tears of pleasure trail down my cheeks. Cillian pulls me against his chest, sliding his soaked fingers from me. I already ache with their absence.

"You did so good, doll," he purrs. He presses a kiss to my curls. "Now, breathe deep for me, please."

I inhale his smell. Nuzzling into the soft fabric of his shirt. Only one single thought in the fuzz of my consciousness.

"Cillian?" I ask, my voice hoarse.

"Hmm?"

I sit up to look at him. "I'd like to touch you. I . . . I need to touch you. Please."

His smile is so soft as he kisses my forehead and nods. With steady hands, he slices the bondage tape with a pocket knife.

I flex my fingers for only a second before immediately reaching for his hair. Carefully, I remove Lucy's hairpiece and tug the tie free.

The strands framing his face are a bit more salt than pepper, I realize. They make the flashes of silver in his beard and dark brows shine a little brighter.

I wander down his neck and shoulders to his torso, working his buttons free with trembling fingers, and slide the shirt off. His chest rises a little faster as I explore, tracing the curve of the black-bird's wing, the sparkle of the silver chain. When the tips of my fingers graze the raised flesh on his left side, he grabs my hand, using it as an excuse to pull us both to our feet.

Turning my back to him, he unbuckles the harness, letting it fall to the floor in a heap of leather and brass. Everything else follows until I'm bare.

"Get on the bed." He gestures to the plush nest of pillows. I crawl into the welcoming softness as he rids himself of his remaining clothes.

Kneeling on the bed, he studies me. I revel in the attention, letting my hands explore the softness of my body as he watches.

"Beautiful girl." He traces the gentle curve of my belly, sinking his fingers into the soft flesh with clear appreciation.

I reach over to the nightstand, sliding open the drawer I

remember him using last time, pleased to find the condoms easily accessible. His breath is ragged as I stroke him before sliding it on.

Bracing himself on the headboard with one hand, the other beside my head. He holds my gaze as he sinks in. I arch up to meet him, my breath catching.

"You take me so well, baby doll." He kisses me as he works himself in and out so slowly it would drive me crazy if it didn't feel so fucking good. Still . . .

"Cillian?" I breathe his name between kisses.

"Yes."

"I . . ." My words fail.

I had been able to ask for what I wanted, what I needed, moments ago. But something about the intimacy of this moment trips me up. Memories of times I'd asked David—a person who, theoretically, knew me better than this man—for what I needed, being met with a sneer or outright disgust, threaten to bubble to the surface.

Cillian's expression softens. He kisses me tenderly, continuing that deliciously languid pace. "Tell me how you want it, Toni."

That's all it takes to banish those memories.

"I want you to fuck me so hard I forget my own name."

He grins wickedly, tongue wetting his lips. "You think you can handle that, baby?"

"Yes. Yes, sir."

With one final rough kiss, he pulls out and flips me over. I let out a small surprised noise as he grabs my hips, pulling my ass up.

One hand grips my hair, pressing my cheek to the mattress. His chest presses against my back as he leans close to say, "Just remember, doll, you asked for this."

I don't have time to respond.

Cillian slams into me and I scream into the mattress, my fists balling into the duvet.

This man gives me exactly what I asked for and so much more, fucking me with feral abandon. The sound of our bodies meeting is rivaled only by the cries of pleasure he pulls from me.

"Gonna come already, baby?"

I can't manage a word, I simply come. Behind me, Cillian rumbles, "Fuck yes."

He wraps his hand around my throat, pulling my body up against him. "Another. Give me another, Toni."

Time falls away. Cillian switches between his cock, his fingers, and his mouth, drawing orgasm after orgasm from me until I'm dizzy with it.

"I wanna see that pretty face." He turns me over once more, the pendant around his neck brushing my cheek. As he sinks back into me, he kisses me slowly, each measured thrust sending shock waves of pleasure through me.

His pace ticks up. "Toni. Doll, I-"

I lock my legs around him, matching his pace and pulling his mouth to mine, devouring the sounds of his release.

CHAPTER 15
Cillian

I PRESS MY LIPS TO TONI'S DAMP FOREHEAD, FEELING small tremors rolling through her.

"So good, baby doll," I whisper into the shell of her ear. "You were so good for me." I sit up on my elbows.

Her arms shoot around me. "Don't go." Her voice is small, distant.

"I'm not going anywhere, doll." I kiss her swollen lips gently, rubbing small circles against her temple.

Her pupils are blown wide, expression airy. "Come back to me."

"I'm right here," she whispers.

"No," I coo. "You're somewhere in outer space, baby doll." I cover her face with light kisses.

She laughs softly.

"What?" I ask, littering more kisses over her neck and chest.

"You're sweet," she sighs.

"Only sometimes."

"Liar," she quickly steals a kiss of her own. Her grip on me loosens, and I lift off her, falling onto my back.

"Come here." I hold an arm open. She eagerly curls into my side, head on my chest.

Another small tremor rolls through her, and I take her hand in mine, kissing her knuckles. "Are you ok, Toni?"

"Mmhmm," she nods.

"Look at me." I tilt her chin up. "You sure?"

Her eyes are sleepy but a little less hazy than before. "I'm blissed out but very much ok." She cups my cheek. "Are you?"

My heart gives a squeeze at the question. I've been in enough situations where my partner didn't ask. Which, considering I typically chose the Dominant position, was fine. But it felt good to be asked.

I nod. "As long as you let me take care of you a little, I'll be just fine."

She smiles. "This is the one situation where I won't fight that."

"Why does that not shock me?"

She feigns an offended face, her mouth open, aghast. I can't help but take the chance to kiss her again, tasting her. I pull back before we're both breathless and before my cock writes a check the rest of me is too damn tired to cash.

True to her word, Toni lets me lavish her with attention in the shower and towel off every inch of her perfect body.

Much like music, the power exchange afforded by this dynamic does something to quiet my internal storm. Something about another person being willing to trust me with their body, their pleasure, their care after the fact, lets me put down some of the weight of my own distrust of myself. If someone else trusted me in this way, how dare I not afford myself the same, at least in these moments?

Back in bed, I pull Toni tight into my side, savoring the warmth of her soft body beside me.

"By the way," she says sleepily, "these sheets are incredible."

I chuckle low. "They better be for what they cost."

"A man who splurges on bed linens, I like it."

"A man who's willing to do damn near anything to try and get a good night of sleep every once in a while." She presses her lips to my chest, just above my heart.

"Do they help?"

I shrug. "They don't hurt."

"That's good." She yawns, snuggling into me.

"Mhm." After a few minutes, I feel her breathing grow steady. "Sleep well, Toni."

✧

Sunlight floods through the window when I finally crack my eyes open.

The clock on my nightstand must be broken. No way in hell it was almost ten. Except my phone also insists it's 9:53 am.

I couldn't remember the last time I'd slept this late. Wallow in bed? Sure. But actually sleep? Years.

Toni is still sound asleep, looking serene with the side of her face against the pillow, facing me, red curls slipping out from her messy bun. My hand moves without thought to tuck a loose curl away from her face.

God, she practically glows. Radiant, like some precious thing from a better place than any I'd ever know.

I swallow hard, writing the static growing in my belly off as hunger.

Pressing my lips to her temple, I gently stroke my hand down the bare skin of her back. "Toni," I whisper into her ear. "Wake up, doll."

She lets loose a small sleepy sound before curling up into me, the button of her nose nuzzling into my chest.

"I'll make you coffee," I try to bribe.

"Hmm, lots of coffee," her voice is sleep-rough and lovely.

"As much as you want."

"What time is it?"

"Late, almost ten o'clock."

"You're a morning person, aren't you?" She accuses.

"Guilty."

"Gross," she whines.

I chuckle. "Too many years in the military, doll."

"Sounds awful."

"Wouldn't recommend it." I kiss her temple and down her neck, earning me a small giggle. She cracks one eye open, the sun catching the strands of honey and auburn, making them look like some earthy gemstone. "There she is."

She grumbles, sitting up, hair wild.

"How do you feel?" I ask, running a finger down the tumble of peonies over her shoulder.

"Great." She pauses, considering. "Sore, but good sore."

"Good." I pull her toward me, unable to go another moment without kissing her.

"Coffee?" She asks the moment we stop.

I laugh. "Doll, you may have a real problem."

"There's only a problem if you lied about making me coffee."

"I would never." I hold my hand out to her, tugging her from the bed to lead her to the rack of robes tucked behind a paper screen.

"Take your pick." I grab a dark green silk number, slipping it on while I watch her run her hands over the myriad of fabrics and prints.

"I thought you didn't drink coffee," she says, pulling the robe I'd laid out for her the first time she was here off its hanger.

"I don't." We make our way downstairs. "But I'm not a

heathen. I always have it." Which isn't entirely a lie. I try to keep some on hand, but when it was clear she'd possibly be here again, I did go and buy some from Jac. Just in case.

"This is possibly the coolest kitchen I've ever seen." She says as we step into the bottom floor of the house.

"It was built in 1865. Somehow it never got gutted by past owners." I explain as I get the kettle going for both of us and assemble her pour-over.

"When did your . . . uncle?"

"Yup." I nod, leaning against the counter.

"Buy this place?"

"In 1980. The neighborhood was still pretty rough. He got it for practically nothing compared to what it's worth now."

A mischievous smirk teases that dimple out as I hand her two mugs. "But he did not buy it with mob money, right?" She teases, clearly referring back to my quip about not everyone in Boston being in the mob.

I bring the kettle and pour over to the table. "I didn't say that."

"So he did."

"Didn't say that either." I pour water over the grounds, briefly remembering with a pang doing this for Kevin every damn morning.

"Don't be a tease." She bats at my arm. I raise a brow, leaning back in my chair to give her a look.

I catch her hand and kiss her knuckles. "All I know is my uncle Bobby is a very gruff, very gay accountant with very good stories." I pour her coffee.

"He sounds amazing."

"He is pretty fantastic." Which was an understatement.

I owed my uncle more than just the roof over my head. He'd been the one I came out to as a confused altar boy at twelve. He pulled some strings to make sure both Lucy and I got easy sentences when we got caught up in the car theft situation that changed the trajectory of my life. Most importantly, he was the one who made sure the people closest to me had and knew how to administer Naloxone. Without that last bit, I wouldn't be here.

"Ok, another question."

I chuckle, leaning her into me. "Shoot."

"What's with the robe collection?"

"I . . . I, uh—" This was the part of meeting new people I hated, the constant mental gymnastics it took to decide exactly what to tell them and how. "Honestly?"

Toni slides her hand over mine, slowing the steady beat I didn't even realize my fingers were tapping on the table. "Always."

My pulse slows.

I tangle my fingers with hers. "After I . . ." *was blown to shit* feels too harsh, "got injured. I was in the hospital for a while. My mom decided I needed a better robe than what they gave me, so she brought me a few. They were reminders of home when that's the only thing I wanted." I clear my throat. "After, they just kept finding their way to me. Gifts, thrift stores, wherever. Just stuck." I chose to leave out that they make me feel less like shit on days I can't bring myself to put on real clothes.

She squeezes my hand. "I promise not to spill coffee on this one."

That tugs a rough laugh from me. "I'd appreciate that. Getting silk cleaned is a pain in the ass." I sip my tea. "Do you have any collections—or hoards, as Oliver calls them?"

"Hold on," she leans back from me, looking at her robe, ignoring my question. "Did you say silk?"

"Yes?"

"Oof. I knew this was too high class for me."

"Nah." I kiss her exposed clavicle. "It's perfect."

"Best not risk it, though." I almost fight her as she pushes me away to stand, but I let her go.

Toni unties the robe, allowing the fabric to flow slowly down, revealing each spectacular curve inch by inch. All thoughts of protest or the question I'd asked flee my mind.

CHAPTER 16
Toni

"WHAT'S IN IT?" I ASK MY BROTHER, BALANCING THE phone between my ear and shoulder as I carry the package inside.

"No clue," he says absently.

I give it a gentle shake. "So it could be a bomb?"

"It was addressed to you."

"Anthrax?"

"That came in envelopes."

"A lot of anthrax."

He huffs an exasperated sigh. "If you want me to open your mail, I will."

"God no." I drop onto the couch, grabbing my keys off my box-styled coffee table to hack at the tape. "Far too risky." A smell that once meant something like home wafts from the box the moment I pry it open.

"Everything alright?" Ben asks. "Toni?" He follows up when I don't immediately answer.

"Yeah." I swallow hard. "It's . . . Just something I forgot about. No big deal. Thanks for sending it. I gotta go." My words trip over themselves as I rush to hang up.

My name, in David's precise hand, is the only word on the front of the card sitting on top of the mystery package's wrapped contents.

I've never hated the look of my own name more.

A slight tremor moves through me as I open the card.

Stop being so dramatic, I chastise myself. It's just a package. Not a threat. Not something to cause me to freak out.

> *Toni,*
>
> *I was cleaning and found some little things that were yours or made me think of you and wanted you to have them.*
>
> *I hope they remind you of all the good parts of us, all the parts I know I don't want to lose forever.*
>
> *Love,*
> *David*

It may not be a cause to freak out, but anger seems reasonable. The fury doesn't have time to sink in before Lucy texts me, letting me know she's here.

Fuck. I swallow hard, trying to force a deep breath and failing.

I had been looking forward to this girls' night with Lucy all week—shopping, dinner, drinks, and a screening of *Romeo + Juliet* at the indie theatre. The absolute last person I was willing to let ruin this was David. And yet . . . my mouth goes dry.

After a few minutes without a response, Lucy calls me, pulling me from my frozen state.

If I don't answer, she's likely going to knock. If she knocks, she may ask to come inside. If she asks to come in, I'd have to find a better reason to tell her no than my place being a disaster zone.

I wish the box had been anthrax.

"Hey." I grimace at the way my voice cracks.

"Hey . . . You ok?"

I softly clear my throat. "Yeah. Dehydrated." My light tone sounds like such bullshit. "I'll be right out."

Tossing the box aside, I slip into my sneakers while trying to physically shake the tension out of my shoulders. The box could be future me's problem. Current me was going to have a fun night.

✧

"WHAT'S WEIGHING ON YOU?" LUCY ASKS AS SHE inspects a deck of tarot cards at the bookstore.

The question catches me off guard. "Nothing," I answer reflexively. I thought I'd been putting on a pretty good front so far. Lucy side-eyes me so hard it's a wonder I don't fall over.

Crossing her arms over her chest, she leans against the wall. "Let's get this out of the way: My two best and oldest friends are reformed Catholic boys, and one had the audacity to become a Marine. I can clock emotional suppression at 100 paces." She slides a pointed nail under the plastic covering the cards. "So either tell me or . . ."

With a Cheshire-like grin, she pulls the deck free, shuffling it with long, agile fingers. "The cards can tell me for you."

I can't help but laugh. "Did you just commit to buying those purely for the bit?"

"Maybe." She winks, continuing to shuffle. "Seriously. Something is up."

I lean against the wall beside her and sigh as I slide to the floor. Lucy does the same, shoulder pressed against mine.

"My ex sent me a box of—I don't actually know what any

of it is. I opened it right before you got to my place, and I didn't look."

"I take it you're not exactly on good terms with this ex?"

"God, no. We're supposed to be no contact . . . until December anyway. But he keeps fucking finding ways around that." I pick at the distressing on my jeans. "Like this package. The card said he hoped the contents would help me remember the good times or something."

"Fuck that!" Lucy stands so fast I'm almost startled. "Come on. Change of plans." I take her offered hand and let her lead me to the counter.

"Change to what exactly?"

"I'm buying these," she holds up the cards, "and we're going back to your place and—"

"We can't go to my place," I blurt.

"That's not suspicious at all."

"It's . . .I haven't finished unpacking and—"

"Oh, that's fine," Lucy waves me off and buys the cards. "You just need to get that box."

Despite my best efforts, including bribery, Lucy refuses to tell me what this mysterious new plan for our evening is. I finally accept not knowing until we pull into a dimly lit industrial park.

"Are we about to commit a crime?" I ask only half kidding.

She laughs, getting out of the car. "Nope. But we are going to play with fire."

Sure, you should likely question something like that, but to be honest, setting some shit on fire sounds kind of amazing at the moment. I follow her to a large padlocked metal garage door without any further questions.

"Welcome to my lair," she says, lifting the door with a clatter.

Lucy's metalworking studio gives equal parts biker femme and medieval blacksmith. Pallets covered in rugs, blankets, and pillows fill one corner to form a sort of DIY sectional next to a well-loved drum set. On the other side of the space, three motorcycles sit uncovered. The back half is all business, with anvils and kilns and tools for her to work her magic.

She tosses her bag onto the pallet-couch and pulls two ciders from the mini fridge. "What's your favorite comfort food?" She asks, passing me one.

"Mexican," I say, taking a deep drink.

She nods, looking at her phone. "Food allergies?"

"None?"

"Fab." Her fingers fly across the screen. "Food will be here in thirty which is enough time for us to get started."

"Doing what?"

She tosses a pair of thick black gloves at me. I barely catch them without dropping my drink. "Purging."

When the tacos arrive, the delivery driver looks at us with more than a little suspicion. In his defense, it is a valid reaction to seeing two women around a metal barrel in an empty industrial park at sundown.

"That man thinks we're dumping a body," I laugh as I pull the gloves off.

"We are." She begins pulling out food containers, setting them on one of the rugs we dragged out. "The corpse of your relationship with this asshole." She holds up the card, sneering at it for at least the third time. "'*I hope they remind you of all the good parts,*'" she mocks. "Who writes shit like this?"

"Fucking David." I take a bite of a swoon-worthy pupusa and pull out a small rectangle wrapped in black tissue paper.

"How long were you together?" Lucy asks.

"Almost three years."

"What made you end it?"

I turn the rectangle over in my hands. "We were on the same page about kids and marriage for a bit at the beginning.

But when our—or rather *his*—friends started doing those things, he changed his mind. I didn't."

"Damn."

"Yeah." Once again, I feel something in me freeze over, the wrapped package feeling impossibly heavy.

"Here's what we're gonna do." Lucy takes the package from me, replacing it with a taco. "You're gonna eat. I'm gonna unwrap this shit. And you can tell me why he's a dick for sending each one of them."

"He's not some kind of monster. Just . . ." I shrug. "Maybe he actually thought I'd want these things."

Lucy gives me an understanding look. "Anyone who ignores your boundaries like this isn't doing it for you. They're doing it for them. He might not be a monster, but he's making it very clear he doesn't respect you."

Was that it?

"What's the story behind this?" She unwraps the rectangle, revealing a journal he'd bought me when we first started dating. He was always mad I didn't use it for my 'doodles', but I explained that while it was lovely, its thin paper and rigid spine made it hard to sketch in.

Venting to Lucy is far more cathartic than I could have anticipated. And as it turns out, she isn't wrong, damn near every single item David sent feels centered around him more than *us*. Like the framed photo from our trip to Mexico with his family. In it, we're smiling and sun kissed, but I remember crying in the shower because he'd let his mom fat shame me the whole trip, justifying her behavior as concern. When the fire turns the photo and frame into a pile of goo and ash, it feels like letting go of all those *pesky pounds* she was so concerned about.

"In front of everyone?" Lucy asks, shocked and clearly disgusted, when I tell her about David's misguided proposal.

"Everyone. And they all let me know I was the would-befiancée who stole Christmas." She hands me a small jewelry box, one of the few things I had from my very unhappy childhood. In the barrel it goes; watching the wood catch fire feels deliriously good. "His mother actually called me crying about it."

"Oh, for fuck's sake!" She grabs a cookbook.

I didn't hate cooking, but it wasn't my favorite thing, and he'd made it clear that the expectation was for me to use it when he "gifted" it to me.

Lucy hands it to me. "Here's to leaving that toxic shit in the past."

My heart twists. "Again. He wasn't some abusive fuck. I never would have stayed if he were." My dad gave me very little, but he did leave me with that lesson. "We were just incompatible people who tried too hard to make it work."

She sighs, plopping down on the rug. "Someone doesn't have to lay hands on you to be an abusive fuck."

I know that. Had said nearly the same to others before. So why did her saying it knock the wind out of me?

A million tiny moments play through my mind as I watch the paper curl in the fire.

"Sorry, that was . . . Sometimes my mouth moves faster than my brain."

"No." I shake my head, pulling my focus from the flames to join her on the rug. "I think I needed to hear that."

Lucy settles one gloved hand over mine, and we appreciate the glow from the fire in comfortable silence until her phone pings.

"Shit," she says, one finger from her glove between her teeth.

"Everything ok?" I ask, nudging my hair from my face.

She grimaces. "Not really. It's an SOS from Cillian."

"What?" My pulse rockets.

"Oh, he's fine, technically, just the bar is short-staffed and they're slammed." She picks up the fire extinguisher. "Would you be too mad if we continue the ritual later? He never calls me and Oliver in to help, so it's gotta be wicked busy."

Relief renders me practically giddy. "A rain check is absolutely fine." I tug the gloves off and gather our trash as she gives the embers of my past a good dousing. "Think they could use an extra body?"

Lucy looks at me, surprise evident on her face. "Are you offering?"

"Yeah?" I help her roll the rug up and carry it inside. "I know my way around a POS, and I'm an excellent busser."

"You're hired."

CHAPTER 17
Cillian

"Hey!" Oliver says. "Where do you need me?"

"Thank fuck," I huff. "We're dangerously close to running out of glasses."

"On it," he says, already grabbing a tub.

A burst of laughter filters down from the side of the bar Dad has been holding down for the past hour. I lay my hands on the back counter and allow my head to hang for a few precious breaths.

"Show's not over yet, boy," Dad says, reaching for a bottle by my head.

"I know."

He nudges me with an elbow. "You alright?"

"Yeah." I manage a half-assed smile alongside the half-assed truth. Maybe together they'd equal something believable.

It wasn't that the bar was packed. Or even that we were short. Both happened on the same night plenty of times in the past. It's just that those times hadn't been preceded by my cousins coming close to blows in the kitchen—their yelling loud enough that the whole bar heard. I'd sent them both home for different reasons. Ginelle was, justifiably, too worked up and Joey too fucked up to finish their shifts.

The worst part was that it just had to happen on a night Michael was covering bar back duties. I maybe could've gotten away with keeping the situation quiet, given Joey one last chance, but as it stood, I was fresh out of free passes.

"The cavalry has arrived. Nobody panic!" Lucy announces as she steps behind the bar.

"Took you long enough," Oliver ribs as he grabs another tub of glassware.

"Shouldn't you be on a date?" Lucy asks him as she passes a half apron to—

"Toni?" My brain cannot comprehend why she's here, why Lucy's handing her an apron, or why she's putting it on.

"That is my name." She flashes that dimpled grin at me.

"I *was* on a date," Oliver answers Lucy's question. "And trust me, I'd rather be elbows deep in stale beer."

"Woof," Lucy says, eyes focused on the table map she's sketching on a piece of receipt paper.

"Understatement," Oliver says as he backs into the kitchen door. "Thought you two were going to a movie?" He asks Lucy and Toni.

"We ended up burning things instead," Lucy says, as if it's the most normal thing to do on a Thursday night. "Ok, so it's pretty easy. Table numbers—" She begins to explain to Toni.

"Hold on," I interrupt. Without further explanation, I gently take Toni's arm and pull her into the kitchen.

"Fuck outta my kitchen unless you're cooking or cleaning!" Michael declares. He switches his focus from the grill to me and Toni. "Oh! Hi. You're . . . Toni?"

She nods. "I am."

"Michael," he introduces himself with a nod. "Nice to meet you. But—"

"Get the fuck out of your kitchen?" she finishes with a good-natured tone.

"Please and thank you!" He tosses over his shoulder as he flips a burger.

"For fucks sake," I grumble leading Toni into the small walk-in.

"I should get out there—"

"Why are you here?" I ask as soon as the door closes.

She cocks an eyebrow. "Lucy said it was a 911 situation. Figured that meant all hands on deck."

"Not yours."

She holds her hands up, examining them. "What's wrong with them?"

I sigh, enveloping her hands in mine. They're soft—the fingers petite and supple—beautiful things. "Nothing at all. But you don't need to do this. You don't—"

Toni lifts our hands, quickly kissing my knuckles, causing my stomach to fill with static. "I know. But I want to." She doesn't wait for my response, just frees her hands and leaves me momentarily stunned in the walk-in.

"You ever wait tables, darlin'?" Dad asks when Toni steps back behind the bar, me hot on her heels.

"Yes, sir," she nods, studying Lucy's map. "Since I was twelve."

"Excellent!" Dad looks over at me. "We got people waiting, son. Let's go!"

"Right." I nod, absently watching Toni grab a couple plates, hopping into the fray without hesitation.

"Don't you have work to do?" She teases as she walks past me.

"Yeah, we're not here so you can slack," Oliver says as he brings clean glasses back.

"Oh, fuck off," I say, rolling my eyes even as a smile pulls at my lips.

To her credit, Toni catches on fast. Within thirty minutes, she's running food and clearing tables like she's been here for years. I try to send her home when we close the kitchen, but she shrugs me off, joining Lucy to knock out the side work for the last hour or so.

As much as I hate that she felt obligated to be here, I'm grateful for the extra hands, and strangely happy that those hands belong to her.

"Sweet Lulu, lock that door before anyone straggles in here!" Dad bellows when the last patrons leave. He grabs a bottle of whiskey off the top shelf, lining up glasses for everyone.

"Get off that leg, boy," he instructs me as he pours.

"I'm f—."

"I wasn't askin'." Dad slides Oliver a shot as he hops onto a barstool. "Far as I know, my name's still the one on all the paperwork. Get out from behind my bar and sit your ass down. Now." His voice drops an octave with the last word.

"Dad voice!" Lucy, Oliver, and Michael all chorus.

By default, Mickey O'Sullivan was the non-confrontational sort. I could count on both hands the number of times he'd raised his voice at me or my brother. Even through the years of watching him run this place, I'd seen him end more bar fights with a joke or gentle word than a shout. That meant when he got stern, it was noticeable enough that the tone earned the moniker of "Dad voice" among the family.

He chuckles, passing Lucy and Toni their own shots.

I scoot the stool beside Toni over and rest an elbow on the bar.

"Stubborn ass," he grouches, passing me my drink.

I could admit that was true, but right now, I'm more worried about my leg deciding to clock out the moment I get off it when there were still closing duties to see to. "You raised me."

Dad chuckles. "That shite comes from your mother's side."

"I'm telling," Michael teases.

"And I'll call you a liar before God," Dad says.

Lucy leans over, saying to Toni in a stage whisper, "It comes from both sides. That's why they're like that."

"Hey!" Michael and I protest in unison.

Dad bellows one of his signature booming laughs. "You may be right, Lulu."

"Ha. Ha." Michael mocks. "One of us has a pregnant wife to get home to." He lifts his shot.

Dad nods. "Thank you to our friends for having our backs tonight. We'd have been cooked were it not for all of ya.

"Here's to cheating, stealing, fighting, and drinking.

"If you cheat, may you cheat death.

"If you steal, may you steal a woman's heart."

My eyes flick to Toni, who watches Dad deliver his toast with a soft smile.

"If you fight, may you fight for a brother.

"And if you drink, may you drink with me."

"Sláinte!" We chorus.

CHAPTER 18

Cillian

Hey. Just making sure you're ok?

REGRET BLAZES THROUGH ME THE MOMENT I HIT send.

Sure, Toni and I have been exchanging at least a text a day over the past month and a half or so, but that doesn't mean she owes me a text or a check in or anything.

But there was always the chance she wasn't okay. Maybe things had gone a bit too far the last time we'd been together. Yeah, that was almost a week ago, but sub drop could hit late sometimes, and I hate the thought that she could be feeling bad due to something I'd done.

I blow out a breath, setting the phone face down. She could just be busy. Possibly even busy with another person—

My stomach drops.

Stupid to care if she was. She should meet other people. It would be best if she met other people. She deserved that. Someone with less—

"You look like a caged animal," Michael says. He and

Ginelle stand in the office doorway, observing the mindless circuit I'd begun to pace around the bar.

"I—" My phone dings.

Ginelle taps into her track and field roots, moving at a lightning pace to grab my phone before I make it a few steps. "It's Toni," she taunts.

Michael grins, "What'd she say?"

"Give me that!" I try to pull it from her hands, but she darts behind my brother, who blocks my way into the office. "Michael. Move."

"It is so cute how you think you can intimidate me."

"Aww!" Ginelle says.

"Gin, give me my damn phone," I snarl over Michael's shoulder.

"She says she's sick."

Michael finally drops his arm, clearing the way for me to barrel into the office and reclaim my phone from Ginelle, who holds it over the desk for me. The screen is already open to Toni's text:

TONI

> Sorry, been a bit under the weather, which has made me slightly narcoleptic the past couple days.

"Remind me to change my password," I grumble, sinking onto the couch.

Ginelle laughs. "You've been saying that for years."

"Yeah, yeah." I wave her off as I type a response, only to erase it.

"That sucks. Tell her we hope she feels better." Michael hops onto the desk, facing me.

I nod absently, finally landing on the most basic response.

You don't need to apologize. Can I bring you anything?

TONI

I'm ok. Thank you, though.

I don't buy that for one second. The woman wasn't exactly an open book, but it didn't take much perception to clock that she wasn't a fan of asking for help.

My leg bounces as I consider. "Michael, remember how you owe me a shift?"

He groans. "Seriously? There's a game tonight."

"There's a game tonight," Ginelle mocks. "Baby."

Michael sneers at her before turning back to me. "You sure you wanna cash that in now?"

"As long as Camille doesn't need you." I wanted to be there for Toni, but not enough to pull my brother away from his pregnant wife.

"Nah," he hops from the desk, "she's got her book club tonight."

"Then yes, I'm cashing in that favor."

"Fine." He holds out his hand to shake.

"Thanks." I leverage his grip to pry myself from the couch.

"Oh. Have you invited Toni to Sunday supper yet?" Michael's question draws me up short, pausing my hand on the drawer with my wallet and keys.

"I think that's a no," Ginelle says.

Michael sighs. "Mom is mad she's the only one who hasn't met her."

"She can stay mad," I say, not looking at my brother or cousin as I grab my stuff.

"I will pay you $100 to say that to her face and let me watch," Ginelle bribes.

The thought almost makes me shiver. "I'd rather chew glass."

"You can't put her off forever," Michael says over his shoulder as he heads back behind the bar.

"I can try."

Michael just shakes his head in response as the door shuts behind him.

"Why don't you want Toni to meet Kitty?" The question once again catches me off guard, both because of Ginelle's surprising sincerity and my lack of a sensible answer.

It wasn't as if my mother were some tyrannical harpy. She could be a bit intense—unsurprising, given that she was the middle daughter of a large Italian family—and didn't share my dad's jovial nature. But my mother was kind, the 'feed the neighbors in tough times with gallons of Sunday sauce' brand of kind.

"We're just friends, Gin." That half-assed answer lands just as poorly as I thought it would.

"People let their *friends* meet their parents. Especially if they've already met one of them."

"She's probably moving in December anyway." I avoid looking at my cousin as I pull my denim jacket off the coat rack.

Still, I can feel Ginelle's eye roll as she says, "All the more reason to humor your mom." I don't respond. "But whatever. Your funeral."

"Don't bring lilies," I say as I open the door. "Too cliché."

⟡

I KNOCK ON TONI'S DOOR A LITTLE OVER AN HOUR later, arms loaded with bags of soup, meds, and snacks.

Whatever doubts and anxieties I'd been harboring around this mission flee once Toni cracks open the door. Her button nose is a painful shade of red while her typically rosy complexion is concerningly pallid. She stares up at me with a mix of shock, disbelief, and maybe a dash of horror.

"I've brought provisions." I lift both my arms, bags hanging from them. Admittedly, I may have gone overboard a little—or a lot.

"I see that." Her voice is rough. "But—" She casts a wary glance behind her.

"If you've already got someone—"

She scoffs, the sound turning into a cough. "Not unless you count the delivery drivers who've kept me alive." I feel a twinge of regret for not reaching out sooner. "It's just my place is . . ."

"Toni." Those big brown eyes flick back to me. "Do you think I give a damn what your apartment looks like? You're sick."

"Yeah. Let's blame that." She huffs a sigh, moving to the side to let me in.

If I didn't know better, I'd think this was the apartment of someone who recently moved in. Boxes still sit at the perimeter of the living room, one clearly serving as the coffee table. No art adorned the walls, though I clock several canvases in the dining room turned studio as Toni leads me to the kitchen.

She gestures for me to put the bags on the kitchen island. "You didn't need to bring all of this."

"I know." I take out two pints of chicken noodle soup from the deli. "Saucepan?" I ask.

"I can handle that." She takes the pints from me, setting them on the counter with a huff. "Seriously, you brought all this, you don't—" I catch her wrist before she can reach to unpack a single item. Her skin feels too warm and a bit clammy.

"Don't you dare."

She pulls away, hands settling on her hips. "I'm fine, Cillian."

"Really? So you're always burning up?"

She opens her mouth to argue, but instead of words, she coughs hard enough to make my own chest ache. I pull a water bottle from the drying rack beside the sink, filling it for her.

Once she catches her breath and downs a few sips, I cup her cheek, pulling her focus to me. "Here's what's going to happen. You're gonna take that water and sit down. I'm going to start heating some soup and bring you some meds. Ok?"

"But the saucepan," she croaks.

"I'm sure I can find it." She gives me a skeptical look.

"I'm not."

"Please, go sit the hell down before I carry you to the living room."

"Fine."

"Thank you."

Without Toni's help, it does take me longer than I antici- pate to locate the right size pan. Although seeing as it was still in a box under some Tupperware, I doubt she would've been able to find it any faster. I set the soup to warm on the stove, the comforting smell quickly filling the air.

If the location of the pan was any indication, there hasn't been much cooking going on in this kitchen since Toni moved in. Coffee prep, though? I shake my head at the significant portion of counter space taken up by one of those $300 drip coffee makers, a small espresso machine, and several accessories I can't name. With an impressive setup like this, I'm shocked she'd ever bother ponying up the $7 for a latte from Jac.

The cabinet above the collection reveals an equally impres- sive assortment of mugs, clearly curated over the years. I pick two and pull out the tea I'd brought. She'd balk, but I was fully prepared for that battle.

I unload the rest of my haul: a fresh baguette and a couple of salty-sweet baked goods from the same deli as the soup, meds, snacks, and . . . the silk at the bottom of the bag brushes against my fingertips, cool to the touch. I set that one aside for now and check on Toni.

I'd half expected to find her frantically unpacking a box or trying to order the artistic chaos of her studio space. But to my surprise, she's curled up in a nest of lush jewel-toned blankets on her blush pink couch. Right where I told her to be.

What isn't surprising is the mug of coffee clutched between her palms.

"Have you even had water today?" I ask. She looks up at me, the diffused light coming from the bay windows behind the couch making her red hair glow.

My heart and my lungs clatter together in my chest. Even in this state, she was a goddamn wonder.

"You saw me—"

"More than three sips?"

She shrugs, looking at her mug. "There's water in coffee."

I pluck the mug from her hands and replace it with the water bottle I sent in here with her. "Drink this."

She pouts. "I'm going to text Lucy and tell her you're being mean to me."

I smirk. "Do that and she'll be over here in five minutes." I pass her a box of cold medicine. "And if you think I'm bad, you've never seen Lucy in mom mode."

"That feels like a threat somehow."

"It will be if you keep fighting me." I point to the water. "Drink."

"I knew I shouldn't have let you in," she says after taking a sip.

"Can't take it back now." I grab an empty box of cold medicine and a few other things that could be tossed from the makeshift coffee table.

"Cillian," Toni says as sternly as she can manage. "Put the trash down."

"Toni," I mirror her tone. "Take your meds."

"I'm being serious, I don't need—"

"You didn't need to come work a whole shift at the bar—for free, mind you—but you did. So unless you want to be a hypocrite . . ."

She groans and falls over into her nest.

I laugh softly at her dramatics. "Friends take care of each other, right?" Setting the bits of trash aside, I coax her upright by her shoulders. "Right?"

"I guess."

"Good enough. Now, do you want to keep arguing with me, or would you like some soup?"

She sighs. "Will saying yes to soup get you out of my apartment?"

"It will certainly speed the process along."

"Soup it is," she concedes.

"Good." I plant a kiss on her warm forehead.

I bring her a small bowl with a bit of the baguette. "Don't worry about finishing it."

While she eats, I inspect what appears to be the only other furniture in the room, a console with a record player on it and two of those cube shelves filled with records.

"Holy shit." I run my fingers along the alphabetized tabs. "This is—"

"Too much. I know." There's a bitterness in her answer I don't like.

"I was going to say impressive." And I mean it. A collection like this takes years and dedication to build. I can't help but wonder who made her feel like it was a negative. "May I?" I gesture to the player.

"Go crazy."

The collection contains a wide spectrum from classical to metal. No single genre appears to take precedence, though one artist does have quite a chunk dedicated to her work.

"Are you a Swiftie?" I ask.

"What gave me away?"

"Oh, nothing, just the multiple pressings of the same album." I pull three nearly identical albums from their place.

"They're not the same," she insists. I raise a brow at that. "They're different colorways and they each have different bonus tracks."

"Right," I tease.

"Careful, I am sickly and bleeding. Blatant Swiftie hate might push me over the edge."

"No judge would convict you in these circumstances, you're right." I slide the records back in their place. "How's the soup?"

"Incredible, actually."

I tell her about the deli, seeing that it's only a few blocks away, as I continue to peruse her collection. "I also brought you some salty snacks and sour candy. Wanted to cover all bases."

"I'm suddenly less mad about letting you in."

"Thought you'd say that. Stick to the soup for now, though."

I settle on a classic, Fleetwood Mac's *Rumors*. The crackle of the record is oddly comforting.

"Oh, good choice," Toni says in approval.

I nod, letting the opening song play for a beat. "My mom is the biggest Fleetwood fan. She says the only reason she gave my dad a chance is because his name is Mick."

"So you owe your existence to Mick Fleetwood?"

"I'd rather not think about it too hard."

Toni sets her empty bowl on the makeshift coffee table.

"You want more?" I ask.

Toni tries to stop me from picking up her empty bowl. "You don't need to take—"

"Do. You. Want. More." I emphasize each word.

"No," she huffs.

CHAPTER 19

Toni

"L ET'S GET YOU TO BED," CILLIAN SAYS AS HE
returns from the kitchen.

"I wish that sounded sexy."

He grins, kneeling in front of me. "Don't think I'm not
tempted, but sleep will get you better faster than my cock
will."

"You never know." God, I hope my blush will be
attributed to the fever. "Endorphins are powerful things." My
body calls my bluff, choosing to hack up the remaining parts
of my lungs.

"Come on. Bed." He extends a hand, pulling me up.

He pauses at the door to my room, looking from my
mattress on the floor to me. "Toni, why don't you have a bed
frame?"

"I do," I say dismissively, plopping onto my mattress.

"Is it invisible?" he asks, crossing his arms.

"Hiding." I motion over my shoulder to the box in the
corner. "I also have all the furniture a well-adjusted adult
should own. It just happens to be in pieces." I'm sure if I felt

less like roadkill, I'd feel more shame at that statement, but I'm simply too tired to care.

Cillian rubs his beard. "Can you nap on the couch?" He asks, looking from the frame to the rest of the chaos of my bedroom.

"Why?"

"Yes or no."

"Yes?"

He nods. "Good. Come on."

"Why?" I ask, batting away his proffered hand.

"Because I'm gonna put your bed together."

"No." My whole body bristles at the thought. Letting him warm me up some soup and toss my trash was bad enough.

"Why not?"

"Because—" another coughing fit racks my body.

He disappears into the living room, reappearing with water in hand. I take it but don't thank him, still prickling at the idea of him assembling my long-ignored furniture. "Because I don't need you to." I could take care of it, I just hadn't.

"Yes, I am aware you don't need me to do anything for you." He holds his hand out once more, letting it hang. "If it makes you feel better, I like putting things together."

"What are you, some kind of carpenter?"

"Technically, yes. I worked in construction for a while before taking over the bar." I glare up at him, trying not to imagine him covered in sawdust. "But I'm guessing this is more of a hex wrench situation. Which I'm also proficient in."

He meets my scowl, unfazed.

"You're not going to let it go, are you?"

"No."

"Fine." I take his hand, and he pulls me up and into him. He tilts my chin up. "Just the bed."

"Sure."

I want to keep pushing, but the soup and medicine have already begun combining forces, making my limbs and lids feel heavy. "You're the worst."

"I know." His lips tenderly brush over mine. "And just think, if I lose our bet, I'm only making my job harder in the long run."

I roll my eyes to mask how the thought of my winning that bet feels a whole lot like losing. It wasn't like I knew what would come next. When I tried to think of a future outside of this place . . .

He tucks a wild curl behind my ear, "Lie down and I'll take care of this."

"Can I at least move the laun—"

"Antionette," he takes my face between his broad palms, squishing my cheeks a bit, "you might be the most stubborn woman I have ever met, and that is saying something. Go. Lie. Down."

It takes me about three minutes to fall asleep on the couch. Hard.

A couple of hours later, Cillian's soft singing tugs me back toward consciousness. I don't immediately move to get up or even open my eyes. His voice washes over me, beautiful and warm.

Just like him. As if in protest, a cough breaks through my comfort.

The singing stops, and Cillian appears at my side. "Hey." He gently pushes a few stray curls from my forehead. "How're you feeling?" Those steady green eyes study me.

Too beautiful. The way his eyes seem to suck in the light, causing them to glow like precious gemstones.

"Maybe a little better," I rasp, throat ragged from sleep and coughing.

He nods, "That's good." The corners of his mouth tick up, crinkling the fine lines at the corner of his eyes in a way that causes my heart to do things I should likely seek medical attention for.

Fuck.

"I'm gonna make you some tea."

That's surprising enough to pull me from my hazy stupor. "Tea?"

"Yes. Tea."

"You brought tea into my home?"

He rolls his eyes. "I did. And you're going to drink it."

"I do have boundaries."

"And I'll respect most of them." He stands, forcing me to roll onto my back in order to glare at him. "Humor me."

I sigh, too tired to argue further.

I snooze a bit more, the music and the sounds of him in the kitchen a surprisingly powerful lullaby.

The record finishes as he steps back in with two large steaming mugs. "Any requests?" He asks.

"Anything you'll sing to," I blurt, cheeks heating.

Cillian pauses, looking over his shoulder, a crooked little smile on his lips. "Was I singing?" I nod. "I hope that didn't wake you."

"It was a nice way to wake up."

He chooses a Hozier album, swaying a bit with the opening notes wafting through the room.

"Hozier fan?" I ask, remembering the band had covered several of his songs when I saw them play. I sit up, making space for him on the other side of the couch.

"Yeah." He takes the seat, his back against the arm, and passes me a mug. "The man writes great music."

I breathe in the steam billowing from the tea. Instead of the tannic notes I expected, a warm spiced scent cuts through my congestion. "Oh." I take another breath. "That smells kinda good actually."

Cillian watches in anticipation as I take a wary sip. Honey

and cinnamon and ginger and other things I can't quite clock soothe their way down my throat.

"And?" He asks.

"You win." I take another sip. "This isn't bad."

"But not great," he teases.

"Not bad is the highest praise I can give tea." I sip once more, trying to suss out the contents entirely and failing. "What is it?"

"A turmeric blend. I had it the last time I was under the weather, worked wonders."

"I could use a wonder." Despite the warm tea, I shiver.

Cillian shifts a bit, holding out an arm. "Come here." It doesn't take any convincing for me to cuddle up to his warmth.

Once I'm settled, blanket wrapped around us both, my back fitting easily against his broad chest, he holds his mug next to mine. "To wonders."

I can't help the broad smile that bursts across my face. "Sláinte."

We slip into an easy quiet. He hums along with the music for a few bars, the vibration soothing, before he begins to sing.

"Are you sure you're not some kind of man-siren?" I ask, the record spinning into silence. I'd been holding his free hand, studying the ink on his knuckles. He wore rings so often I rarely saw the words—*Hell Bent*—spelled out across his fingers.

He snorts, "That's giving me too much credit."

"It's not." I shift a bit to be able to look at him. "I saw you on stage, remember? You sing and people can't help but listen."

He rolls his eyes.

"False humility isn't a good look on anyone."

"It's not humility." He takes my empty mug in his free

hand, setting them both on the windowsill behind the couch. "I know where I stand is all."

"Did you ever want to do more with it? Really pursue something?" I feel him tense behind me. Rather than push him for more, I offer something of myself. "I never let my art be plan A. That was a path for people with a safety net. So it always got pushed to the back burner. A show here, a mural gig there, but never something I let myself commit to." I pause. "I think that's why it was easy to let David convince me it didn't matter."

"I'll say it again, he's an idiot. Your work is stunning."

I shrug, letting the back of my head fall onto his shoulder. "Stunning isn't enough."

"Neither is being able to carry a tune."

"Oh, come off it. You're good with instruments, you've got stage presence, that voice, you could've... I don't know."

"Been a rockstar?" He asks with a hint of levity.

"Why not?"

"Maybe in a different life."

"Scholarship domino?"

"Yeah." He sighs as I tangle our fingers together. "Maybe the version of me who did the Berklee thing would've tried to make a career of it."

After a few beats, I nudge, "But?"

"But, first month of senior year, Lucy and I got caught with some other kids stealing a car."

"Fuck."

"Yeah," he laces his fingers between mine. "My uncle helped us dodge the felony, but it still cost me that full ride. And being a dumb kid, I thought it was the end of the world." He takes a moment before continuing. "I decided to drop out, get my GED, and enlist."

My stomach twists. I move my back against the couch

while still being in Cillian's lap, needing to take him in. "Wait, how old were you?"

"Seventeen," he says.

"You were a baby." A lump rises in my throat.

He huffs something too sad to be a laugh. "My mom would agree. But no one could tell me that, and my cousin—who I thought was the coolest motherfucker I'd ever met—was in the army . . ." He swallows hard, "Joey told me it would be the easiest way to get outta Boston and get my degree." His gaze shifts down to our entangled hands. "And I believed him like the dumb kid I was."

Since meeting Cillian, I'd struggled to understand how someone like him ended up in a war zone. Not only because he didn't look the part, but there was a gentleness to him, something at the core of who he was that didn't align with 'soldier' to me. Now I understood.

Faces of people from my hometown flash through my mind. Like Cillian, they'd believed in the promise of something better, something bigger, too young to wonder what the price really was. From the sidelines of social media, Belle and I had watched as obituaries rolled in over the years, losses to a machine I'd assumed mostly targeted poor kids in towns like ours. Realizing just how wrong I was is harrowing.

"How long were you in the army?" I ask.

"Marines," he corrects. "Eight years." He releases a shaky breath. "It's kind of ironic that by the time I got out, the last thing I wanted to do was play music much less get a fucking degree in it."

"What changed?"

"The school thing never did—sitting in a room while people tell you how to create sounds miserable—but playing . . . I don't know." I let the silence hang, giving him space to find the words. "Time, I think. I needed time to come back to it, to let myself find joy in it again."

"I'm glad you were able to find your way back to it."

"Me, too."

Words don't feel sufficient, so I press a kiss to his knuckles and rest my temple on his shoulder. Cillian nuzzles his nose into my hair, and we allow the silence to hold us for a few moments.

"How are you feeling?" He asks, voice soft as though he doesn't want to break the serenity.

"Better, actually." My skin had lost the static ache of fever, and my lungs seemed a little less insistent on exiting my body.

Cillian rests his palm on my forehead and moves to press the back of his hand to the side of my neck. "You don't feel as warm." His lips brush my hair. "Why don't you hop in the shower, and I'll heat you up some more soup."

"I don't know if I should be offended by that suggestion."

He chuckles. "Come on."

⋄

THE SHOWER IS LIFE-ALTERING, MADE EVEN BETTER by the shower-melt thing Cillian brought.

I linger, letting the steam soak into my pores, scrubbing my skin pink. Honestly, I take so long I almost feel bad for leaving Cillian alone. That is, until I come out of the bathroom to find him vibing to a record, completely content on my couch, all the blankets neatly folded, setting his mug of tea on a freshly assembled coffee table.

Admonishing him will clearly do nothing, so I opt to shake my head in dramatic disapproval as I pass by, shutting my bedroom door behind me.

"Soup is ready," he calls, amusement coloring his voice.

I almost quip something back at him about not wanting soup, but the words get stuck behind the lump in my throat that forms the moment I see a familiar silk robe on my bed.

My knees feel less stable than usual, and my heart beats that concerning rhythm again.

Maybe I'd stroke out right here and not have to deal with how fucking considerate this and every goddamn thing he's done today has been. I force myself to take several breaths, as deep as I can in the circumstances, and change.

"I'm going to need you to stop being so nice." The silk of the robe is soothing against my skin.

Cillian grins, setting two bowls on the coffee table. "Don't worry, I'm sure I'll be an asshole in the future." I was beginning to seriously doubt that.

"Where is my former coffee table?" I ask as I take a seat.

"Over there," he thumbs to the collection of other half-unpacked boxes on the other side of the room. "Figured this would be better than a slowly collapsing box."

"Maybe I liked my collapsing box."

"Is that the aesthetic? Cardboard fort chic?"

"Unstable-core is all the rage." I tuck my legs under me as Cillian joins me.

We enjoy our soup and more of that incredibly good baguette for a few songs before he asks. "Why haven't you unpacked?"

The spoon freezes halfway to my mouth. My nervous system malfunctioning at even considering the answer to his simple question.

This was why I didn't want to let him, or anyone else, in here. Outside of these walls, I could perform the role of someone who knew, at least a little, what she was doing. In here, the hurricane was impossible to ignore; in here it was all too clear what David meant when he said I was unreasonable.

"You really wanna know?" I ask.

Cillian rests a warm hand on my exposed thigh. "You don't have to tell me." God, I needed him to stop being so . . . him.

"I'm fucking terrified." Tears burn at the backs of my eyes, and I manage to blink them back, swallowing down a few spoonfuls of soup as a distraction.

"Of what?"

I snort something like a laugh, keeping my eyes on my bowl. "Everything." I move a carrot around my bowl for several long moments until Cillian takes it away, setting it beside his own unfinished soup on the coffee table.

The table that he built for me.

My teeth sink into my lip, hard enough to sting.

"Hey," he coos, reaching over and pulling my lip free. "It's ok."

"Is it?" I snap. I tuck myself as far as possible into the corner of the couch, needing distance from his tenderness. "Because I'm not an expert, but I do think living out of boxes for several months—not because you want to but because you can't manage to bring yourself to do anything about them—is sort of not ok."

He doesn't react, just leans back agains the opposite arm of the couch, voice level. "I think you may be being a little hard on yourself."

I scoff, "You would."

"What does that mean?"

"It means you're too fucking nice and . . . stable and well adjusted," I spit out like an accusation. The rest falls out of my mouth in a torrent. "It means I'm an asshole for coming within six feet of you because I'm a goddamn hurricane of a person, and you don't deserve to be in the path of my disaster."

My chest aches. I'd been holding that in for the last two months, pushing it away, letting myself get comfortable around this man and the life he'd welcomed me into. But I couldn't keep letting this continue without being honest.

"Who made you believe that?" The severity of Cillian's tone forces me to meet his eyes.

"Experience," I admit. One only had to look at my history to see it. Constantly in motion, never settling. Well, until David . . .

"Bullshit," he rumbles, expression hard. "That's something someone sold you."

"Maybe." I shrug, feeling the fervor from my earlier outburst fade, replaced with a heaviness that seems to weigh me down. "Doesn't mean they're wrong."

How do you function? That was the first thing David had asked when he saw my studio space in the apartment I'd been living in for about two years.

What's the point? The question was asked when I'd said I didn't really intend to sell my art.

Hurricane Toni strikes again. Any time I did almost anything he disagreed with.

"Look at me." Cillian reaches for me, cupping my cheeks. "There is a difference between a disaster and a force of nature." His expression is intense, laced with determination and something softer. "You are a force, not a disaster. And if some people are too stupid to realize that, it's their shortcoming. Not yours."

Speechless.

I am, for possibly the first time in my life, rendered truly speechless. Devoid of words, all I can manage is to sit here, slightly slack-jawed.

"I . . ." He rubs his beard, pulling back. "I just . . . You deserve to see yourself the way—" He cuts himself off, sighing before looking back at me. "You deserve to see yourself as you are, and not through the lens of someone who's trying to make you feel smaller for their own sake."

My hold over the emotions that have been threatening to pour out of me since Cillian showed up on my doorstep this afternoon finally slips. Tears spill down my cheeks. A small sob breaks through before I can catch it.

"Toni." In a split second, he closes the space between us, calloused fingers delicately brushing the tears away. "I didn't mean to—"

I shake my head, words tumbling out. "No. No. It's not— You. You're wonderful. And that was possibly the nicest thing anyone has ever said to me." I try to get myself to stop but only manage a choked cry. "I'm not, I don't usually—" I cover my mouth.

Without another word, Cillian gathers me in his arms, cradling me against his chest. All better judgment flees me, and I cling to him. "I've got you. Let it out, doll."

And I do. I give myself over to the tears. Letting all the stress, fear, and anxiety that built up over the last several months out.

Cillian doesn't shush me or try to feed me empty platitudes. In fact, he doesn't say anything at all. He just holds me, an immovable object for my storm to crash against.

When my crying slows, he pulls me upright, tissue ready to dry my tears.

"I'm pretty sure I got snot on your shirt." I take a stuttering breath. "Sorry." The gentle warmth in his face almost brings on a new wave of tears.

"Doll, I've had far worse things on my shirt. Don't worry about it." He holds up the tissue box, and I take a couple, trying to gather the shattered pieces of my dignity. His broad hand runs up and down my back.

"Fuck," I sigh. "I'm sorry, I promise I'm not always an emotional basket case."

"Everyone gets to be a basket case sometimes."

I force a sardonic laugh. "I have a hard time seeing you break down because someone said something nice to you."

Cillian laughs. "Look, whatever you perceive as—what did

you say—stable and well adjusted, is one part a front and several parts years of therapy." He brushes an errant tear from my cheek. "Trust me, my fault lines are the size of the fucking Grand Canyon."

"People really like the Grand Canyon."

"It's still just a giant hole in the ground."

I roll my eyes.

He pecks a kiss on the tip of my reddened nose.

I let my cheek rest against his chest, a wave of exhaustion washing over me.

Some time later, he coaxes me awake with tender care.

"Let's get you in bed."

I sleepily nod.

Cillian leads me to my room and slips the robe off my shoulders. He picks one of my ancient sleep shirts from the laundry he'd folded earlier, sliding it over my head.

Half asleep and emotionally drained, I am out of any fucks that may have prevented the next words from coming out of my mouth. "Will you stay? Just—" I yawn. "Just for a little bit?"

Cillian smiles, kissing me softly. "I'll stay as long as you like."

Forever, a traitorous part of me whispers. I ignore it.

Cillian strips to his boxers and slides into bed next to me, pulling me into the broad warmth of his chest. My hand rests over his heart, fingers grazing the jagged circular scar.

I fall asleep to the steady beat of his heart beside me and dream of the Grand Canyon.

CHAPTER 20
Cillian

MY LEG BOUNCES AGAINST THE CRACKED BOOTH, making the tea in my mug vibrate like that one Jurassic Park scene, a warning of something big and vicious close by. Except, rather than a T-rex, it's my wrecked nervous system threatening to send everything to shit.

My phone vibrates. For once, I'm grateful Joey is a goddamn hour late, so there's no one around to notice how something as small as a message from Lucy is enough to make me flinch.

A picture of Toni holding up an almost too perfect apple, damn near the size of her face, dimples popping with her bright smile fills my screen.

LUCY

Baby's first apple.

That's where I should be. Enjoying the sunny fall day. Eating apples until my stomach hurts with my friends and my . . . and Toni. Not in this drab diner, drinking mediocre tea.

Across the restaurant, a toddler shrieks, their plate clattering to the ground.

My pulse is too loud in my ears.

Tension pulls every muscle in my body tight enough to snap.

I want to scream, maybe at the kid or with them, I don't know. But it's the only thing I can think of that might get this misdirected, senseless rage out of my body.

Get out. Need to get out. Out!

I slap a $10 on the table, not caring that it equates to essentially a $7 tip. Better to lose out on a few dollars than losing so much more by ripping this booth from the fucking wall.

Early October air pours into my lungs with each desperate breath I force into my tight chest. I should count, hold the air, let it out with some semblance of control, do any of the things I've learned over the years to bring myself back to center. The best I can do is breathe.

There will be times when all you can do is take one breath, and if you're lucky, another after that. Allow it to be enough. I let that nugget of wisdom from my first therapist play in my head over and over again until my heart rate slows down. Until I can begin a count.

In... 2, 3, 4—

"You about to hurl or something?" Joey's voice cuts off my count.

"Yeah." I hadn't fully registered until this moment that I'd crouched down, elbows on my knees, and head in my hands. "Move a little closer so I don't have to aim."

"Very funny." He reaches down, grabbing my upper arm as if to pull me up.

"Don't fucking touch me," I snap, pushing him away with far more force than necessary.

Joey makes a knowing sound. "So it's that kinda day." It isn't a question. "Here," he holds out a cigarette.

I take it. Joey smoked the shittiest menthols money could buy but I almost appreciate the way the smoke sizzles into my lungs. Almost.

"If you mean the kinda day where I sit in a shitty diner waiting for my asshole cousin to show. Then, yeah, it's that kinda day."

He takes a long drag, his too thin cheeks sucking in further, before crushing the half-smoked cigarette under his boot. "We going in?" He doesn't wait for my answer.

"Dick," I say, smoke streaming from my nostrils as I follow.

"Welcome back," the same waitress greets me once I settle into a different creaky booth. "Another tea, sweetheart?"

"Yeah, thanks." Maybe my previous tip would earn me a less shitty cup.

"Coffee," Joey adds.

"You got it."

He leans across the table a bit, lowering his voice, a shit eating grin on his face. "Think I should tell her you called this place shitty when she gets back?" Instead of words, I land a kick to his shin under the table, garnering something between a hiss and a chuckle.

"You look like shit, man." I know it's harsh, but it's also not a lie. Besides, I'm still bristling.

"If I wanted a fucking crayon eater's opinion, I would've asked," he grouses. The waitress deposits our mugs and takes our assurances that we're good for now.

"Crayon eater?" I hadn't heard that particular jab in a while. It insinuated that all Marines were more brawn than brains. "You can do better than that."

He snorts into his coffee. "For your information, some of us had to take a third shift gig because we got fired."

My hackles rise. "Maybe you wouldn't have gotten fired if you showed up on time every now and then."

"Yeah, I'm sure that would've kept you from giving me my pink slip."

"I didn't fire you." I can hear my voice tilting a touch too loud and try to rein it in. "I went to bat for you more times than I should've."

"You want another fucking medal?" he spits.

"Oh, fuck you."

Tense silence falls between us, the diner's sounds seeming to grow louder with each moment.

"Why'd you wanna talk, Cillian?"

I shrug. "Wanted to check in."

"So you can tell my sweet sister how great I'm doing?" Bitterness drips from his words.

"What the hell, Joseph?" I can't pretend that shit doesn't sting. "I've never—"

"I know," he waves me off. "That kinda day—" He sighs. "Month, year . . . life for me, too."

That wasn't true. For several years after he got out, Joey seemed good. He got a job and a house—did the dad and husband thing. In comparison to the absolute dumpster fire that was my life after discharge, his was what most of us dream of—a vision of stability.

But at some point, the wheels started to come off.

"You talk to anyone?" I ask, eyes on the tea bag floating in my mug.

He scoffs. "What, so some PhD can tell me how fucked up I am? No, thank you."

"Plenty of therapists don't have a PhD," I say into my mug. Unfortunately, my tip had done nothing to improve the quality of the brew.

"Smartass."

"Thought I was a crayon eater."

"You can be both."

I could keep this going. Settle into the easy, if shallow,

back-and-forth—nothing but me and my cousin shooting the shit. But Joey's bloodshot eyes and gaunt figure won't let me.

"I wasn't talking about that, anyway. There's a group—"

"Cilli," he groans. "I'm fine, man."

Bullshit.

"I'm not." I didn't admit that to many people, it was easier than worrying them with shit they couldn't fix. Even saying it now, to someone who would understand more than most, feels like turning my back on a firing squad.

Concern knits his brow as he studies me with a fresh intensity. "If you're using again, I—"

"Fuck no." I shake my head. "I'm good there. It's just . . ." I tap my temple. "Loud. Louder than usual."

"It's the fuckin' weather." He takes a swig of the coffee, grimacing, before reaching for the sugar. "Always makes shit worse."

"Yeah," I agree. The thing is, as a kid, I loved the cooler months. They ushered in the joyful chaos of Halloween, holiday breaks, snow days, and my birthday. But ever since I was 17, it felt like this time of year was cursed or something.

"That's why I wanted to ask you to come with me," I say.

"Since when have you needed me to go with you to shit like that?"

"I didn't say need. Just thought it would be better than going alone." I don't add, *for both of us.*

Joey lets out an exasperated sigh, the kind you'd direct at an annoying kid. "Cillian, if you wanna sit in a circle and listen to a bunch of guys—"

"There are women there," I interject.

"Veterans," he corrects with a bit of snark. "Bitch about their feelings, more power to ya. It's not my thing."

"Nah, your thing is downing a fifth of cheap whiskey before breakfast," I say it like a joke, but I'd smelled it on him the moment he walked up earlier.

"Like I said, late night," he tries to deflect.

"And the times before?"

"Sometimes you just need a little something to get through it, ya know? I'm not some drunk sleeping on the street or nothing."

"Maybe not but going around smelling like the morning after St. Paddy's isn't exactly a good thing." I didn't need him to fully admit to having a problem, just accept that maybe he'd been hitting it a little harder than normal. It would be a start.

He settles back into the booth, looking smug. "Better a little whiskey stink than a needle in my arm."

The immediate urge to punch that fucking sneer off Joey's face turns my hand into a fist in a split second. But I keep it on the table, barely managing to pull in a breath.

"Good talk." I toss another $10 on the table and get up.

He doesn't follow me, and I don't bother to look back.

✧

EVEN THOUGH THE GROUP SESSION WAS HELPFUL, I'M grateful to be closing down the bar tonight. The familiar space, the white noise of patrons, the methodical nature of the work keeping my hands busy; it's exactly what I need.

Just after last call, I lift my head up to find a small bag of apples on the bar.

"I will have you know I kept myself from making a 'how 'bout them apples' joke," Toni says, hopping up onto a barstool.

"You deserve a reward for your incredible display of self-control." I try, and fail, to restrain the smile that just seeing her brings to my face.

"Can the reward include gin? I feel like I need gin."

"Oh no. What did they subject you to?"

"Ye of little faith. Ooo, Negroni," she coos. I chose that

over her usual gin and tonic since the color goes with her mini dress and cardigan. "Thank you." She takes a sip, looking pleased. "They subjected me to a picture-perfect day."

"So why the need for gin?"

She sighs. "My fucking ex called me."

My hackles rise. "The one you asked to have no contact with until December? That ex."

"Yup." She drags the word out, popping the 'p.'

"One second." I close a few tabs and set Sean on some closing duties. "So he called?" The question tastes foul on my tongue.

"Yeah. We'd already gotten back and were hanging by the fire pit at Lucy and Oliver's duplex." She runs a finger around the rim of her cocktail. "It was a number I didn't know, but the area code was Houston, so I picked up, like an idiot."

"That doesn't make you an idiot. It makes him an asshole." She shrugs. I reach across the bar and grab her chin. "You didn't do anything wrong."

"I know." I let her go even though all I want is to gather her in my arms. "Just haven't heard his voice in a while and it was . . . weird."

"I'm sorry." I lift her hand from the bar and press a kiss to her knuckles. "If you want to talk more after we close, I'm free." She nods.

After a few minutes, Toni pops up beside the register, one foot sliding behind the bar. "Want help?"

I block her entry. "Employees only."

"Oh, come off it," she tries to push past me.

"Aww, cute." I scoot her to the other side. "Go drink your cocktail. We'll be locking the doors in ten." She huffs but settles back at the bar, whipping out her sketchbook.

With the last patrons out the door, I round the bar and wrap an arm around her middle. The spicy floral notes of her perfume and the feel of her in my arms settle something in me so thoroughly and suddenly that I almost sigh with relief. "What 'cha working on?"

"Just doodling."

"One day you're gonna have to explain what constitutes a doodle in your eyes," I say. There's a full-on portrait of Lucy on one corner of the page and a clear sketch of the barn at the orchard in another.

"Cillian, you want me to finish the dishes?" Sean pokes his head in from the kitchen. "Hi, Toni!"

"Hey," she returns his greeting.

"Don't worry about it." My fingers flex against Toni's waist.

"You sure?"

"Mhm, go on and head out." His brows rise. "Goodnight, Sean."

"Night!"

"Such a generous boss," Toni says.

"Sure." I press a kiss below her ear, dragging my mouth down her neck, relishing the way she relaxes into me. "Generous." I pull her cardigan aside to reveal a sliver of shoulder, sinking my teeth into her skin before covering it with a kiss. "So generous."

The sound of the back door closing lets me know we're alone.

"I'll be right back." I run to the office to slide the bolt on the back door, not wanting to risk someone deciding to come in for any reason. When I come back, I almost barrel into Toni on the opposite side of the office door.

She grabs my hips to steady herself, laughing, and I pull her closer. "I said I'd be back."

"You know I'm not good at waiting," she says, looking up at me, her body pressed against mine.

"Yeah. Maybe that's something we should work on."

She slides her hands up my torso, brows knitting. "Wait, I'm the worst, I didn't ask how your day was."

I cradle her face in my hands, shaking my head. "I don't wanna talk about it." All I want is her and to make her forget the sound of her ex's voice—make sure some selfish asshole's intrusion doesn't taint her picture-perfect day.

Toni yields to my kiss, lips parting at the barest flick of my tongue.

"What do you want?" She asks, breathless after a few moments.

Was I also a selfish asshole? Because if I'm being honest, this isn't just for her. I want my world to reduce to one singular focus. I want to let go of everything—all the noise in my head, all the bullshit this day brought—and lose myself in her pleasure. If that made me an asshole, I'd repent later.

Pushing her back against the bar, I grab her hips and lift her onto the bar top, reveling in her little gasp. "You," I say.

I plant myself between her legs, teasing her through the barrier of her panties.

"Cillian." Fuck, my name has never sounded as good as it does when it comes from this woman's mouth. "Someone could see."

That was true. We were fairly far back in the bar, but the few lights that remained on and the light from the street meant if anyone were to look in, they could likely make us out.

I yank her panties aside, more than a little satisfied at how quickly she soaked them for me. "Let them look," my desire for her turns my voice to gravel.

She doesn't protest; in fact, she rocks her hips forward, opening herself further to me. I take the invitation, sinking one finger then another into her tight pussy. Toni fists the front of my shirt with both hands, holding onto me as her head falls back, the most beautiful cry spilling from that perfect mouth.

"You like that, doll?" A slow grin fills my face as she drags her gaze to me, nodding, lips in a perfect "O". "Good."

Cradling the back of her neck with my free hand, I kiss her savagely, swallowing her sounds of pleasure until I feel her walls pulse around my fingers. "Already?" I tease.

"Oh, fuck you," she pants. I curl my index and middle finger just a touch more. Her body jerks toward me.

I consider the merits of working on her patience problem now. Holding off her orgasm until she begs. But my own lack of patience gets in the way.

"Eyes on me, Toni." She locks in without hesitation. "Good girl," I purr. "I wanna see that pretty face when you make a mess all over my hand."

She sucks in a breath. "Cillian, I—" A whimper cuts her off.

"Go on. Show me how much you like being fucked on top of my bar." Gooseflesh pebbles her arms, her breath catches, her sweet mouth opens, but no sound escapes. "Come for me, Toni," I demand.

God, she does.

I brace her with my free hand, working her until the aftershocks begin to fade and she wilts against my chest.

If I could bottle this feeling, take little hits of it throughout the day, I'd be a much happier man. Seeing as that isn't possible, I settle for drinking this moment in, happy for what time I have with this glorious creature.

Once she catches her breath, I coax her upright, gently pulling my fingers free. Toni watches with rapt attention as I taste her, savoring her pleasure. She licks her lips.

"You should know how good you taste." I press my fingers to her lips, she takes them into her mouth, sucking them clean. My cock presses painfully against my jeans. "Fuck," I huff.

A reckless part of me wants to turn her around and fuck

her right here. My place is simply too far, and if the whole city wanted to watch on in envy, let them. Instead, I pull her in for another possessive kiss, the taste of her dancing on our tongues.

Better demons ultimately prevail.

Gripping her hair by the roots, I pull her head back, breaking the kiss. "We're going to your place. And I am going to make you come until the only thought left in that pretty head is how good it feels to be mine."

CHAPTER 21
Toni

"I LOVE BEING RIGHT," JAC SAYS, SOUNDING ALMOST wistful.

"About what?" I hang another painting, stepping back to assess if I like the placement.

One green eye peeks intensely from the center of a sculpted 3D flower. I almost didn't show this one. The realism of the eye juxtaposed with the not-quite-real individual petals, their color vibrant at the center but just beginning to darken and curl at the edges, feels unsettling when paired together. An effect I appreciate, but one that may not be for everyone.

Not to mention the non-zero chance the owner of that green eye would clock it as his own.

But Jac and I found a frame at the thrift store that fit it perfectly, so I couldn't resist.

"I said I doubted your art was terrible." They gesture at the wall. "I was right."

"Approximately how long will you be smug about it?"

They take a thoughtful sip of their cold brew. "Indeterminate."

"I'll be putting that on my cons list for sticking around."

"She has jokes!" Jac teases.

A customer comes in, drawing Jac's attention, and I finish hanging the few remaining pieces.

If I were being fair to myself—and I rarely was when it came to my work—this wasn't a bad showing for only a couple of months. A curator would scoff; the collection wasn't what most could call cohesive. But to me, the threads connecting the works are clear in the glimpses of people I'd met here, slivers of the city popping up in color and texture.

"Be serious," Jac returns to my side. "Are you still thinking of leaving me?"

"It's a consideration."

They grab my hand, tilting my face toward them. "I thought we had something special." We stare into one another's eyes, dripping with dramatic faux sincerity, until we crack, bursting into laughter.

"But you should know, this is absolutely triggering my abandonment issues," they say.

I take a seat. "It will just give you something to talk about with your therapist."

"Yes. I do find myself running short on trauma to work through."

"You're welcome."

"When do you need to make a decision?"

I sigh. "Technically, a couple of weeks ago. But my landlord is giving me more time to decide."

"That's surprisingly nice for a landlord." They take the seat across from me, keeping a watchful eye on the counter.

"They're really great."

"So that's in your pros column. What else?"

I go through a few highlights. "And the seasons actually changing is nice. I have so many sweaters waiting for their moment."

"Huh . . ."

"What? Not a fan of the colder months?"

"I mean, I could live without it being the dead of night before 5 pm, but I grew up in Buffalo. Cold and I are old friends." The bell above the door jingles as someone walks in. "I'm just surprised a certain bartender hasn't made his way onto that list."

I don't justify that with a response and instead busy myself by packing up my hanging supplies and tossing my trash. However, the activity doesn't do much to keep me from rolling Jac's words over and over in my head.

Cillian had been putting in the work to win our little wager, that was for sure. Even if it wasn't something he could take me to, like apple picking a couple of weeks ago or Provincetown at the end of the summer for a gloriously queer beach weekend, he'd been making sure I clocked in as many quintessential New England experiences as possible. Not to mention, since the day he steamrolled me into letting him assemble my furniture, my apartment had begun morphing from a place some animal went to ground, into a place someone actually lived. I'd even had Lucy over for a girl's night this past weekend.

My phone buzzes in my pocket.

CILLIAN

How's the gallery coming along?

I snap a few pictures to send over.

Not too shabby.

CILLIAN

I can't wait to see it later. :)

Will you be around?

> I was gonna go into the city and get some work done there, wanted to see the park in the fall.

CILLIAN

> Great idea.

> Still coming to mine tonight?

> You've offered to feed me. So yes.

CILLIAN

> Good.

"He's definitely on the pros list," Jac says from behind the counter.

"You don't know who I'm texting." I shove my phone into my jeans pocket.

"With that smile, I would bet," they grab their tip jar, "this, that I do."

I roll my eyes. "Well, for your information, you're also on that list."

"I know. But I'm your caffeine dealer, so I don't count." They set my usual on the counter.

"That just means you count more."

✧

As the Red Line trundles over the Longfellow Bridge, I take a picture, sending it to Cillian.

Jac's claim that they knew who I was texting by the look on my face echoes in my memory when I realize I'm grinning at the three dots indicating Cillian was working on a response.

Fixing my face, I shove my phone deep into my bag, ignoring the vibration.

Yes, he was on the pros side of the equation. Of course he was. He'd been so kind and welcoming, sharing his city, his friends, his bed . . . I shake my head, trying to clear my thoughts.

And, yes, we'd been spending more nights together than apart lately. But with Two Sons being so short-handed, it only made sense. My apartment was within walking distance. It was convenient. It didn't have to mean anything more than that.

And the nights you go home with him? A traitorous voice in my head asks.

My stop comes up before I have a valid answer.

Instead of going to the park, I pivot in the opposite direction. The park was something Cillian shared with me and I don't want to think about him, about us.

I don't want to think.

Abandoning my good intentions to get some work done, I wander. With each new block, the city unfolds in cobblestones and concrete, one thing after another demanding I pull out my sketch book. By the time my tired feet and empty stomach are welcomed by Chinatown's gate, I'd captured a tour guide in a tricorn hat, a cemetery with graves older than the town I grew up in, and the brutal angles of modern buildings.

Not wanting to look at my phone, I choose the first bakery that catches my eye, grab a mix of sweet and savory bites, and settle in at the pocket park in the gate's shadow. Most of the tables are filled with older folks playing games and carrying on lively conversations. They pay me no mind as I let their banter wash over me, pencil lazily capturing snippets of the scene between bites.

"You're very good," someone says behind me. I jump a little, startled to find myself being observed by an elderly couple.

"Thank you," I say. The woman is decked out in an almost dizzying array of patterns and colors that somehow manage to work while the man on her arm wears a sensible grey tracksuit.

They give the impression of a rainbow and the cloud that brought it on.

She takes a seat across from me as the man beside her protests in a language I don't speak. They bicker back and forth for a moment until the man tosses his hands up in defeat.

"You do what you want," he grouses.

"I will," she says with a smile. Clearly, this was a familiar dance between them. "You could draw us?" She asks as though she already knows the answer.

"You don't have to—" He begins.

"She'd love to. Wouldn't you?"

I laugh. "I'd be honored."

The man shakes his head as he sits down, but still, he immediately takes her hand in his as if it were a habit—automatic.

We begin chatting as I start to sketch. Or, rather, Miss Lily begins chatting, leading introductions for herself and Mr. Tae before slipping into their story. She tells me how they both immigrated from Korea, how they'd lived in Boston for almost forty years. Lily explains how she left her abusive husband when she was 30 and how wild she was until she met Mr. Tae. He makes sure I know she's still wild with a smile that crinkles the lines on his face.

"He asks me to marry him every year, for twenty years," she says with a twinkle in her eye. "Every year I say no. You know why?" I shake my head, the mention of proposals still enough to make my teeth grind. "Because husbands are useless. Boyfriends are better." We all have a laugh at that.

"Why do you keep asking?" I ask Mr. Tae.

He beams at Miss Lily, "So she knows I would. If she wanted." He turns back to me. "But being a boyfriend keeps me young." This earns him a peck on his cheek.

I take care to capture their matching smile lines, white

hair, and the shared spark of adoration in their eyes—little things that speak to lives well-loved—as they continue to tell me their story.

Using the pencils Cillian bought me, I finish with some touches of color. Partially because color is clearly important to Miss Lily, and also because I just want to keep listening to them.

Finally satisfied, I sign the bottom corner and carefully pull the page from my book.

"You made us look old!" Miss Lily exclaims.

My cheeks heat. "Oh, I didn't mean-"

"We are old," Mr. Tae chuckles.

"Exactly. Young people are too obsessed with being young. Age is a wonderful thing." She turns a sparkling smile on me. "Thank you." She says something to Mr. Tae, and he reaches for his wallet.

"Don't you dare."

"You can't do work for free."

I shake my head. "Your company was payment enough." They narrow their eyes at me, clearly ready to argue. "If you'd like, you can tell me your best recommendations for food in the city. I just moved here not too long ago and don't know what's good."

We spend ten more minutes together, Miss Lily giving me a comprehensive list of dos and don'ts of Boston's restaurants.

They thank me again, and I watch them walk away, hand in hand. Sure, their ease together could be decades in the making, but something tells me, at some level, it's innate. Two people who simply fit.

It's a nice thought, the idea that someone out there could mesh with all your jagged edges. And I've seen people in my life find that—Belle and her late husband, my brother and his wife—I just can't seem to envision the same for me.

I finally pull my phone out and start to walk in what I

think is the direction of the stop I got off at, testing my navigation skills.

Before getting to Cillian, I tend to every other missed notification from the past few hours, even pausing at a bench to watch a random cute cat video from Belle.

He sent a heart reaction to the picture from the bridge, and a few messages.

CILLIAN

> I really should just print this out and tape it to the office door. Something to keep me sane, lol.

> We're going up to my cabin in New Hampshire in a couple of weeks. If you're interested in roughing it for a weekend.

> 'We' being Lu, Oli, and a few others. In case that matters.

A couple of weeks would put us just into November. Then would come December. Then Christmas...

The thought settles like a brick in my stomach.

It wasn't just the question of where to go next that I needed to answer. I had to figure out the David of it all. Even now, almost a year out, the thought of sitting face to face with him sets me spiraling.

When David insisted we take the year apart, I initially turned him down. If Ms. Lily and Mr. Tae were pieces that simply fit, David and I were the opposite. But like kids determined to finish a puzzle, we shoved the pieces together until they broke.

So what was left?

I wasn't sure then, and I certainly wasn't sure now. However, a few friends sat me down and pointed out my history of 'cutting-and-running,' insisting I owed David—someone who was just trying to love me—another chance at making us work. What they didn't say, but heavily implied, was that they had chosen their side. I could either take his generous offer of a year to gather myself and come back or find myself mostly friendless and alone.

With friends like those . . .

The unknowns fill my mind like a goddamn swarm of cicadas. Not buzzing. Screaming.

It's not until I find myself standing above the Charles, the sound of the train and traffic, and pedestrians breaking through the cacophony, that I realize how far I'd walked past my intended stop.

You should see it at sunset. That's what Cillian had said about this place. He wasn't wrong.

Above me, a watercolor sky of magenta and gold burns bright, gilding the river and the glass facades of modern buildings. Along the water, a palette of autumn shades coat the trees.

I drink it in, letting the beauty chase away everything else until I feel . . . grounded.

⟡

"Toni!" Oliver greets me from behind the bar at Two Sons.

I wave as I make my way over, hopping onto an open bar stool. "How do you find the energy to do this after dealing with children all day?"

He shrugs. "The tips are almost better than my salary some nights."

"That . . . is depressing."

"I know." He pulls a pint, delivering it a few seats down. "Cillian's in the office."

I nod. "Can I grab a water, actually?"

"Of course." He passes me a glass.

"Thanks." I take a deep drink before asking, "So, this cabin. When Cillian says 'roughing it,' how rough are we talking?"

Oliver considers. "Indoor plumbing, no wifi, questionable cell service."

"I can handle that."

Familiar warm arms wrap around my waist. "Is that a yes to my invitation?" Cillian asks. Without meaning to, I relax into his embrace.

"Hold on." I tilt my head to look at him. "How big is this cabin. If it's you, me, Oliver, Lu—"

"Oh, we camp," Oliver clarifies.

"'We' better not include me," I say.

"Do you not like camping?" Cillian asks, surprised.

"Sleeping on the ground for fun has always seemed deranged to me." I look at Oliver. "No offense."

"Only a little taken," he teases.

Cillian sighs. "I knew there had to be a flaw."

"Hey, you not drinking coffee is far more of a red flag than me preferring to sleep on an actual bed."

"The woman isn't wrong," Oliver agrees. Cillian chuckles, moving to lean on the bar beside me, clearly taking weight off his bad leg.

"You ok?" I ask, taking his hand in mine.

"Yeah," he dismisses.

I raise a disbelieving brow at that.

He kisses my knuckles. "Just sore. Promise."

"I can cook tonight," I offer.

"You? Cook?" he asks, shocked.

"I am capable of cooking." Judging by his expression, he doesn't believe me. "I am."

"Ok, ok." He laughs. "We can do it together. How's that?"

"Fine."

He gives me one of those delicious slow grins before

kissing me briefly. If I weren't seated, my knees would be liquid. "And to be clear, we can sleep in the cabin. Owners' rights."

"Should've led with that."

"So you're coming?" He asks.

"I guess." I sigh, rolling my eyes dramatically.

"Brat."

"If you'd like . . ."

"Maybe later." He kisses my cheek. "Let me finish a couple things, and then we can leave."

"Ok."

Cillian slips back into the office as Oliver moves over to me. "Off the record," he begins in just above a whisper. "The trip is sort of for Cillian's birthday."

I don't hide my surprise. "When is his birthday?" I realize neither of us had asked the other.

"It was the 17th."

"As in last week?" I hiss, guilt making my cheeks burn.

"Yeah. But he's . . ." Oliver trails off. "He isn't big on celebrating it."

"Why?"

"That's his story to tell." Sadness flickers in Oliver's honey brown eyes. "But we've been going to the cabin in early November for a few years now, and everyone just sneaks him gifts."

"Stealth birthday."

"Exactly," Oliver says, his warm smile matching mine.

CHAPTER 22
Cillian

"Antoinette Joy, don't you dare hang up on me!" A woman's voice I don't recognize says from Toni's phone as she opens her front door.

"Joy, huh?" I tease.

"Middle name privilege is earned," Toni says, ushering me inside.

"Put him on the phone," the woman demands.

Toni lifts her phone up. "Belle—"

"Now."

"Ugh. Fine." Toni holds the phone out to me. "Cillian, this is Belle. Belle, Cillian."

A brunette with striking blue eyes greets me on the screen. "Finally," she huffs. "I wish we could have met under better circumstances, but can you please tell this woman she doesn't need five sweaters for a weekend in the damn woods?"

I look up from the screen, cocking a brow at Toni. "Five?" She shrugs by way of response. I follow her into her room while Belle continues.

"And tell her that she needs to bring real pants," Bell continues.

"I thought we were past the leggings are pants debate," Toni says.

I look back at the screen to see Belle rolling her eyes in a way that reminds me of Oliver so much I almost laugh. "They are technically pants. But if they're the only thing you're wearing, your Texan ass will freeze."

"She is right. It's gonna be pretty cold this weekend."

Toni pouts her lip a little. "But the sweaters look better with the leggings."

"Won't matter if you're miserable," Belle says. I nod in confirmation.

"Ugh." Toni begrudgingly fishes a pair of jeans from the pile of clean clothes on her bed. This wasn't the first time I'd seen her effortlessly extricate an item from what, to me, looked like total chaos. It's an impressive feat. She tosses them in her bag. "There. Real pants."

"And the sweaters?" I ask. Bell sniggers from the phone.

"I knew I never should have let the two of you talk."

"Doll," I lean on the door frame to take some weight off my leg, "we're gonna be there for hardly 48 hours. You need maybe two sweaters."

"Exactly," Belle says.

"I just appreciate options." Neither Belle nor I respond. "Fine." Toni pulls a couple sweaters from her bag, bringing it to a much more reasonable level of full.

"Thank you for the support," Belle says.

"Anytime," I say, grinning.

"Not anytime." Toni tosses a shirt at me. I bat it away with a laugh. "I can't have the two of you conspiring."

"It isn't our fault you're too extra for your own good sometimes," Belle says with affection.

"I refuse to believe that," Toni says.

"This is why you and Lucy get along so well," I sigh.

"Because she's a delight?"

"In case you're curious, yes, she has always been like this," Belle says.

I laugh. "Somehow that doesn't surprise me."

"Ok, enough of you two," Toni reaches for the phone, but I pull it away.

"Oh no, I'm having far too much fun," I tease. Belle's answering laugh is good-natured.

Toni huffs. "Tell her to get her ass out here and she can share all my embarrassing teenage stories with you."

"Tempting," Belle says. I bring the phone back to eye level. "You two have fun. Good to meet you, Cillian!"

"You're avoiding the offer!" Toni yells.

"You, too," I say.

Toni takes the phone back. "You're the worst," she directs to Belle.

"That's Toni for 'I appreciate you,'" Belle says loudly. "She's only half as prickly as she wants you to think."

"Goodbye, Isabelle!"

"Bye, Antionette!" Belle's laugh gets cut off as Toni ends the call.

"Attacked in my own home," Toni says. She shoves the phone into the waistband of her leggings, the cropped length of her T-shirt leaving it half-exposed.

I take a seat on the edge of her bed. "Yes. You've been horribly victimized by people hoping you stay cozy."

"Sweaters are cozy," she protests as I pull the phone from her waistband.

"They are." I grab her exposed waist, pulling her between my legs. "But unless you're going to wear three at a time, you still don't need that many."

"What do you know?"

I hold her gaze as I press my lips to the soft skin of her midriff. "I know you look best with no sweater on, much less

191

three." Playfully, I tug on the waistband of her leggings with my teeth.

Toni shakes her head, laughing. "I still have to pack."

"Mhm," I agree, hands slipping down to give her ass a squeeze.

"We'll be late," she protests.

"They can wait."

✧

"About time!" Lucy accuses, looking down at us from the deck as we get out of the car. We deserved the call-out. The sun had already dipped below the tree line, casting the sky in a wash of warm colors.

I would feel bad about just how late we are if all the people here didn't have full access to everything on the property. Not that there was much to access. There's the elevated cabin with barely one room that was here when I bought the place; a large outbuilding, which mostly held firewood and camping supplies; and a tiny pre-fab cabin Michael and I finished last summer, which is arguably nicer than the original cabin.

"Someone wasn't packed when I got to her place," I say, catching Toni's accusatory glare in my periphery.

"More like someone wanted to stop and look at the leaves every few miles," she rebuffs.

Neither was a lie. We just left out the part that included her soaking my beard.

Oliver laughs as he joins us to help with the bags. "You're both full of shit."

"I take offense to that," Toni says, letting him take her bag only after a brief tug of war.

"I didn't say it wasn't cute," he teases.

"Personally, I believe her," my sister-in-law, Camille, says.

The sunset and that pregnancy glow make her dark brown skin absolutely radiant. "We know Cillian has a thing for leaf-peeping."

I drop the bags beside her on the raised deck. "I had to show Toni the ropes."

"Sure you did." She pulls me into a fierce side hug, her belly now big enough to provide a significant barrier. "I haven't seen you in forever."

"Sorry, work has—"

"I'm well aware," she cuts me off. "Who do you think Michael complains to?" She winks. "I'm just glad to see you before I'm in mom mode."

"How is the cooking going?" I ask.

She rests her hands lovingly on top of her bump. "Rowdy. He's been using my kidneys as punching bags."

"He?!" Oliver, Lucy, and I bellow in unison.

"He," Michael confirms. He wraps Camille in his arms from behind, hands resting over hers.

"Do mom and dad know?" I ask them.

Camille nods. "Your mom swears he'll be here before Christmas, but I'm holding out for a Capricorn."

"Not a Sagittarius fan?" Toni asks. She'd been hanging back a touch, watching our excitement without any trace of impatience or discomfort.

"I try not to discriminate," Camille says with a smirk. "But as a Capricorn, I'm biased." Her face shifts to concern, "You aren't a Sag, are you?"

Toni laughs. "Nope. I'm the more aggressive of the fire signs."

"You being an Aries actually makes so much sense," Lucy says, eyes flicking between us.

"I'm taking that as a compliment."

"I would never give you anything less than praise, darling."

Lucy loops her arms between Camille and Toni. "Let's go enjoy the fire I painstakingly started inside."

"You?" Oliver protests. He picks up Toni's bags and tries to grab mine before I snatch them away. "I'm pretty sure I brought in the firewood."

"Yes," Lucy says over her shoulder as she leads the other two women inside. "But I lit the match."

We get settled in, and I thank Oliver and Lucy for making the place cozy. They'd already wiped down the kitchen and tossed the canvas drop cloths I used to cover the old couch and collection of floor cushions.

"Honestly, I feel kinda bad," Oliver says as he puts on a pot of coffee.

"Why?" I ask.

He shrugs. "I've been out here more this year than you have, and it's your place."

"I consider it everyone's place these days." Ever since I moved into my uncle's house, it made sense to keep the invite open to the family if I wasn't using the cabin or property.

"Still. You should—"

"If you're about to say 'take time off,'—" I sigh. "I know."

"Oh, God," Camille groans. Oliver's face mirrors my own as my stomach drops to my knees for a fraction of a second. "Is that coffee?"

"Cam, you're too pregnant to start anything with 'oh, God,' nearly gave us a heart attack in here," Oliver chides.

She laughs. "Believe me, if something was happening with the baby, I'd be screaming something with more bite than 'oh, God.'"

"You should have heard what came out of her mouth when she was having Braxton Hicks contractions last week," Michael says, slipping his jacket off to hang by the door. "Could've made the devil blush."

"I'm excited to see what I come up with when this little guy decides he's ready to come out. I may invent new words."

Michael smiles at Camille tenderly, kissing the top of her head as he passes by. "You want some tea, babe?"

She sighs as I bring Toni a mug of coffee and perch on the arm of the couch. "Sure. Maybe if Toni lets me smell her coffee, I can pretend it's as good."

Toni holds the mug under Camille's nose. "Breathe it in."

Camille doesn't hesitate, wafting the steam rising from the mug toward her face, inhaling deeply. "I miss you," she whispers.

Lucy looks down at her own mug. "I almost feel guilty drinking this in front of you."

"Don't." Camille accepts the tea Michael brings her. "Trading coffee... and sushi, and charcuterie, and-" She pauses.

"That's a lot of things." Toni pats Camille's knee.

"So many things," Camille dramatically pouts. "But, it feels like a fair trade for a tiny human."

The rest of the evening is filled with easy banter and good food. But the combination of a long week mingles with the crackling of the fire and the cool autumn night and begins lulling us all to sleep earlier than any of us anticipated.

Michael and Camille tap out first, retreating to the tiny cabin. Oliver and Lucy aren't far behind, committed to sleeping rough rather than bringing their cots into the living room.

"I will never understand it. Inside is better than outside." Toni says around a yawn, her body relaxing against me on the couch.

I chuckle, "You like the park and the beach, and didn't you spend a whole day apple picking?"

"I'm not entirely opposed to the outside, but I got plenty of the—" another big yawn cuts her off, "outdoors and the country as a kid."

"Fair enough." I plant a kiss on her cheek. "Come on, let's get you to bed."

"Just me?"

"Not just you."

CHAPTER 23

Toni

WARM SUN POURING IN FROM THE BIG WINDOW beside the bed and the gentle sound of Cillian's light snores beside me coax me awake earlier than usual.

I crack my eyes open, sit up slowly, and look over at him.

Cillian lies on his back, one arm under his head, that mess of dark brown and silver hair splayed around him. He looks peaceful, his pink lips slightly parted, the sunlight emphasizing the freckles across the bridge of his nose.

Even though we've spent quite a few mornings together at this point, I've never seen him like this. He always managed to be up before me, blaming his years in the military for breaking him of the habit of sleeping in.

I burn the image into my mind. Not wanting to forget a single line or strand of hair. The soldier in repose.

How long is it acceptable to stare at someone asleep before you enter into Edward Cullen levels of creep? I decide I'm getting too close for comfort and pull my eyes away. Determined not to interrupt his rest, I try to slide from the bed.

Unfortunately, this mattress isn't his plush dream back in

Charlestown, and it gives a slight creak. I grimace as a warm hand wraps around my wrist before I can get up.

He still looks peaceful, eyes heavy with sleep, lips soft and welcoming in a gentle smile.

If I've ever seen something—someone—so beautiful, I can't remember it.

"Where you goin'?" his voice thick and drowsy.

Rather than attempt a response, I lean into him, kissing first his strong brow, then the tip of his nose, and finally those lips. He hums with satisfaction, pulling me in closer and deepening the kiss.

We stay like that for a while, kisses languid and unhurried. When we finally part, I feel drunk on it. On him.

"Good morning," I say.

"Good morning." He pushes my hair from my face, cradling my cheek in his hand. I lean into his touch for a moment before planting a kiss on his palm.

"Since I'm never up before you, I was going to make you your tea, but . . ."

His smile broadens. "I'm a light sleeper, doll. But you can still make me tea even though I'm awake."

"That does mean you have to let me get out of bed."

"Hmm . . ." Cillian pulls me in for one more kiss and releases me.

The cold seeped into the cabin overnight, leaving things just a bit too chilly to roam in my usual sleepwear. I change into leggings and a sweater before heading into the kitchen to start tea for Cillian and coffee for those of us with better taste.

Cillian isn't far behind. He steps into the open main room of the cabin in grey sweats and a black hoodie, looking far better than anyone who just woke up has a right to.

"What is this?" he asks, lifting up a large flat rectangular package wrapped in butcher paper.

"No idea," I say, turning back to the task of beverage

assembly and trying to keep the nervous flutter from my voice. Lucy must've snuck it in here last night.

"Why don't I buy that?"

The kettle clicks, and I pour water over his tea before answering. "Sounds like trust issues to me." I set his mug on the metal workbench, turned-kitchen-island. "Your leaf juice is soaking."

"Toni," he says, dragging my name out like an accusation.

"Cillian," I say in the same cadence. That earns me a raised brow. "You brought me here, remember? I think you would have noticed if I had some large mystery package with me."

A wolfish grin narrows his eyes. "True. I guess I can just toss it—"

"Oh, just open it!" I break, my anticipation overriding my patience.

He laughs and leans against the back of the heavy old sofa. Carefully, he tears away half of the paper before going so still I can't be sure he's even breathing, and when his eyes meet mine, wide and slightly glassy, I know I'm not.

Looking back at the canvas, he pulls the rest of the wrapping away. Again, that stillness.

Unsure, I finally break the silence. "Oliver told me everyone just kind of foists not-birthday birthday gifts on you." I chew my lip. "I hope it's ok . . . I just thought—"

"It's stunning, Antoinette. I—" He shakes his head, clearing his throat. "I don't have words," he says, huffing something close to a laugh.

Cillian gently places the canvas against the back of the sofa. His eyes linger on the sunset view from the Longfellow Bridge, rendered in vibrant colors, with gold leaf making the windows of the skyline glow. I even had to admit, it was one of my better pieces.

"Your tea," I say, gesturing to the mug as he makes his way into the kitchen.

He doesn't acknowledge it, just pulls me into his arms, his fingers fluidly cradling the back of my head as he kisses me. When he pulls back, the look in his eyes is—

Alarm bells begin to sound in the back of my mind. A voice insisting that I needed to run while I could, while my knees still held me upright, because the moment they finally gave way, I'd be done for.

"Thank you," Cillian's voice is rough. He smooths a calloused thumb across my cheek.

"It's just a painting," I say, hoping to quiet the fluttering in my chest.

He cocks a brow. "Just a . . . that is the most beautiful gift I've ever received." He grabs my chin, just firm enough to make a point. "And if I ever hear you downplaying your talent again, I will figure out a way to make you regret it."

"Promise?" I ask.

"Promise," he purrs, pulling me in for another kiss.

"Ok, enough of that. I don't like puking first thing in the morning," Ginelle says as she walks in. She closed the bar the night before but still made her way out here. I wasn't sure where she'd spent the night, but I had my suspicions.

"Can we help you?" Cillian asks.

"Not unless you want to help me take a piss."

"Can't rough it?" he teases.

"Why piss behind a tree when there's a perfectly good bathroom inside?" She closes the door just as Lucy comes in, confirming where Ginelle had spent the night.

"Gin beat you to the bathroom," Cillian tells her.

"I'm good. Haven't given up the perk of pissing standing up for a reason."

"Kinda jealous of that, not gonna lie," I say as Cillian reluctantly lets me go.

"You should be, it's convenient," Lucy says, giving me a

playful wink. She notices the painting against the couch. "Found the delivery from your fairy dyke mother I see."

"You were the co-conspirator," Cillian accuses fondly.

"Of course," Lucy says.

"Will Gin want coffee?" I ask Lucy, passing her a mug.

"She will." I set another mug beside hers as she pulls a sweetened coffee creamer from the fridge, doctoring one mug. She notices my curious expression—I'd mostly seen her take her coffee black unless it was a specialty drink at a coffee shop. "Don't ask."

"Wasn't gonna." I take a deep drink, filing that conversation away for a later date.

"It's freezing in here," Ginelle says, stepping out of the bathroom, rubbing her arms.

"Coffee will help," Lucy says, holding the mug out to her.

"Thank you." Ginelle takes the drink, but I notice the intentional distance kept between the two women. "Cillian, fire, please."

I look over to see Cillian loading wood into the cast-iron stove. "What do you think I'm doing?"

"Just making sure," Ginelle says, shivering.

It doesn't take long for the cabin to warm, especially when everyone else joins us and the O'Sullivan brothers put their short-order cooking skills to good use, doling out breakfast plates to everyone.

"Is this all y'all do out here?" I ask, full and cozy. "Eat and talk shit?" Ginelle had just finished a deserved and amusing tirade about the worst customers of the week.

"And hike," Lucy says.

"No, thank you." I scrunch my nose.

"Same," Camille agrees with me. "I just bring a stack of books."

"See, I can get behind that activity."

"When it's warm, the lake is great for swimming," Oliver says.

I grimace. "I don't trust lakes."

"What?" The whole room choruses.

"There are too many unknown creatures!" I defend myself.

"Sure, there are fish, but nothing that will eat you," Cillian says from his place beside me on the couch. "Unlike the ocean."

I narrow my eyes. "Water moccasins?"

"Do I even want to know what that is?" Ginelle asks.

"A poisonous snake," I clarify, confused.

Cillian smiles. "Oh! No. Water's too cold up here, doll. No snakes."

"Another for the pros column," Lucy says with a grin.

I don't disagree. In fact, this morning has potentially added several pros to the list.

CHAPTER 24

Cillian

"I THOUGHT WE HAD SOMETHING SPECIAL," LUCY chokes out in response to the draw 4 card Toni lays on top of the deck, demanding Lucy take the hit.

Toni shrugs. "There are no friends in Uno, my love."

"Color?" Camille demands, pounding her hand on the coffee table.

Toni narrows her eyes at the very few cards in Camille's hand, as though she is trying to see through them. "Blue."

Camille slams down one of her two cards. "Uno, bitches!"

"That's it. We have to take my wife down." Camille throws a pillow at my brother. "I'm sorry, babe. I love you. You're the mother of my child, the most beautiful and radiant woman I've ever known, but this is war."

"Michael Arthur O'Sullivan, if you plot against me, we're getting a divorce."

"Oooo," Oliver and I sound at once.

"Middle name level of trouble," I taunt.

"Cillian Daniel," Camille pins me with a glare, "You're the one I suspect he'll plot with. Don't. You. Dare."

Oliver lays an innocuous blue 3.

"Sorry. Brotherly loyalty and all." I drop a reverse.

Michael lets out a villainous cackle, and Toni punches my shoulder. "Excuse you, that fucked me, too!" She gestures to Lucy, tittering behind her stack of cards.

"Sorry, doll. Like you said." I pull her toward me, kissing her temple.

Soon enough, the game ends with Camille, once again, claiming victory over us all.

"Who wins three in a row?" Michael grumbles.

"Don't be bitter, just be better, baby!" She teases, blowing him a kiss he still performatively catches despite the scowl on his face.

"You coming?" I ask, waiting for him to join me on the deck for his one permitted smoke.

"Yeah." He grabs his glass and kisses his wife before heading out.

Our glasses clink as we let out twin clouds of smoke.

"I know we just ignore your birthday generally, but how's thirty-eight so far?" He asks, leaning on the railing.

I can't help the smile that rips across my face, so wide it practically hurts. "Can't complain."

Emotion sparkles in my older brother's eyes as he clasps a hand on my shoulder.

"Don't look at me like that," I say, shrugging him off.

It was Michael who found me almost ten years ago, half dead from a heroin overdose. Michael, who, any time they allowed him to be, was by my side. Michael who reminded me I'd promised not to make him bury me before my first deployment, a promise that, according to him, didn't end with my service.

My brother was the reason I was here for this. And gratitude doesn't begin to cover it.

"Thank you," I say, my voice thick.

He nods, leaning his shoulder into mine.

A delighted squeal of laughter draws our attention back to the house. Through the slider, we watch as Camille sprays Toni with the sink nozzle, her face lit with delight.

Toni's rich laugh reaches us, and my chest practically splits open. She grabs Lucy as a shield, while Oliver and Ginelle hide under a blanket.

My brother and I soak in the laughter and golden light spilling onto the deck from inside.

"We're lucky assholes aren't we?" he asks, eyes on Camille.

For the first time in a long time, I feel like that just might be true. "Yeah," I breathe.

Michael puts out his cigarette, and I follow suit. "Let's intervene before my wife makes this a home insurance issue."

⬧

I TEAR MYSELF AWAKE FROM A DREAM, SLAMMING into consciousness so abruptly it takes time for my mind and body to reconnect, leaving me frozen.

Typically, I loathe this feeling, being trapped in my body while my mind screams. But, as I register Toni still sleeping soundly beside me, for once, I'm grateful. Though my heart is slamming against my rib cage with such force, I'm shocked that alone doesn't wake her.

The fear of Toni seeing me like this is enough to bring me back into my body. Enough to propel me from the bed on shaky legs and out into the cold night.

Sucking in lungfuls of crisp air, I grip the banister so tight my palms ache, watching my breath form clouds that float out toward the shining lake.

Today had been a nearly perfect day. No reason for my mind to fall into dark places, nothing that would've triggered the nightmare. Not that any of that mattered.

Sometimes, the mind didn't need a reason to fling open

doors you'd rather stay closed. And sometimes, good times—or rather the fear of losing them—was trigger enough.

"Cillian?" I jump at Toni's voice, so lost in my spiraling thoughts that I didn't even hear her open the sliding door. "What're you doing out here?"

"Um . . ." I start to answer, reaching for something reasonable to say. Instead, my fuzzy mind latches onto the fact that she's out here in nothing but her sleep shirt. "Doll, it's cold, go back inside."

Considering I'm only in my boxers, she gives me the look that statement deserves. "I have more on than you do."

"I'm good."

She closes the space between us, resting her warm hands against my chest. I begin to shiver. "You're freezing," she says, voice laced with concern.

I want to reassure her, tell her I'm fine. This is fine. I'll be fine. Anything to keep her from seeing the fault lines this exposes. But when I open my mouth, nothing comes out.

Toni slides her hands down my arms, tangling our fingers together. "Come back to bed."

I don't let go of her hand until she pulls me onto the mattress with her. And that's where we stay, her arms around me, our foreheads pressed together, long enough for my skin to forget the cold and for the fog of unwanted memories to lift.

"What're you thinking?" she whispers, one finger tracing the lines between my brows.

For a heartbeat, I consider lying, afraid of what her answer may be. "I'm wondering what you see." Saying it feels like opening an old wound, inviting her to pour salt into it. All I can do is hope she won't.

Rather than give me a fast answer, she moves to sit on her knees beside me. I reposition, propping my back against the pillows to better see her.

Toni studies me, her sharp gaze peeling back my defenses with each passing second.

"You," she says matter-of-factly. "I see you, Cillian."

Not all of me. I've held back, kept the things I feared were too much packed away. But, for the first time, I let myself wonder if maybe she could. If I showed her, would she reject me as others had?

I don't have the chance to linger on that question. The feeling of her fingers tugging the tie from my hair, quickly followed by her lips on mine, grounds me in this moment.

She trails that pretty mouth down my jaw to my neck. I shiver as she nibbles at my pulse, tracing her tongue along my collarbones. When her lips press against the scar above my heart, I suck in a breath.

"Sorry. I—"

I press a finger to her lips, cutting off her apology, shaking my head. "No. It's . . ."

Most people I'd been with avoided the scars, especially once they knew their origin. Even Kevin, whom I spent years with, rarely acknowledged them, his hands always skirting around their edges. A strange desperation takes hold of me, a need for Toni to not only be someone at my edges.

Words failing me yet again, I take her hand, pressing her palm to the map of scars along the left side of my torso. I guide her touch down over my boxers and to the wreck of my thigh. Inviting her, intentionally, to the places where I'd been torn open.

Toni doesn't recoil when I release her hand. Her fingers travel over the uneven skin as though she could read the story from the marks it left. My own dialect of Braille that only she'd been willing to learn.

She scoots down, her lips now following the path her fingers had. Methodically, she kisses every ridge, every bump, from my side, down to my hip, slipping my boxers off as she makes her way to my thigh.

My lungs and eyes burn with the effort of holding on to some kind of composure. Part of me wants to weep. Part of me wants to run.

Once more, she studies me, moving to rest between my thighs. In the low light, her brown eyes are dark pools.

"I see you," she repeats. "And Cillian, you're beautiful."

I open my mouth—to say what, I don't know—but she presses her fingers to my lips, silencing me. Saving me. "Shh."

She drags her hand from my face down my chest to my Adonis belt. The caresses and light touches trigger a lightning storm under my skin. My cock jumps, my hips rise.

"You don't always have to be the one in charge, you know." It's not a question. Her hand wraps around my shaft, rubbing the bead of moisture across the head. I let out a strangled sound of pleasure.

Satisfaction sparks in her face, and my god, she's the most spectacular thing I've ever seen.

When she lowers her mouth to me, I swear I nearly come. She takes me slowly, working me with her lips, tongue, and hands. Sitting up, she has one hand on my cock while she presses the fingers of the other against the tender spot just behind my balls, pulsing and rubbing.

I moan, my body shaking with the need to come, but I refuse.

"Stop," I manage. She does without hesitation.

I pull her to me, needing to feel her body against mine, tearing her shirt off. Our teeth clash in my haste to kiss her, to taste her, my fingers roughly moving her panties to the side. I growl against her mouth with satisfaction when I find her already soaking.

"I need to be inside you. Please." I'd beg if she wanted. Get on my knees right now and beg her for the privilege of letting me feel her.

She nods, shifting her legs to straddle me.

"Do you care about these?" I ask, fingers wrapped around her lace underwear.

"No," she says, shaking her head.

The delicate fabric gives way to my fingers as I rip them off. I grab her hips, pulling her to me and kissing her neck, her breasts, her nipples, letting my hands wander up the curve of her soft belly and digging my fingers into her. I can't get enough; I can't touch enough of her.

What a beautiful problem.

Her warmth envelops me, blotting out everything else. There's only this. This incredible woman.

"Cillian," she groans, her head falling back as she takes all of me, her hips rolling, seeking her pleasure.

"That's it, baby doll." I lift my hips to push myself deeper. "Take what you need." *Take all of me*, I think.

She does. God, she does. In every way, whether she knows it or not.

I'm awestruck watching her ride my cock, her hair falling free around her shoulders, the dawn light slowly slipping around her, outlining her in a golden aura.

She looks ethereal. Holy. Something good and right and mine.

No. Not mine. Not really. Not yet.

But I want her to be, I allow myself to accept that. I want every morning to be this. I want every day to taste like her kiss. I lo—

Fuck.

Love.

I feel her tighten around me.

Fuck.

The sun breaches the hills, flooding the room with light

just as clarity floods all my senses with joy and fear in equal measure.

This woman. I love this woman. All of her. Her mess, her chaos, and her stubborn strength.

I love her.

She comes apart, her body shaking with release, glowing and rapturous.

"Antionette," I breathe her name like a prayer, a rite, something sacred.

I pull her face to mine, needing her mouth to keep me from saying something stupid. Gripping that perfect ass, I move her at my pace.

"Look at me," I demand. She does. "Fuck." My voice is gravel.

"Come for me, Cillian."

I cry her name as I come, my body practically convulsing with the force of it.

Both of us lay there, slick with sweat and shaking, neither willing to move, but one thought clangs in my skull.

What the fuck am I going to do now?

CHAPTER 25
Toni

Too much. This feels like too much.

The look in his eyes, the way his hands touch me like he's holding something precious, how fucking good this feels.

It's too easy to let myself fall into him. Into this. Too easy to get too comfortable. Too easy to say too much.

My heart stumbles over itself, tangling in my chest with all the shouldn't and can't and want.

All the things that I know I am and that I'm not.

All the ways I have ruined good things in the past.

All the reasons I know that I cannot let myself have him.

"Hey," Cillian breathes. He pushes my hair behind my ears. "Where'd you go?"

"Nowhere." I shift my gaze from his, too afraid that he'll see the lie.

"Look at me." That gentle command in his tone sends tingles through my body, and I do as he asks. "Stay with me."

I study him, wanting to untangle what he means by that.

Stay in bed? Stay . . .

Don't. I chide myself.

I bite my lip and nod. He reaches up, freeing it and pulling me down for a kiss.

My head settles into the place where his neck and shoulder meet. I breathe him in. His fingers trace patterns on my back, and I doze, the steady rhythm of his heartbeat and breath as good as any lullaby he could sing.

Better, even.

We stay like that as the sun rises higher, until we hear a mumble of voices in the living room.

Slowly, without words, we untangle and dress.

As my hand wraps around the doorknob, his appears above my head, holding the door closed.

I turn, looking up into his gently smiling face. He tilts my chin up, kissing me so tenderly.

"I'm gonna shower," I say when he releases me.

"Ok." He kisses my forehead. "I'll make sure there's still coffee when you come out."

In the bathroom, I study my reflection. The woman in the mirror should look blissed out. Instead, she looks desperate. I just wish I knew for what.

Desperate to stay?

Stay with me.

Desperate to run?

It wasn't just my penchant for clutter that earned me the "Hurricane Toni" moniker. My twenties were littered with proof of my inability to stay anywhere for too long. I moved through people and places quickly.

A chorus of voices fill my head like static. Friends chiding me for my inability to commit, my unwillingness to compromise on topics like children and picket fences. Confused at my consistent dismissal of people who seemed 'perfectly nice.' Exes I left after a first fight, or ones who never even had the chance to become more than a fading memory of a few decent orgasms.

Then there was David. Nice, stable David. And I decided to try. I tried to be something more refined, less chaotic, less loud. Less. Because maybe everyone was right. Who could be expected to handle all my mess, and noise, and . . . everything?

But just like all the times before, my storm broke. My unwillingness to change, my unreasonable nature, won out in the end.

"Don't do this to him," I whisper to myself.

Cillian said his fault lines were there—Grand Canyon-sized even—but if so, he'd managed what I never could and filled in the holes. Built reinforcements, worked on an infrastructure of healing, and found a way to cope.

If I let this continue, Hurricane Toni would rip through those reinforcements.

Lucy's laugh cuts through the sound of the water.

Breaking things off with Cillian would also mean losing these people. Without meaning to, I'd begun to feel like they were my friends, too. And for the second time in less than two years, I'd find myself alone.

I press my forehead to the tile.

Did it have to be over, though? We were adults. Couldn't we stay friends? Just friends. Friends who kept their hands to themselves and who didn't have incredible, soul-moving sunrise sex.

Fuck.

Everyone but Ginelle—who heads out before I'm dressed to be back in time to open the bar—spends the morning lazily preparing to leave. Thankfully, the banter and activity keep me occupied, drowning out the low-grade panic clawing at the back of my mind.

Right up until we say our final goodbyes.

It's just an hour and a half, Toni. You can keep your shit together for an hour and a goddamn half, I say to myself over and over.

Except, I'm not 100% convinced I can. Holding my tongue, especially with anxiety buzzing through my body, has never been something I've excelled at. But I couldn't tell Cillian, "Hey so that was amazing and you're so wonderful and your family and friends are a delight and thank you for bringing me along but maybe we should see less of one another you know just to be safe because I'm scared I'm going to ruin your life," out of the blue.

An hour and a half. I repeat again as I slide into the passenger seat.

"Before we hit the road, we need to talk about something," Cillian says, in a tone that feels perhaps a touch too serious. My stomach drops. He holds the AUX cord out to me.

A laugh bursts free before I can tone it down. It's not entirely warranted, but some of my fear floods out with the sound.

"Don't laugh!" he says, grinning. "This is a very serious moment of trust. I don't let just anyone play music in my car."

"I'll be sure to make you regret it," I say, composing myself.

An hour in, my concerns about loose lips have been washed away with a steady flow of early 2000s pop and pop punk. Though the last 15 minutes had been nothing but Taylor Swift.

I can't help but stare in disbelief as Cillian sings along.

"What?" he asks as the song fades out, noticing my gawking.

"That is the fourth Taylor Swift song you've known almost every word to."

"And?"

I can't help but laugh. "And, I'm pretty sure you gave me shit when you saw my record collection."

"No." He tosses me a bright smile as he slows to turn. "I gave you shit for having multiples of the same album. Not for being a Swiftie. I respect it." He takes my hand, planting a kiss on my knuckles, and slides his fingers between mine.

The next song starts but is quickly interrupted by the Bluetooth announcing a call from "Ma."

He ignores it. "I'll call her when we're back."

A few seconds later, another call cuts through.

Cillian's brows knit. "Sorry, I should—"

"Don't apologize," I reassure him.

"Hey, Mom."

"Hey, sweetheart." Cillian's mom—Kitty, as I'd heard others refer to her—answers, her accent thick. "Sorry to bother ya, I know you're on your way back but . . ." she fades off, muffling the mic before continuing. "Have you heard from Joey recently?"

His jaw flexes beneath his tight, cropped beard. "No. Not for a few weeks. We . . . We had words. Why?"

"Oh . . ." More muffled voices from off the line. "Will you give me a damn minute, Tina?" Cillian's mom says to someone, frustration clear in her tone.

"Mom?"

"Hold on, sweetheart." In the shuffling silence, Cillian and I exchange a tense look. "Sorry, impossible to talk with my sister in the room in the best of times." Kitty sighs. "Tina hasn't heard from Joey in a few days. He's not taking her calls. Julie and the kids even tried to call him and got nothing."

Cillian releases my hand, gripping the steering wheel so tight his knuckles turn white.

"She's getting worried. Wants to call in a wellness—"

"Do not let her call the cops, Mom," Cillian cuts her off.

"I know, I know. I talked her down from it . . ." She trails off for a moment. "He's probably fine. Right? Just having some bad days."

"Yeah. Probably." Cillian pulls into a gas station.

"Anyway, just wanted to check with you. She said she wants to go over there today, so I'll just go—"

"No." Cillian snaps, his voice rough. He drags in a breath. "Just . . . tell her I'm on my way."

"Cilli . . ."

"Mom, please." He rubs a hand over his face. "Do not go over there. Don't let her go over there. Let me handle it."

There's a tense pause before she replies. "Okay." Cillian's body visibly relaxes. "I'll do my best to stall her, but she's gonna try to get over there."

"Give me at least an hour if you can. Tell her I'm on it and I'll give you a call when I talk to him."

"Alright. Be safe, sweetheart."

"I will be."

"I love you, Cillian."

"Love you, too."

As soon as the call disconnects, the music starts playing again, its poppy tune incongruous with the heavy atmosphere that has settled over the car.

Cillian turns, the volume down, his eyes fixed forward.

After the silence hangs a little too heavy, I speak. "I've got nothing else to do today. Wherever you need to go, I'm good to come along."

He nods stiffly. "Thanks. I . . ." He heaves a sigh, letting his head thud against the headrest.

"You don't need to explain." I reach over, giving his thigh what I hope is a comforting squeeze.

He covers my hand with his, returning the squeeze, as he looks over at me. "Thank you."

Rather than plunge us into total silence, I let the music keep playing at a low volume as we head out, hoping it can bring a bit of levity to the drive. But as we get closer to our destination, the tension radiating from Cillian only seems to increase. When his mother texts him, a half hour later, letting him know she and his aunt are on the way to Joey's, the tension and our speed ratchets up even higher.

We pull onto a residential street, and he stops the car suddenly, his breathing ragged. Before I can ask if he's ok, Cillian turns to me, gathering my hands in both of his. His expression is hard, but it's what I see in his eyes that scares me.

Fear.

"I need you to listen to me," he says, tone stern.

I nod.

"You're going to get in the driver's seat. I'll direct you the rest of the way. When we get there, you are gonna lock the doors, and you're not to get out of this car for any reason whatsoever." He pulls a breath in through his nose, jaw visibly tightening. "And if you hear anything or see anything that seems out of pocket or suspicious, you're going to leave and call the cops. Understood?"

"Cillian—"

"Promise me you will not get out of this car, Antionette. Please."

I nod again, the urgency in his voice silencing any questions.

"Say it."

"I promise." That seems to soothe something in him.

He takes a deep breath, nodding. "Good."

We switch positions, and he guides me just a few streets down to his cousin's house.

Everything seems normal. Just a standard small single-family home. Empty driveway. Nothing amiss.

Cillian pulls the pendant he always wears from under his sweater, pressing it to his lips before letting it fall against his chest.

"Cillian?" I lay my hand on his shoulder, unsure what to say.

"He's probably fine. Just on a bender." Something in his tone tells me he doesn't believe that.

He looks at me, a storm of his own raging in his green eyes. It makes my heart ache, longing to somehow make this easier, knowing I can't do anything beyond what he's already asked of me. Cillian pulls me to him, pressing a kiss to my forehead before letting go.

"Stay in the car," he commands as he gets out.

"Be careful," I say after him.

"It'll be fine," he says, trying to force something like a reassuring smile but falling short.

When I was a kid, I'd always get this 'calm before the storm' feeling right before things would get bad at home— usually meaning my dad had gotten fired again or was going to come home drunk. It was like some survival mechanism gained from growing up in a war zone. As an adult, it never went away, and the last time I felt it was the night David proposed. And now, sitting in Cillian's car, watching him knock and wait before using a spare key to let himself in, that feeling creeps over me again.

A storm was coming. I just didn't know what kind.

I keep my eyes on the house, scanning from the windows to the garage to the front door and back again. Every muscle humming with tension.

In the side mirror, I see a car pulling up along the curb.

A petite woman with Ginelle's blonde hair leaps from the passenger side, while a tall woman with honey brown hair rushes after her from the driver's seat. My heart falls into my stomach.

Cillian hadn't said there was danger. Not explicitly. But I had read his order to stay in the relative safety of the car as a warning all the same. A warning that his mom and aunt hadn't received.

I don't hesitate to get out of the car, figuring a broken

promise is better than a potentially worse outcome. Before the two women manage to cross the postage stamp of a lawn, I intercept them.

"Hi!" I say, attempting something like a smile. "Cillian went in a few minutes ago. I think he wants to check things out first. Just give him—"

"Who the fuck are you?" The petite woman asks, trying to push past me.

"Toni, I'm Cillian's friend." I move to block her as her sister lays her hands on her shoulders.

"Tina, why don't we give Cillian a minute? No one wants their family barging in—"

"Get off me!" She tries to shrug Kitty off but whirls on her instead. She flings a finger back at the house, barely missing my face in the process. "If it was Cillian—"

"I know," Kitty says, grabbing for her sister's hand. Her tone is even and soothing, "If it were, you'd be telling me the same thing. Give them a minute and then we'll go in and—"

Behind me, the door opens, drawing our attention to Cillian as he steps out onto the small porch.

His face is white, his expression stoic.

"Cillian . . ." Tina's voice is crystalline, sharp, and strangely delicate. She pulls from her sister's grip, shouldering past me, moving toward him. "Is . . . Is Joey home?"

His mouth opens, then closes, eyes moving from his aunt to his mom, looking for a moment like a lost boy.

Kitty sucks in a breath, her hand flying to her mouth.

The storm I'd felt in the car makes landfall.

"I . . . I'm sorry." He shakes his head. "Tina, I'm sorry."

"Sorry?" Tina asks. She sounds confused, as if she doesn't understand, or refuses to understand, what Cillian's words imply. "Get out of my way." She makes a shooing motion, trying to move past him. He grabs her arm, drawing her short.

"Excuse—Don't you fucking touch—" She tries to pull free. "Joseph! Get your ass out here! Joey!"

"Tina, honey . . ." Kitty says, taking a step toward her sister.

Tina throws her a wild glare. Her eyes are wide and shining with fear, fury, and something deeper. She jerks her arm painfully hard, but Cillian doesn't budge.

"I can't let you go in there, Tina," he says, his voice rough. She looks up at him. Cillian shakes his head. "He's not . . . He's gone. I'm sorry."

"No," she says so quietly, I almost miss it. "No," she declares louder. "No. He's . . ." She looks over at me and Kitty, frozen in place on the lawn. "He can't. No." The word feels heavy.

Tina takes a step back, away from the house, and Cillian releases his hold on her. Taking advantage of the moment, she tries to bolt for the door, but Cillian catches her once more, wrapping her tightly in his arms as she fights until her back is pressed against his chest.

"I'm sorry," Cillian says again.

"Let me go!" she howls. "Let me see my son." The final word is anguished.

"He wouldn't want you to see him like this. I can't—"

"You don't know!" she cries, fighting like a trapped animal.

"I do," Cillian's voice cracks, his eyes finding his own mother. The implication makes me shiver. "I do."

Something about this breaks Tina's fight. She goes limp in Cillian's arms, and he guides them both to their knees in the grass, finally letting her go.

Kitty unfreezes, moving with almost shocking speed toward her sister and son. She lays a hand on her sister's back while cupping her son's cheek, trying to be what they both need, pulled in two impossible directions.

Tina howls a sob, a guttural, near-primal sound that vibrates somewhere in my bones. The unnatural sound of a parent mourning their child.

It's the worst thing I've ever heard.

Cillian shuts his eyes against the sound. His mother's hand delicately stroking his cheek.

I can't imagine what she must feel. Her boy, still here while her sister's is gone. Her boy, who clearly got close enough to know what he would and wouldn't want his mother to see.

Kitty looks over at me, and I produce my phone. "Should I?"

She nods.

I feel guilty wanting both to be helpful and utterly desperate for an excuse to step away from the heartbreaking scene before me.

I've barely hung up the phone with 911 when a car I recognize squeals onto the street. Ginelle barely parks before getting out and freezing, the sound of her mother's sobbing carrying down the yard to where I face her on the curb.

"Toni?" she asks, breathless, eyes begging me to lie to her.

All I can manage is to echo Cillian. "I'm so sorry."

She reaches behind her, fumbling for the car, anything to lean against. I step forward, reaching out to steady her. Ginelle falls into me, accepting the support, her body shaking but not quite crying.

"Baby?" Tina's ragged voice pulls our attention back.

"Mom . . ." Ginelle's voice breaks.

The woman rushes to her daughter. Ginelle meets her halfway and they embrace, sinking to the grass, holding one another tight.

Across the lawn, I meet Cillian's eyes, finding them surprisingly cold.

Kitty remains at his side, arm wrapped around his.

Seeing mother and son together completes something in

my understanding of Cillian. While he has his dad's coloring —the dark salt-and-pepper hair, the green eyes—everything else is Kitty. She stands only a few inches shorter than her son; her features are defined, with full lips. For a woman who has to be in her 60s, she's incredibly striking.

"You ok?" He asks as I walk up to them.

"Relatively."

He nods. "I need a smoke." He pulls away from Kitty's hold on his arm and walks to the car.

We both watch him, our shared worry humming between us like static.

"Toni," Kitty says, and I turn my attention to her. "Kitty." She holds out a well-manicured hand. "Sure, you figured that out by now, but still."

"Good to finally meet you." I give her hand a squeeze.

"Wish it was in better circumstances." She looks over to the tangled pile of her niece and sister.

"Me, too . . ." I chew my lip. "I'm so sorry for your loss." The words feel grossly inadequate.

She purses her full lips, swallowing hard. "Thank you." Her fingers curl around a crucifix hanging over her sweater, eyes moving to her son, his back to us, a curl of smoke rising from his cigarette. "It's a mother's worst fear." Her voice is distant. "That she'll bury her babies."

Before she can say more, the cries of sirens cut through the air.

Everything becomes a blur, punctuated only by the moment when they bring Joey out, a man whose name I'd heard but whose face I'd never seen.

Tina's howl of grief redoubles, the impact rattling through everyone in range.

Unable to watch, I keep my attention on Cillian. His eyes remain fixed on some distant point miles away, even as he holds Ginelle tight, keeping her on her feet; his mother presses a hand to his lower back as she soothes her niece as best she can.

I feel like an interloper. But with nowhere else to go, I'm trapped hovering at the edges, trying to remain close enough to help if needed but not so close that I'm intruding.

When the responders finally clear out, the silence they leave is suffocating.

"Ginelle, sweetheart," Kitty coaxes Ginelle to look at her. "Why don't you leave your car here and ride with your mom and me?" She wipes a quiet tear from Gin's pale cheek.

She shakes her head. "I can drive."

"Gin, I could drive your car back if—" I begin to offer.

"I . . ." She sniffs hard, looking over at her mom, who is sitting on the steps of the porch, eyes fixed on her hands. "I think I need the time alone. Before . . . before we go tell the kids." Her jaw clenches as she visibly tries to contain a sob.

"Gigi," Cillian says softly, a name I'd never heard anyone use for Ginelle before. "I can handle that."

"You've done enough. You don't have to do this."

"I know I don't have—"

"I've got it." Her voice is suddenly steady, firm in her stance on this.

"Ok, sweetheart." Kitty gives her shoulder a squeeze.

"Mom," Ginelle kneels at her mother's side. "You're gonna ride with Kitty. I'm gonna follow, ok?" Tina only nods blankly.

Without prompting, Cillian goes to Tina's other side, and with tender but effective hands, he guides his aunt to her feet. Ginelle stands, taking her mother's other side.

Kitty clears her throat, taking my forearm to draw me a little closer as the others lead Tina to the car. "I know you haven't known one another for very long and that this . . . has been a lot." She looks over at her son. When she returns her focus to me, there's a near-desperate fire in her eyes. "But please don't let him be alone right now. Please. I'll give you my number, or I assume you may have Lucy or Oli—"

I cover her hand with mine, giving it a firm squeeze. "Kitty, I'm not going anywhere. I'll stick with him, I promise."

I've never meant anything more in my life.

The truth of what I said must've shown through because she visibly relaxes. "Thank you." She looks over at him once more. "If it . . . If anything is too much, though . . ."

"I've got him."

She gives me a warm smile, her shoulders dropping the barest bit. "Just call if you need to, ok?"

I nod, handing her my phone. Cillian walks up, as she hands it back to me, hands shoved in the pockets of his jeans.

"You know you're welcome to go to the house if you'd like," Kitty says to Cillian. "Your Dad is at the bar, but I think he's gonna close early."

Cillian looks at the ground. "Yeah. Maybe."

Kitty cups his face in her hands, pushing stray silver and dark brown strands from his face. "You don't have to. If you just want to go home, that's ok, too."

He nods, avoiding looking her directly in the eye.

"Look at me, Cillian." He hesitates but complies, his expression momentarily vulnerable before the hardness returns. "This is not your fault, baby."

"Mom, don't—" He pulls away from her, but she grabs his shoulders, holding him in place as though he were a little boy and not a six-foot-three man.

"No," she snaps, voice low. "I need you to hear me. You couldn't have changed this, Cillian." She drags in a shaky breath. "Do not let this undo you."

"I won't." Cillian's voice wavers. "Promise."

"Good." She pulls him into a tight hug. "I love you so much, my sweet boy."

"Love you, too, Mom."

Kitty turns her attention to me. "I'm so sorry you had to be in the middle of this, but I'm so grateful for your help."

"I didn't really do anything, but you're welcome," I say, trying to give her a warm smile.

"If you need anything . . ."

"I'll call."

She nods and, without warning, wraps her arms around me with the same force she applied to her son. I return the embrace, partly because it seems rude not to and also because that maternal warmth, even borrowed from someone else, feels so good right now.

Releasing me, she sighs. "And by the way, I know my son hasn't passed along my Sunday supper invite. I'll send you a text." It's a small moment of levity, but we latch on to it.

"Mom," Cillian sighs.

She laughs a little. "You two drive safe."

Cillian turns to me, after his mom drives off, looking at me head-on for the first time in a while. He briefly strokes my cheek, but his eyes remain cold. "Let's get you home."

"I'm not going home unless you're coming with me," I say, matter-of-factly. His eyes narrow. "Cillian, I'm not—"

His jaw clenches, neck muscles tightening. "Did my mother—"

"She didn't have to." It's not a lie. I stare up at him, unflinching.

He rolls his eyes.

"Cillian, what you just went through, that—it's not something I'm going to leave you to sit with alone. If you'd prefer someone else, that's—"

He laughs. It's dark and humorless. "I promise you, I sit with worse every day. I don't need a fucking babysitter."

"Don't be an asshole."

"I am an asshole."

"Sure, you are."

"Toni," he growls.

"I'm not arguing with you. And I don't need anything from you. We don't have to talk, hell, we don't even have to be in the same room. But you're stuck with me."

And maybe I don't want to be alone either.

To say Cillian softens, worn down by my defiance, would be an overstatement. Still, there isn't any malice in his tone when he says, "Fine. Let's go."

⟡

WE RIDE BACK TO CILLIAN'S IN SILENCE.

His eyes remain firmly ahead, both hands on the wheel.

I gnaw my lip until I taste copper, so I switch to chewing at the inside of my cheek and picking off my nail polish.

Despite not wanting to be alone, in the silence of the car, I consider texting Lucy and Oliver. They'd be better equipped to deal with this than I am, and if he'd prefer their company, I could cope on my own. But while I figured it was safe to assume they already knew, I'd rather throw myself out of the car than risk being the one to break the news of Joey's death to either of them.

So instead, I arrive in Cillian's red brick driveway with my mouth raw and fingers devoid of any color.

Given his overall demeanor, I expect a door slam or snide remark. But there's none of that.

"You want your bag?"

"I can get it."

He ignores me, grabbing both our bags and the canvas.

Every move as we go through the motions of unloading the car, going upstairs, and depositing our bags in the primary bedroom feels like a step on a tightrope. On the surface, everything is calm, yet just one incorrect wobble and one or both of us will teeter over into the abyss.

When we begin to head back downstairs, I brace myself and ask, "Would you like me to stay up here, or do you want company?"

"You can be wherever you want." He tosses the words over his shoulder. "I'm getting a drink."

I swallow the petty retort burning on my tongue and follow him down to the dining room turned study just off the living room.

Over the past few months, I'd come to love this room. Books—some are Cillian's and some were left by his uncle—spill out of the built-in shelves. Two old plush chairs face the fireplace, one of Cillian's well-loved guitars in permanent residence beside them. Usually, the space is the pinnacle of cozy and comfortable.

As we walk in, it might as well be a meat locker.

Cillian heads straight to the antique buffet tucked in one corner. Cut crystal bottles I'd never seen him touch sit in a cluster with a few glasses beside them. He pours a hearty amount of amber liquid into one of the tumblers, downing it in one go.

I watch his shoulders heave as he drags in a deep breath, laying his palms flat on the buffet. Several long moments pass before he pours another.

He takes a sip, his back still to me as he says, "I'd rather you not observe me like a zoo animal. Make a drink, sit down, go upstairs, anything but just standing there."

I eye the bar as he drops heavily into one of the armchairs, tempted by the prospect of a drink, but decide against it. Generally, I try to avoid alcohol when emotions are this high. Sure, I'll imbibe some sadness wine here and there, but my fear of being my father's daughter makes me keep my distance from anything harder.

"Toni," he prompts.

"Sorry," I shake my head. "I'm not sure what the right thing to do is."

He sighs, looking tired. "There isn't a right thing. Do what you want."

"I want to be here for you. I just—"

"And here you are."

I roll my eyes at that, unable to stop myself.

He looks at me, his face a blank mask, void of the Cillian I know. "Look, if you expected hysterics, I'm sorry to disappoint."

My jaw tenses, the urge to tell him once more to not be an ass is strong. "I didn't—" I take a breath, leaning against the thick molding around the pocket doors. "If this is how you need to process, that's fine."

"Not to be crass, but this isn't new for me. Plenty of people I knew have . . ." He trails off, letting the unspoken words hang. "He won't be the last."

"I'm sorry."

"Me, too."

"But he is—was family. It's ok if this is harder—"

"I don't expect you to understand this, but the others felt a lot like family, too."

"But you didn't—"

"Find them?" He finishes his whiskey and makes another. "No, but a dead body also isn't something new to me." His voice drops so low I almost don't hear him as he mumbles into his glass, "At least I'm not directly responsible for this one."

My breath catches, loud enough for him to hear.

Immediately, I regret it. I want to explain that it isn't that I'm shocked; I did the math and inferred what eight years as a Marine meant. It was that my heart hurt for him, that I hated he carried this, that—

"And to be clear, I've been directly responsible for more than a few." There is nothing but disgust in his words. Disgust aimed solely at himself. But the way he pins me with his eyes feels like a challenge.

"Why are you doing that?"

"What?" He settles back into the chair, setting his foot on the small ottoman. "Telling you the truth?"

"Cillian . . ."

"Toni."

"If you think this is going to scare me off, you should let that go."

He shrugs, taking a slow sip. "I think you'll do whatever you want."

I hold on to my composure with gritted teeth and pull the ottoman from under him to perch on. "Care to explain what you mean by that?"

"Not really."

For several long minutes, we sit in tense silence, the settling of the old house and Cillian's methodical swallowing the only sounds filling the void.

By default, I'm good at showing up, at getting shit done, but I've never been the most nurturing person. When Belle's husband was in his final weeks, I made sure meals were arriving at the ranch, helped her mom get the paperwork in order, and performed other similar tasks. But the comfort portion, the parts of being there for someone that involve stillness, those I'm less adept at.

Even so, if the only thing I can do right now is be present, I will. However, I will not be someone's dartboard.

Cillian empties his glass and rises to refill it a third time. Before he takes a step, I latch onto his forearm with as much strength as I can muster. It manages to bring him to a stop, though I'm under no illusion that I'm actually holding him in place.

Stern eyes slide from my hand to my face, one dark brow raised in silent question.

"I know you're hurting." He says nothing. "And I want to be here for you. But if you have an issue with me being here, I can go." I leave out that if I do go, I will be texting his best friends before I'm even out the door.

He remains silent, pulls his arm away, and stalks to the bar.

I sigh, looking to the ceiling as if it holds some wisdom that will help me be of any use in this fucked situation.

The slam of the heavy-bottomed decanter slamming into the top of the buffet makes me jump, drawing my attention back to Cillian.

His hands are braced on the buffet, head hanging as he draws in slow, deep breaths. Beside him, his glass remains empty.

"You were supposed to stay in the car." His voice is a restrained rumble.

"What?" I ask, genuinely unsure if I heard him correctly.

"The fucking car, Toni!" he snaps, frustrated, but I don't sense any anger in the words. "You were supposed to stay there. To stay out of—away from anything."

"Cillian," I keep my voice calm, "your mom and aunt—"

"It wasn't safe. You weren't—" A fissure sounds in his voice as a shiver shakes his broad frame. "None of you were."

"It was a bad situation." I try to soothe.

He shakes his head. "If you'd all just listened!" He slams a palm against the buffet, crystal shaking.

"It wouldn't have changed anything."

He scoffs. "And if it had been different?" He spins to face me, eyes burning with something I don't think is anger but can't quite clock. "If he hadn't—If . . ." Cillian runs a hand across his face, pacing to the bookshelf and back to the doors. "If he'd come out armed or swinging, what then, Toni? What if something—If he—If you . . ."

Fear. It hits me all of a sudden. It isn't anger. He was, hell, is afraid. My heart twists.

"Fuck!" His fist slams into the brick of the fireplace with a painful thud. My whole body tenses, muscle memory more than anything, because despite his actions, I don't feel threatened. He lets his hand fall away, a tiny speck of red smearing the white painted bricks.

"Cillian . . ." I slowly rise, but don't move toward him.

"You have to listen to me sometimes," he says, voice again low. He braces himself on the mantle, not turning to face me as he speaks. "I know this was different. I know you were doing what you thought was best. I just . . . I need to know you'll listen because if I . . ." His shoulders shake with a swallowed sob, and I can't keep my distance any longer.

I lay a hand on his shoulder, but he shrugs me off, stepping away toward the corner.

"Don't." He shakes his head, hand again rubbing across his face. "I need you to understand. I . . ." He looks to the ceiling, the window, the floor—anywhere but at me.

"You what, Cillian?"

"That I am not ok!" His eyes are wild, desperate.

"Of course you—" I stop my forward motion at his gesture to remain back.

"No. Not this. Not just this." He leans his back into the corner, letting his head thud painfully against a shelf of books. "What happened today could have been me." I open my mouth to protest, but he cuts me off. "It almost was me. And . . ." He swallows hard. "There are still days . . . That it's hard. It's so hard." His face contorts as he fights back tears.

His eyes lock on the curtains. "Days that I'm not . . . I'm not here. I'm not me." When he looks back at me, I feel like someone is ripping my sternum open. "It's too much. I-I'm too—"

"You are not too much," I say with all the conviction I can muster.

"You don't get it. I am fucked up, Toni. The shit in my

head . . . this isn't just 'oh, I don't put the laundry up,' kinda fucked." It's a statement meant to push me back, but it's weak at best. He gestures to his chest. "It's 'I may not be safe to be around' kinda fucked. I could—"

"I'm going to stop you right there, because I need you to hear me." I pause for protest, but he doesn't issue any. "I promise you, I will listen to you. I'll always listen and take you seriously. But Cillian," I meet his eyes, squaring my shoulders, "I will not let you be a threat to me."

He opens his mouth to protest, but I don't let him.

"I'm not done. I knew how to scent violent men before I could spell my own name." Concern flickers on his brows. "I need you to trust that I know when to run. It's hard-wired in me. And if I ever for one second thought you were a threat to me, I wouldn't be here."

I take a half step toward him and then another, slowly closing the distance between us. "And I'll gladly hold space to talk about safety, and what will make you feel comfortable. But Cillian, right now, I think you're just using that to avoid what happened today. Because it was awful and it shook you and you're scared." His eyes squeeze shut. I cup his cheek cautiously, expecting him to pull away, but he doesn't.

"And that makes sense. And I know you wanted to keep me from it. But I was there, and I'm here now, and you're not alone with this."

A tremor rocks through him. He holds my hand against his. "And I'm not going anywhere right now. So stop trying to push me away. I'm incredibly stubborn, so you will not win."

He huffs, almost a laugh, but on its heels comes a small sob.

It's as if that one sound sucked his strength away because he sinks to the floor, back pressed into the corner.

I kneel before him, unsure how to offer comfort to a hurt so vast. With a hand on his knee, I say, "I'm here."

A brutal sob racks through him, and my hesitation flees. He pulls me into him, and I settle into his lap. I do my best to gather as much of him into me as I can, my legs around his hips, holding him tight as he weeps against my chest.

"I've got you." I realize how many times he's said those words to me in the short time we've known one another, how many times he's been willing to carry me literally and figuratively.

Rubbing his back and stroking his hair, I repeat it like a mantra, like a prayer. Begging him to trust me enough to let me carry some of his burden for a little while.

CHAPTER 26
Cillian

BEYOND THE CURTAINS, THE LIGHT HAS FADED, leaving the room dim and quiet.

I know we should get up, should let the blood flow back to our legs, should . . . Shit, there were plenty of things I should do right now, people to call, arrangements to help with. But all I want to do is hold onto Toni.

The weight of her in my lap, the warmth of her body, her gentle reassurances—the whole of her—is keeping me here. And, as much as I don't want to admit it to myself, there is a part of me that does not want to be here. Or anywhere. It's the part of me that is so goddamn tired of pain and loss. The part that is screaming to feel nothing.

So I tighten my grip. Rest my forehead against her chest. Squeeze my eyes tight.

"Breathe," she coos in my ear.

I suck in a ragged breath. And another. Her scent mixes with the much-needed oxygen.

"Sorry," I rasp.

Toni coaxes me to look at her. "Don't you dare."

"I did say there wouldn't be hysterics." I try to make my

voice sound lighter than I feel, a poor attempt to hide the twinge of shame curling in my gut.

She rolls her eyes, shifting a bit. "Not to change the subject, but I think my legs are numb." The awkward grin on her face brings a genuine smile to mine.

Blood flow restored, Toni walks toward the living room. "Come on." She waves for me to follow.

"For what?" I ask.

"You need to eat."

I follow, not because I agree, but because I don't want her out of my sight. Despite my dismissive words earlier, the thought of her being away from me right now makes the ground shift beneath my feet, not unlike the moment I saw her outside the safety of the car when I walked out of Joey's house.

"I don't have much of an appetite," I say, needing to focus on anything other than Joey.

"Too bad." She opens the fridge, studying the contents. "I'm Southern. My impulse in these situations is to cook . . . something."

For a moment, I'm entranced, watching her pull things out. "No offense, but I've never so much as seen you turn the stove on, doll." My thigh cramps angrily, informing me that I would be paying for having my breakdown on the floor rather than someplace more sensible. I pull out one of the old dining chairs, stretching my leg out in front of me.

"Liar."

"Oh?"

"I turned the stove on when we cooked together a couple of weeks ago. Not that you let me do anything more than that." I raise a brow at her. "I can cook," she says. I can't restrain the way her heavy emphasis on 'can' brings out that Texas twang in her voice. "When the spirit moves me."

"And the spirit is moving you in the direction of?"

"Chili?" she asks.

"Sounds great."

As Toni cobbles together our meal from whatever is in my kitchen, we chat about small things. She tells me how she learned to cook from watching her mom in the kitchen. I tell stories about my own mother teaching Michael and me to cook, because she didn't want her boys to be as useless as her brothers.

For a precious couple of hours, it feels like there is no world outside of this bubble. No painful memories. No grief. Just warm light, good food, and this woman.

"That was very good," I say. "I'm pleasantly surprised."

Toni glares at me. "I feel like that was meant to be a compliment." She stands, gathering her bowl and reaching for mine.

I grin, stopping her from taking my bowl and pluck her's from her hand. "It was." Grabbing her by the hips, I pull her closer. "Thank you."

"You're welcome," she says, kissing my forehead.

"But, since you cooked, you're not allowed to do the dishes. House rules." I scoot away from her, bracing myself on the heavy wooden table as I stand.

"House rules my ass," she scoffs. She yanks her dishes back from me. "You never let me do dishes when you cook."

"Guests aren't allowed to do dishes either." I try to take the bowl back. "Hey, I don't make the rules."

"This is quite literally your house."

"Technically, it's my—"

"Uncle's. Don't blame him." She tries to pull it free from me, but we're in a standoff. "Ugh!"

"Did you just stomp your foot at me?" I chuckle.

"Maybe." She pulls at the bowl. I smirk, pulling the bowl up until she's forced to release it. "You're being so difficult!"

I grip her chin with my free hand, kissing her pursed lips. "Now you know how it feels."

Her jaw drops open with an offended gasp.

My laugh catches me off guard, the sound a bit too big for the low-ceilinged kitchen. I set the dish down and try to pull Toni into me. To my delight, she fights me.

"Absolutely not." She pushes against my chest. "You just called me difficult." Playfully, she bats my kiss away.

I get around her defenses. This time, her lips soften against mine. "I like that you're difficult," I say softly.

An emotion I can't quite clock flutters behind her eyes, so fast I may be imagining it.

Toni clears her throat a little before saying, "So does that mean you'll let me do the dishes?"

We ultimately split the task, falling into an easy rhythm of me washing, her drying. When I rinse soap off the final spoon, I've never been so disappointed to be done with the chore.

Before my mind spirals into thoughts of what to do next, Toni asks, "What's your go-to comfort movie?"

I consider. "There are a few."

"Nope." She shakes her head, folding the dishtowel. "You can only pick one."

"*The Lord of the Rings,*" I say without hesitation.

She grins. "That's three movies."

"One trilogy."

"Loopholes," she sighs, rolling her eyes playfully. "Fellowship is one of my all-time favorites, so I'm game."

"Extended edition?" I ask.

"Is there any other way?"

We settle in on the couch, Toni cradled between my legs, her cheek on my stomach. Somewhere around the Lothlorien mark, she drifts off.

I feel the steady rise and fall of her breathing, every shift her body makes. The rhythm of her sleep paired with the comfortingly familiar sounds of the movie soothes me to my core.

✧

"CILLIAN!"

The sound of my name, followed by a banging on the kitchen door, wakes us both. I clutch Toni, momentarily too flooded with fear and adrenaline to register that it's my brother's voice.

When he calls my name again, accompanied by the slamming of the kitchen door, the fog clears enough for me to let her go. I haul my stiff body off the couch as Michael barrels up the stairs.

"What the hell?" I ask, intercepting him in the hall.

"I could ask you the same fucking thing." He shoves my chest. I can't tell if his intention is to move me out of the way or, given the force, if it's an alternative to hitting me. "Do you not know how to answer your goddamn phone?"

I hadn't even thought about my phone since pulling into the driveway yesterday. Today? I can't be sure what time it is, seeing as it's still pitch black outside.

"I—" He doesn't let me answer.

"No one has heard shit from you since yesterday. Since . . ." He drags a hand over his face, a tick we share. "You can't just—You can't drop off the planet!"

"I didn't. Mom knew I was—"

"Yeah. And how many times did you lie to her before?" He spits the question at me.

If I were in a better, clearer headspace, I'd be able to acknowledge that he wasn't wrong. But at the moment, I am not in a clear and balanced headspace.

All I'm seeing is red.

"You think I'm lying?" My voice is dangerously low.

"No. I . . . I don't know. You disappea—"

"Ask the question you really wanna ask, Mike." His mouth opens and snaps shut. "Go on. Fucking ask me." I shove him just as he had me, his back thudding into the wall.

His face flushes red. "Fuck me for worrying I'd find you with a needle in your arm, Cillian!"

Michael's words should have been the thing that snapped my reality back into full focus, but they aren't. It's the sound of the floorboards creaking behind me.

"Toni . . ." Michael's face falls, the shift from anger to dread jarring. "I didn't—I'm sorry."

"It's ok," Toni says. I can't bring myself to look at her. "I'll give y'all some space."

As soon as I know she's far enough up the stairs, all the fight drains from me in a rush. I brace myself against the wall with one hand. "Fuck."

"Cillian, I . . ."

I shake my head. Without a word, I slink back down into the kitchen, wanting whatever was left of this conversation to take place as far away from her as was possible.

The clock on the microwave reads 5 am.

Guilt pummels me. I should've called or at least texted someone. But I'd wanted to narrow my world to Toni.

I sit in the same chair I had last night, my elbows on my knees, eyes on the floor. Michael leans against the newel post.

All I see are his sneakers as he says, "If I'd realized she was right there, Cillian, I wouldn't—" He sighs heavily. "I don't know what I would've done, actually. I was so . . . am so . . . Fuck." His voice cracks as he slumps to the stairs, his pose mirroring mine.

I look up at him as he says, "I'm sorry. I was . . . scared." He rubs his hands together nervously.

No matter how old you get, seeing your older sibling

afraid will always be unsettling. More so when you know you're the cause of that fear.

"I won't lie to you and say I don't want to." The gnawing, hungry ache for release undermined every comfort Toni provided, or tried to, since we walked in that door.

The voice insisting, *Just one. Just a bit. A moment to breathe. A moment of peace.*

"God," I say on a heavy breath, "I want to. But I am fighting it, Michael."

"I know. I know you are." His eyes remain focused on the terracotta tiles. "I shouldn't have said that about Mom."

I shrug. What he'd said stung, but he hadn't been entirely unjustified. I had lied. For years. To him, to our parents, to myself. Lies that I convinced myself I was telling to protect them, to not burden them with how bad things really were. That kind of thing leaves wounds, ones that, even after all these years, were bound to reopen sometimes.

"You been over there? To see them?" I ask, voice sounding hollow.

"For a bit last night." He massages the bridge of his nose. "Going back in the—Well, I guess it's already morning," he says, looking at the clock. "I told mom and dad I'd be over around 9."

"You can stay here if you want." He looked like he hadn't slept.

"You sure? With Toni—"

"It's not like we're gonna fuck in the stairwell or some-thing," I cut him off, my tone a bit more biting than I intend.

"Ha. Ha." Michael deadpans. "I'm only saying I don't want to cause more issues than I already have."

"You're assuming—"

"Cillian, you wouldn't have reacted like that if she already knew about . . . everything."

He doesn't use the words addict, or addiction, or overdose, but I feel them all the same.

Recovery is a winding thing. It's a journey that doesn't have a destination, not really. Some days, I don't feel shame around them; they're a part of me, but they don't define me. Other days, they feel just as damning as all the rest of my many mistakes. The weight of them is heavy around my neck, dragging me down.

"She's not Kevin," Michael says, accurately diagnosing the source of my hesitation to be honest with Toni.

Old affection makes me want to defend him. Not because I missed or wanted Kevin back, that was a door that should have closed long before it did. But because I couldn't hold his decision that *recovering addict*, no matter how long I'd been sober, was over the limit of baggage he was willing to carry against him.

"I know." I stand up, ignoring the twinge in my leg. "Crash here. It's fine."

He nods, following my lead, and stands. "I'll call Cam and let her know." It's code for, *I'll sit in my car for a bit to give you guys space*, and I appreciate it.

CHAPTER 27
Toni

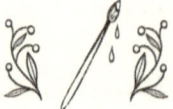

ANXIETY HUMS THROUGH MY BODY AS I PERCH ON the loveseat in Cillian's room. While it wasn't my fault that I'd been in the living room when Michael said what—from the look on his face when he'd seen me—was clearly not meant for my ears, I still feel guilty.

How many times in twenty-four hours can I be in the wrong place?

I may have been moderately useful yesterday, but still, it wasn't a scene or situation I had any right being a part of. And once we made it back to Somerville, I should have just texted Lucy and Oliver. Gone back to my apartment.

Just like the first night I spent in this room should have been the only time I was here.

What was I doing? In this house? In this city?

Just go home. A judgmental voice in my head says as if I have ever had any clue where that is.

The stairs of the old house creak, and I turn as Cillian appears at the top of them.

"Hey," I say, cringing internally. Hey. Like nothing has happened. Hey. Like everything is fine.

The corner of Cillian's mouth twitches up just a smidge. "Hey." He sits on the other side of the small couch.

It's still dark enough outside that our illuminated images are reflected in the window. A hazy still life.

Every empty comfort and pointless thing I could say trip over one another on their way to my tongue, causing a pile up at the back of my throat. I look at my reflection, convinced I'll be able to see the mass they're creating there.

"I'll be ten years sober next year. On my birthday." He doesn't say it like a celebration; he says it like penance.

I can't bring myself to look at him directly, so I choose the still life version. The edges are smudged, fading in the growing dawn, but I can make him out still, elbows on his knees, eyes on his hands. Those beautiful hands.

"I—He—Michael. He found me. Saved my life. That was the last time."

Now I understand why Oliver didn't explain the why behind Cillian's birthday avoidance, why no one had let so much as a whisper slip about it around the actual day.

I shift my eyes from his fading reflection. His position hasn't changed, but now, in full focus, I can see the weight of everything he's carried, all of it as clear as though it sat on his hunched shoulders.

I don't know what to say to take some of that burden off him. All I know is that I can be sure I'm not adding to it.

"If this . . ." He trails off. I hold my tongue. "If this is all too much, I get it."

Indignation flares hot in my chest.

How could anyone make him feel like his healing was too much? As if his survival was a thing to be ashamed of.

"Why would you being honest be too much?" I try to keep the heat from my voice.

Cillian's jaw flexes, teeth grinding. "I know it's another thing. Another tick in the cons column."

"Next to what?" If I had a pros and cons list for this man, that column was decidedly empty.

"Plenty." He stares out the window, fiddling with his necklace.

"Your sobriety is something to be proud of. That's not a con."

He shrugs. "Maybe, but when 'recovering addict' sits beside 'combat veteran,' I know it implies—"

"It implies nothing," I cut him off. "And it doesn't have any impact on our friendship either."

I feel a shift in the space between us and hold my breath.

"Friendship?" Cillian asks.

He looks at me, and I wish I could disappear.

It had to be that. Friendship. Just that.

The only thing Cillian telling me about his recovery did was resolve the thoughts I'd had in the shower this morning— or was it yesterday? Regardless, he'd worked too damn hard for me to roll in and wreck shop.

"Yeah? At least I thought—" I cut myself off, looking toward the stairs as I hear a door close.

"Michael's going to crash here for a few hours before we head to our parents' place."

"Ah." I know 'we' doesn't include me.

"And you thought right." Cillian takes my hand in his, giving it a gentle squeeze. "I'm sure you're ready to get home."

There was that damn word again. Home.

"I can call a car."

"I can take you."

"It's ok," I say, fingers already moving across my phone screen. "They'll be here in five."

Time folds in on itself as I gather my things. Five minutes feels both like an eternity and a millisecond.

We make our way downstairs, Michael's snores from the couch making it clear he's dead to the world.

As we stand in the foyer, I realize with a pang, this is the only time I've gone out the front door since the first night we spent together.

Cillian sets my bag down and pulls me to him. "Thank you for everything," he says into my hair. I rest my ear above his heart, breathe in his scent—evergreen and tobacco today—squeezing my eyes shut to hold back the tears.

My phone vibrates in my pocket, informing me of my driver's arrival.

With a tender touch, Cillian tilts my chin up to kiss me. Slowly. Intentionally. When we separate, I know the shine in his eyes matches my own.

"If you need anything . . ." My voice trails off.

"I know where to find you." He tucks one of my curls behind my ear, pressing a kiss to my forehead. "Goodbye, Toni."

My heart cracks.

⟡

Sparse early morning traffic makes the ride across town blessedly short, so I manage to hold on to my composure right until my door closes behind me.

The sob doubles me over. Hot tears soaking my cheeks in a breath.

Some selfish, unreasonable, part of me is screaming to get in my goddamn car and go back. Beg him to . . .

What?

Love me?

Bitter laughter bubbles up through the tears. I let my knees sink to the floor and lean against the wall, dragging in stuttering breaths.

A knock at the door sends my heart into a panicked,

hopeful staccato. Furiously, I wipe at the tears, knowing there's nothing to be done about my overall state.

With one final steadying breath, I haul myself up and open the door.

My landlord stands on the porch, a vase of flowers in hand.

Not Cillian.

Of course.

"Hey!" She greets me with a smile. "Everything, ok?"

I sniff. "Yeah. Just . . ." I shrug.

"Life does that." She holds the vase out. "These came for you on Friday, didn't want them to die before you came back."

"Thank you," I say, accepting it. "I'll put them in something else and give you your vase back. One—"

"Don't worry about it. You can give it to me later."

"Thanks again."

She gives me an understanding smile. "And if you need a little more time to think about the lease, that's fine. We're not in a rush."

I finger the card, still attached to its little plastic holder. "That's . . . really nice of y'all."

She shrugs. "It leases pretty fast. Not a big deal. Have a good day!"

"You, too."

She opens her door, disappearing up the stairs as I step back inside.

In my kitchen, I set the vase on the island, studying the flowers while my coffee brews.

A generic assortment of mums and daisies.

Bracing myself, I open the card.

Toni,

Couldn't stop thinking of you. I hope these bring extra beauty into your day.

Always yours,

David

Over our three years together, I could count on one, maybe two, hands the number of times that man got me flowers. Too impractical, he'd say. But that wasn't what had my hand shaking.

This wasn't a forwarded package from my brother's address. Somehow, he figured out where I lived.

I shudder.

After college, I moved to Atlanta. I'd gotten a job at a marketing firm and was ready to get out of Texas. I hopped on Craigslist—much to Belle's chagrin—found a roommate, packed my car, and left. I had a great time . . . until a hookup turned into a stalker.

I moved apartments twice, and somehow, that guy kept finding me, sending flowers and gifts, insisting we pursue something more serious. Eventually, he threatened me if I didn't. It didn't stop until I put several states between us.

David knew all about that experience. And still, he sent these.

It was either intentional cruelty or extreme negligence. I wasn't sure which one hurt more.

Exhaustion washes over me, drowning my heartache and my rage, leaving me numb.

Coffee forgotten, I throw the flowers in the trash and retreat to my bed.

Maybe tomorrow I'll wake up a better woman. One who isn't running from her past. One who doesn't want what she can't have. One who knows what the hell to do next.

CHAPTER 28

Toni

Much to my disappointment, the next sunrise doesn't bring answers. Neither does the one after nor the one after that.

They also don't bring any word from Cillian.

In fact, that's how most of the month trudges on.

Clarity and Cillian both avoid me.

The latter is for the best. At least that's what I remind myself every time I pick up my phone to send him a text—a habit I'd developed over the last few months without realizing—while with each passing day, the former becomes more and more pressing.

With Cillian around, it had been easy for me to forget the purpose of coming to Somerville in the first place. It was supposed to be a sort of self-imposed exile, a way to get my head straight before I was forced to come face to face with David and my own uncertain future.

I tap my pencil against the page, eyes focused on the pattern of rain against the coffee shop's window and not the green and gold sign across the street. Even though I'd been working from here a couple of days a week, I avoided Two

Sons with almost comical intensity: crossing the street early and making sure I came in either before or after Cillian usually went to work. The last thing I wanted to risk was an awkward run-in.

Well . . . maybe not the last thing.

"I've been meaning to ask what your Thanksgiving plans are." Jac plops into their seat across from me, leaving the other barista to handle the lone customer at the counter.

"You know, until Lucy invited me to the O'Sullivan's, I'd forgotten about it." Holidays were always a bit fraught. Even as a kid, they rarely left me with any good memories.

"You gonna go?"

I shake my head. "It feels . . . weird? It is weird, right? We —Cillian . . ." Blowing out a breath, I stir the ice in my cold brew.

"He still hasn't said anything." Jac saves me from having to say it.

"Yeah." I fight the urge to look across the street. "And I get it; he's got a lot going on."

Jac scoffs. "I mean, it's not hard to send a text."

"Maybe not, but grief makes even easy things a million times harder." I'd learned that lesson at Belle's side, the way grief could make even something as simple as opening a piece of mail feel impossible.

"I guess." They cast a glance out the window, as though admonishing Cillian from a distance.

I sigh, "I'm probably just gonna rewatch something over some wine and whatever takeout is available."

"No, you're not." They casually sip their drink.

"I'm not?"

"Nope. You're gonna come to my place and have Thanksgiving with the rest of the misfit queers." I go to speak, but they cut me off. "I'm not taking no for an answer, so don't even try."

A grin breaks across my face. "Fine. What time?"

"Around one. Bring whatever you want." They look up as a few customers walk in. "Or nothing. We always have too much anyway."

$\diamond$

MY SISTER-IN-LAW'S THICK SOUTHERN LOUISIANA accent fills my kitchen the next morning, "I promise you, browning the butter is gonna make all the difference."

"But, like, how much of a difference?" I ask, staring at the butter in the pan, slowly turning a darker shade. It was barely 8 am, and as much as I didn't want to show up empty-handed to the day's festivities, I was beginning to doubt the validity of my plan.

"Toni Joy, don't question me."

"Ok, ok," I laugh.

"He won't say it, but your brother is so happy you're not alone today. The man's been grumbling about it for the last two damn weeks."

"Why?" I ask, eyes glued on the pan. "I've had some good solo Turkey Days. He doesn't have to worry."

Dianne makes a dismissive noise. "Family is supposed to worry." For a moment, the sounds of the hospital cut through the background. "I gotta get back to it." She'd be spending her Thanksgiving at work, being Super Nurse.

"Thanks for the help."

"Any time, sugar! Happy Thanksgiving!"

"Happy Thanksgiving."

Just as I pull what I have to admit is a beautiful pecan pie from the oven, I notice a text from Jac.

JAC

About today . . . The basement flooded because our neighbors are idiots. So we have no water.

Oh shit!

JAC

Yeah. Still trying to figure out where we're going. It's not looking great, but I'll let you know.

I look around my apartment. While not massive, I could easily move my easel and supplies into my bedroom, leaving the dining room free.

Jac answers on the second ring. "If you're calling to tell me you're somehow a plumber, I'll become the embodiment of thankfulness."

"Tragically, not a skill I possess. But, depending on the size of the RSVP list, I'm happy to host."

"Ten . . ." They drag the word out, uncertain, "ish."

"Think people could BYO chair?" I ask.

"Girl, we can BYO table, chairs, all of it."

"Great! Might be tight, but we can make it work."

"You sure?" They ask, excitement barely restrained.

"I'm sure."

They let out a joyful screech. "When can we head over?"

Within the hour, Jac and I are hanging cheesy Thanksgiving decorations around my dining room while their nesting partner Finn—the frohawk guy I'd seen at the craft store and met at Jac's drag show—fills my kitchen with better food than I ever would.

"Wanna taste?" he asks, holding out a wooden spoon with homemade cranberry sauce.

"Sure!" My eyes pop open as orange, cranberry, and spices dance across my tongue.

"Good?" His anticipation for my approval is adorable.

"Incredible."

"Isn't he?" Jac says as they wrap an autumn leaf garland around my light fixture. "At this point, I don't think I'll survive without a chef in my life."

"Spoiled," Finn teases.

As expected, I don't know anyone who walks in my front door throughout the afternoon. They arrive with food and wine and booze and games. My record collection serves as the soundtrack of the day, people excitedly taking turns picking the next album. By the time everyone leaves later that night, my heart and my belly are full in ways I didn't know I needed.

I settle on my couch, the echoes of laughter and Jac's ridiculous decorations still clinging to the walls around me.

For all the jokes that had been made about a pros and cons list over the last several months, I hadn't actually made one. I flip open my big sketch book to a blank page and begin writing. When I'm done, one side is significantly longer than the other.

The pros column is brimming with many things Cillian had a hand in, but my choice to stay or go never could have been determined by him alone. No matter how much I cared for him, the truth was I'd been using him as an excuse to put off this decision that was mine alone to make. I couldn't stay for him just like I couldn't—shouldn't—wait for life to force my hand as it had so many times in my past.

It was time to choose whether I would build a life that was full and vibrant. One that I could be proud of—just for me.

I set the sketchbook aside and grab my laptop, opening the lease agreement my landlord sent me weeks ago.

CHAPTER 29

Cillian

THE FAMILIAR SCENTS OF ROSADO'S GYM—LEATHER, bleach, and decades of sweaty bodies—cocoon me. They blot out the scent memory of Joey's house and Toni's perfume.

Music blares in my headphones. Loud enough to drown out the echoes of my aunt's grief and Toni's laugh.

Sweat drenches my body, stinging my eyes. I don't wipe it off, hoping the salt will burn away my final image of Joey and how radiant Toni looked that last morning at the cabin.

Each hit sends the bag swaying, the impact reverberating up my arms. Easier to focus on that than what it felt like to comfort Ginelle at the funeral or to cradle Toni against me at the end of a long day.

My muscles are tired.

My leg is screaming.

I keep going. I need to keep going. I need there only to be this, not a past filled with mistakes and bad calls. Not the compounding heartbreak of the last few weeks.

Just one hit after another after another . . .

I stumble forward half a step when, for some reason, the

bag isn't in range of my next swing. Confused, I finally wipe the sweat from my eyes.

Oliver's annoyed face appears from behind the bag. He gestures for me to pull out my earbuds with his free hand, the other keeping the bag pulled back.

I oblige. "What?"

"You trying to break your knuckles or just bloody my bag?" He asks.

My hands flex in response, pain registering for the first time. I look down, my wrappings red-stained, gloves abandoned on the floor beside me.

"Both."

"Nice." He pushes the bag back at me with jarring force.

"Oh wow, he is alive," Lucy snarks.

"Looks like it," Oliver says. He tosses his button down over the ropes, picking up my roll of tape to wrap his own knuckles.

"Did you forget how to use your phone or something?" she asks.

"I've been busy." It's not a lie.

With Ginelle focused on helping with Joey's arrangements, we'd been down a manager, making things tough, even with the two new people we brought on. This meant I'd been spending almost every day and night at the bar. And that wasn't looking like it was going to change anytime soon.

"I haven't been called in," Lucy points out. "Have you?" she asks Oliver.

"Nope."

"Huh." She crosses her arms over her chest. "Can't be that busy."

I bristle, my emotions an unstable cocktail sloshing far too close to the surface. Before I can spit a response about how not needing them didn't mean we weren't busy, Oliver grabs my forgotten gloves, throwing them at my face.

He slides between the ropes into the ring, his own gloves in hand. "Come on." That's all he says, rolling his neck and shoulders, hard lean muscles tight beneath his undershirt.

"Oli—" Lucy starts.

"Get your ass in here, Cillian," he cuts her off. Lucy and I exchange a look, both confused and cautious.

"Nah, I'm good."

Oliver settles a hard gaze on me. "Didn't ask." When I don't move, he adds, "Or you can give me your key."

"What?" I ask, not trying to hide my disbelief.

Not having a key to Rosado's made about as much sense to my brain as not having one to Two Sons. I grew up here as much as the bar, and the same was true for Oliver and Lucy.

"You heard me." There's no heat in Oliver's words. Just cool, level command. Teacher voice. It makes me furious.

"Fine," I snarl. "You wanna go, we can go."

Whereas Oliver flowed into the ring, I lumber. My leg, size, and irrational incandescent rage make grace inaccessible.

"Boys, let's not have bloodshed, ok?" Lucy says from the floor.

Oliver tightens one glove with his teeth. "He already bled all over my bag."

"It's held together with duct tape and a prayer, a little blood ain't gonna hurt it."

"Maybe I could afford a new one if I was here instead of helping run your kitchen." He snipes back.

My hands protest being shoved into the gloves. "As you pointed out, we haven't had you there in a minute. What other excuse you got?"

"Cillian, bro, come on," Lucy chides.

"He started—"

"It's fine, Lu." Oliver takes his stance. "Let him run his mouth. Won't help him."

"Cocky." I try not to wince, the muscles in my left thigh

making their displeasure with me, and the choices I'm about to make, evident.

"Correct," he shoots back with a fox-like grin.

Unfortunately, for both my body and my pride, he is right.

Within minutes, he lands a few hits. Nothing hard, just proof that he can.

"So," he asks as we move around the ring, "You know how to use your phone, but maybe it's not working."

"If you wanted to talk—" I land a hit. "Should've stayed out of the ring."

"Too easy." He practically dances around me.

Show off. I think bitterly.

"It must be broken." His glove slams into my right side with enough force to send me stumbling, my left leg throwing off my balance. "Only reasonable cause for you to have not said shit to either of us since the funeral."

He lets me land my next hit. Which only manages to piss me off even more.

"Not feeling very reasonable lately." I make a reckless move, completely missing him and leaving me open.

Oliver only pulls his punch a little, his glove slamming into my jaw, sending me to the ropes.

"Sloppy." His teeth flash white, but the gleam doesn't reach his eyes.

"Fuck you."

He ignores me. "You done already?" Wiping a glove across his forehead, he studies the leather. "I've hardly broken a sweat."

I should say yes. I should just grab my shit and leave. Instead, I slam my gloves together, "Let's fix that."

Nothing else is said until we're both panting.

"Are you two done?" Lucy asks, looking up from her phone.

My body sags against the ropes, the slightest taste of copper on my tongue. Must've bitten my cheek.

"Don't know," Oliver huffs. "Up to him."

"Me? You threatened to evict me. This is your fucking game."

He shrugs. "Thought if I could get you to throw some punches, you'd at least hang around for a minute." That fucking grin again. "Worked."

"Can confirm, his phone appears to be working by the way." Lucy holds my phone up.

"Put that dow—" I lunge for the opposite side of the ring, and my leg finally gives out. Pain slams through me as my knees hit the mat. "Fuck," I gasp.

I hear Oliver's gloves hit the vinyl as he rushes over to me.

"Don't fucking touch me," I hiss through gritted teeth.

He ignores me, laying a hand on my shoulder. I throw him off with enough force to send him to the mat.

"Cillian!" Lucy hurls my name like an accusation as she slides through the ropes to check on Oliver.

"I'm fine," he says.

She spins on me, "What the fuck, man?"

"Give me my phone." I clench my jaw as I reposition to rest against the ropes, gripping my thigh. Rather than hand it to me, Lucy slides it across the mat.

"I didn't open it," she says. "Just happened to look down when Kitty called."

"Who you've also hardly spoken to since the funeral," Oliver says.

"Guess there's a group chat I'm not in." I set my phone face down, not wanting to think about the missed texts and calls from the last few weeks.

"Not like you'd respond if you were," Lucy says.

"Sorry, I'm not feeling chatty since finding my cousin after he ate a bullet. I'll fucking work on it." Silence hangs. "That what you guys wanted to hear? No?"

"We don't expect you to be chatty," Lucy says.

"But we do expect you not to shut everyone out again," Oliver adds.

"I'm not—"

Lucy cuts me off, "What would you call missing Thanksgiving?"

"Taking a day off," I grumble.

"That's bullshit and you know it," Oliver says.

The silence hangs between us like a wall.

Surprising no one, Lucy is the one to knock it down. "If it seems like we're coming on too harsh, I'm sorry. We're scared, Cilli. Scared we're gonna lose you."

Oliver meets my eyes and nods his agreement.

The words hit me harder than any physical blow.

"I—" My voice cracks. "Fuck."

Any fight left in me floods out in a rush. I squeeze my eyes shut, massaging the bridge of my nose, forcing a steadying breath into my lungs.

Before I can open my eyes, I'm surrounded, Lucy on one side, Oliver on the other.

"Come here." Lucy wraps an arm around me, and I let her pull my head to her shoulder. Oliver takes my hand in his, and we stay like that for a time.

No words.

Just me letting my friends be there.

"For what it's worth," I say once I feel less on the verge of shattering, "I wasn't trying to shut everyone out, it was just . . . Everything felt like it was caving in. Joey, and Toni, and keeping the bar running and—"

"What about Toni?" Lucy asks.

"I'm in love with her." Saying it out loud feels like being shot in the chest all over again.

Oliver snorts. "Obviously. Ow!" He exclaims as Lucy reaches behind me and flicks him hard on the ear.

"Shut up," she hisses.

I can't help but laugh. "I'm that transparent, huh?"

Lucy grimaces. "Crystal clear."

"Why is that a problem?" Oliver asks.

"She doesn't feel the same." I feel, rather than see, the look the two of them exchange. "She doesn't. She views us as just friends. And I wanna be okay with that. I'd be lucky to be her friend. It's just hard."

"That sucks, man," Oliver says.

I shrug. "It is what it is."

"But have you—" Lucy begins.

"Let it go, Lu," Oliver cuts her off. Lucy sighs. "Is the bar struggling?"

I'm so grateful for the subject change, I consider flinging my arms around the man. Shop talk was an easier pill to swallow. "Business is good—great even—but getting new people in and schedules worked out, and with Ginelle leaving—"

"Leaving?" Lucy asks.

I look at her, a bit surprised by her confusion. "Yeah . . . She can't exactly commute in from Denver."

Gin told Michael her plan to go stay with some friends in Colorado a few days ago. She hadn't specified when she'd be back, only that we should probably find someone to replace her.

"Oh . . ." Hurt drips from Lucy's voice.

"Lu . . . I-I'm sorry. I thought you knew." Had I been more in touch with everyone, I might have realized this wasn't something Gin had shared widely. But then again, of all the people she should have told, I'd have thought Lucy would be near the top of the list.

Lucy shakes her head. "It's ok. It's . . . she needs to do what she needs to do. It's fine." Oliver and I exchange a look, one that says we both know it's anything but fine.

My stomach decides this is the perfect time to inform everyone how I'd neglected it today. I press a hand to my middle as Lucy and Oliver shoot surprised looks my way.

"Not to change the subject, but I am starving," I say.

"Pizza?" Oliver suggests, getting to his feet.

"I kinda want wings," Lucy says, following his lead.

"Both?" I ask.

"Both." They agree as they each hold a hand out to me, helping me to my feet.

✧

THE NEXT DAY, DESPITE MY ACHING LEG AND THE obscene amount of food consumed, I feel lighter than I have in weeks.

I still can't bring myself to face the graveyard of missed notifications my phone has become, but I do call my mom on her lunch break and hold a conversation with my brother as we switch off at the bar. Progress, however small, is progress.

After lockup, I let the newbies go home a bit early and handle a few of the more menial closing duties myself. Of course, they think I'm just being a generous boss when, in reality, I want the time alone to wind down before going home.

I'm wiping down the bar when Ginelle lets herself in the front door.

"We're closed," I say as she locks the door behind her.

"Very funny," she drawls and tosses the keys on the bar as she hops onto a stool. "Meant to bring these to Michael earlier, but I lost track of time packing."

I pick them up, looking from the keys to my cousin, worry pressing down on my shoulders.

Ginelle was the kind of person who, even on her worst

day, looked at least a bit polished. So to see her in this state—hair dirty in a nest on top of her head, no makeup, circles under her hazel eyes rivaling my own—is more than a little jarring.

"How is the packing coming along?" I ask, pulling a glass out for her.

"Fine." She picks at her cuticles, a habit I hadn't seen her do since she was a teenager. "Never know how much shit you have until you move. You know I've been in that apartment for five years?" She shakes her head.

I nod, pouring grenadine. "It really has been a while. Kevin and I helped you move in."

"That's right." She pauses, tracing the woodgrain in the bar top. "You're like a whole different person now."

"Thanks?"

"It's a good thing. I feel like I . . . Like I'm the same. Like I've been the same."

I set a bright red drink in front of her, plopping three cherries on top.

She huffs a small laugh. "Shirley Temple."

"Sprite, not ginger," I add. "And if you want it dirty, just ask."

"Nah, this is perfect." She pops a cherry in her mouth.

"Remember when you drank so many of these, you hurled?" I ask.

That brings a real smile to her face. "Oh god! Your dad tried to cut me off, but I begged, and he caved so easily. My puke was an unholy color, and Mom thought I was dying."

"I remember hearing her yell over the old landline in our kitchen."

"Mickey still snuck me them all the time. Always with a, 'don't tell your mother.'" Her attempt at replicating my dad's accent cracks me up.

Ginelle takes a sip, eyes roaming around the dim bar. I

watch a tear gather on her lashes before she dashes it away. She sniffs hard.

"You don't have to go, Gin. Not right now."

A shiver shakes her shoulders. "I do, though. If I don't . . . I'm scared I never will."

"Is that so bad?" If looks could kill, I'd be on the floor. "I'm just sayin'," I hold up my hands in surrender, "there are worse places."

"And better ones," she spits.

"Sure."

"But everyone else has-has gone somewhere else. Tried something else. Even Jo—" She swallows the back half of Joey's name like a bitter pill. "I have to," she almost whispers.

I want to tell her the grief will follow her, that she can't outrun it. But I know she's not in a place to hear me.

"Do what's best for you, sweetheart. We'll be here if you need us."

"Of course you will be. Toni's here." She almost sounds like her usual self, so much so that I feel bad bursting that particular bubble.

"I'll be here. Not sure about Toni."

"What? Why?"

"Far as I know, her lease is out at the end of the month." And then she'd be gone. I have to believe it's for the best.

Ginelle looks genuinely confused. "You sure? Lucy was literally talking to her about winter coats a couple days ago. I mean, I've never been to Texas, but I'm pretty sure that's not a need there."

I hate the hope flaring hot and bright in my core at the thought of her staying.

"Wait." The hope takes a backseat as Lucy's pained expression from last night flashes in my mind. A couple of days ago would be just after Thanksgiving. Ginelle had told Michael about her plans to move before the holiday. "You were with Lucy a couple days ago?"

"Yeah . . ."

My voice drops, "And you didn't fucking tell her you're moving across the goddamn country?"

Ginelle doesn't look at me. "'It's complicated."

"It's not." I run a hand over my face. "Ginelle, I support whatever you need to do. But I won't forgive you if you don't cut her loose before you leave."

"Just because you're friends, doesn't make what happens between us your business." It's an old line from an older argument.

I lean over the bar, not in her face exactly, but I need her to hear me. "It is my business. It's cruel to let her keep believing there's a future with you when there isn't. And she's dealt with enough cruelty in her life."

She drags in a shaky breath. "I don't know what the future looks like."

"No one does. But the least you can do is be honest with her. She deserves that."

"Like you've been honest with Toni?" She scoffs.

"What does that mean?"

"I'd bet money you haven't told her how you feel."

"You have no idea how I feel." Lucy could be a loud-mouth, but I knew that wasn't something she'd blab to my cousin in less than twenty-four hours.

"Whatever." Ginelle finishes her drink and hops down. "Maybe handle your own shit before you try to tell me how to handle mine."

"Ginelle, wait!" I call as she storms away, through the office door, and out the back before I can make it around the bar.

CHAPTER 30
Toni

I STEP BACK TO STUDY THE PORTRAIT OF MY brother and his family I'd been working on all weekend. Each of the boys has a Starfleet insignia on their shirt, and rather than poised expressions, everyone looks like they're mid-laugh —or in my brother's case, lovingly annoyed.

It feels distinctly them.

Ben wasn't exactly giddy when I told him I'd decided to renew my lease, but he was supportive, which was enough for me. Apparently, my choice had ruined his planned Christmas surprise of bringing the family up to all help me pack, but they're still coming.

In a way, I'm still surprised, both because I hadn't been expecting to do much for Christmas and at how excited I am to see them. Me. Excited for Christmas? What a wild concept.

I should get a tree.

A knock at my door barely registers over "Bennie and the Jets." I turn the music down, catching another round of knocks.

"Just a minute!" I call out.

I look through the peephole. A slender white man stands

on my porch, his back to the door as he rubs his hands over his arms. His chestnut hair is a bit shaggier than usual, but I don't need to see his face to recognize him or the jacket I bought him last Christmas.

David.

How fucking dare he. Anger rises in my chest, quick and hot.

I consider ignoring him. Leaving him on the front porch to freeze in the early December chill. But when he turns back, softer memories of our time together tease the corners of my mind. Gentle, almost bittersweet, nostalgia tempering my rage.

Familiar brown eyes, wire frames perched on his nose. Angular features I'd loved to draw at one point, though the thick coat of stubble was new.

He raises his hand to knock once more, but I open the door before he can.

"Toni," he says, hand frozen in the air.

"What're you doing here?" Just because I was willing to open the door didn't mean I had to be pleasant.

"Good to see you, too."

I cross my arms over my chest, leaning in the doorway, perfectly willing to wait for a valid answer.

"Would you believe I booked a last-minute flight because I needed to see you?"

"No."

David smiles knowingly. "Fair." He looks at his sneakers, scuffing them on the wood before looking back at me. "It's true, though."

I don't know what to say to that.

He shoves his hands into his pockets. "You're letting your heat out."

The statement is so quintessentially David that I can't help but grin a little, rolling my eyes. There's no malice or judgment in his words, only a sort of sincere practicality I'd found endearing at one point.

"Come in, I guess."

I lead him into my home feeling both proud and protective of this space. The walls hold my art. A few Thanksgiving decorations still linger. My pink couch is cluttered with jewel-toned pillows and an abundance of blankets. The overstuffed chair I just picked up from the local buy-nothing group completes the living room nicely. Then, of course, the dining room is filled with canvas and supplies—my creative chaos on full display.

None of it would be to his taste. But all of it is perfectly mine.

"This is a unique place." He stops to study a smaller version of the view from Longfellow Bridge I'd painted for Cillian. "You did this?"

In this version, the colors are almost neon—a sky and city made of light and color. I'd done it as a test before deciding to go in another direction.

"Yeah. Best view in the city." An arrow of longing lances straight through me.

"Wow," David breathes. "I . . . wow."

"Not bad for a pointless hobby," I snipe. Without extending the invitation to join me, I take a seat on the couch, leaving him standing awkwardly with his duffel bag still in hand.

"I didn't . . . I never meant it like that, and you know it." There's that cutting tone I remember so well. "At least . . . I wish you knew." He wilts into the chair, letting his bag settle beside his feet. "I should've made sure you knew. I'm sorry I didn't."

I try to blink away my shock, force the image of the man I knew to mesh with this version. One who bought a—no doubt expensive—plane ticket and who apologizes for things like misunderstandings.

"But that?" He gestures to the painting. "That's not pointless. Someone would pay good money for that."

My head spins again. Annoyed because what someone would pay for it was always the point with him. Things couldn't just be worth something for the beauty of it.

"Make me an offer," I say cooly.

David meets my eyes, and like flipping a switch, that charming smile of his transforms him, softening all his hard edges. "Whatever it costs to break your lease."

"What?"

"Name the price, and I'll pay it."

"You cannot be serious."

"I am." He's so still, I'm not sure he's breathing. "Whatever it takes to get you home."

Home. As if what we shared had ever felt like a home.

"Jesus Christ." I get up from the couch. Despite it being barely noon and my rules around drinking when emotions are heightened, I suddenly need a drink to get me through this.

He follows me to the kitchen. "Is it so hard to believe that I want you home? That I'd do anything to—"

I laugh bitterly, cutting him off. A half-empty bottle of white from Thanksgiving is conveniently in the door of the fridge. I flick the cap off and take a deep drink before answering. "Yes. It is."

He looks genuinely hurt. "Why?"

I take another drink. "Because you don't make unreasonable decisions, David." I spit his name like it tastes bitter. "And according to you, that's what I am. Unreasonable. A hurricane. A disaster."

He pulls the bottle from my hands and finishes the remainder.

"So you want me to believe—" I begin.

267

"I was an ass!" he blurts. "I am an ass. And I'm here because I recognize that." We both cringe as he sets the bottle on the counter with a little too much force. "Won't you at least hear me out? I came all this way."

"I didn't ask you to," I practically growl. "In fact, I asked you to give me space, and instead you've found literally every way you could to—"

"I was desperate, Toni!" His voice cracks on my name. "I . . . you left, and this blackhole opened in my life. All I could think was, 'she should be here.'" Tears roll down his cheeks. "I just want to talk, please. Please, Toni."

I finally look at him. Really look at him. This is the man I spent three years of my life with. Hell, I thought I'd spend the rest of my life with him. He flew across the country to beg for a conversation in my kitchen.

David, who was, if I was honest with myself, easy to be with. And if I was even more honest, some part of me missed that, missed his predictable plans, his routines, and his cut-and-dry manner. Again, that bittersweet nostalgia softens my resolve.

"You want some coffee?" I ask.

CHAPTER 31

Cillian

TONI

Just checking in.

Here for you if you need me.

Lucy told me the funeral is this weekend. If y'all need help at the bar, happy to volunteer.

Hope you're ok. Or as ok as you can be.

Happy Thanksgiving!

I'D IGNORED TONI. SHUT HER OUT ENTIRELY. ALL the while, she'd kept the door open.

It was a kindness I didn't deserve.

But if Ginelle was right. If she was staying . . .

The idea that I may have the chance to make it up to her. Prove that I could be worthy of her friendship. Because having her in my life, in any way, was better than not having her at all.

"Earth to O'Sullivan!" one of the old men barks at me from their usual perch at the end of the bar. They all hold up empty pint glasses.

I accept their good-natured jabs and promises to 'report me to the boss'—aka my dad—when they all go bowling with him later in the week. They were, at least at their core, understanding, no doubt chalking my distracted demeanor up to grief. Other patrons were another matter.

My staff must think I'm losing it, muddling through the day like I'd never done this before. Forgetting orders, mixing up tickets. An entire mess. And I can't be bothered to care. All my thoughts are on Toni.

Would she forgive my cold shoulder?

Would she understand?

What if I were honest with her?

Would I lose her?

That last one takes the wind out of me.

Despite it being fully dark, it was only five-thirty. That meant at least six more hours before I could . . . What?

I get one of the newbies to cover me while I duck into the office.

Lucy doesn't answer, but Oliver does.

"What would I need to pay you to come in and cover me?" I ask, desperation evident in my tone.

"You ok?"

"Technically, yes. I . . . I need to talk to Toni, and—"

"I'll be there in twenty."

"You are my goddamn hero."

"I know."

Being on time anywhere in the Boston area is a damn near impossible task, but, somehow, Oliver always manages to pull it off. Exactly 20 minutes after we hang up, he's walking behind the bar.

I waste no time, thanking him as I practically run out the door.

Once in my car, I spiral.

The coffee shop is long closed for the day. Flowers feel like both too much and not enough. And while I could sing Taylor Swift from her stoop, that feels far too eighties romcom, and even I have an ounce of dignity I'd like to hang onto.

Still, I don't want to arrive empty-handed.

Praying to whatever traffic gods who have Oliver's back, I head toward my place. They listen well enough, but I still sprint up to my room, cursing whoever thought building a house with this many stairs was a good idea.

At least I know the exact robe I'm looking for.

I insisted I didn't need it back after giving it to her when she was sick, that it was a gift, but she kept sneaking it back onto my rack. It became a game, me bringing it to her place when I stayed over, her bringing it to mine. Seeing as she almost always chose to wear it here, I knew it wasn't a matter of taste.

Even if she decided, rightfully, that she was done with me, as far as I was concerned, this robe was hers.

CHAPTER 32
Toni

HOURS LATER, I'M TIRED, HUNGRY, AND THE certainty I'd barely grasped over the last several months—hell, the last few days—was beginning to fog over.

David takes my hand in his from across the coffee table. The coffee table Cillian assembled for me. My heart gives a squeeze.

"I want you to be happy, Toni."

"And if that means staying here?" I ask. We'd been dancing around this for the last hour, and I was sick of it.

He barely hides his grimace. "I mean . . ."

"Would you come here? If that's what it took to try again?" I don't know what I want him to say.

"We could certainly consider it."

"I asked if *you* would move. Not we."

His posture stiffens ever so slightly, and I feel my own body tense reflexively. "Well, if we're trying to rebuild, we want to do it sustainably, right? And you may be able to make some extra money from your paintings, but not enough to make up the cost-of-living difference."

I'd actually sold a number of my pieces from the coffee

shop show, but I don't feel compelled to tell him that. "How would you know?"

"Toni." He says my name like he's speaking to a child. I pull my hand back, recoiling. "Don't be like that. Besides, our friends—"

"Your friends," I correct him

"They're your friends, too. I told you everyone misses—"

"Yes. You told me that. But you know who hasn't? Who I haven't heard anything from in almost a year?"

He makes a dismissive gesture. "That's not abnormal. People don't know how to navigate this kind of thing. And, I mean, you did leave."

"I left—"

He continues as though I hadn't begun speaking. "Watch, once you're back, things will go back to normal."

Normal. His normal.

I'd traded vinyl for a shuffled playlist, not willing to have this 'conversation' without some kind of background noise. Like a goddamn lifeline, a Taylor Swift song, one Cillian and I had sung along to before everything went to shit, starts.

David groans like he's been injured and demands the smart speaker skip to the next song.

"Seriously?" I blurt.

"You know I can't stand that shit."

"So sorry not everything can be fucking lo-fi."

"What's with the attitude?"

"Is disagreeing with you considered attitude now?"

A knock at the door prevents him from answering.

"Oh, for fuck's sake," he grouches. "I said they could just leave it on the porch. How hard is it to read the delivery instructions?"

I let him get up, silently apologizing to the delivery person for any attitude they may receive for the sin of knocking.

"Leave it by the door," David says loudly in the entry, over annunciating the syllables. "Thank you."

"Toni?" A muffled, yet all too familiar, voice reaches me.

My heart leaps into my throat.

David opens the door in a huff, "I said—Oh, you don't look like a Vicki."

"Not on most days," Cillian replies. "Is Toni here?"

I scramble to my feet, my brain, heart, and body buzzing with terror and excitement . . . and dread.

"And who are you?" David asks.

"I could ask—"

"Cillian," I say his name on a breath.

His smile is immediate, warm, and welcoming like the sun breaking through the clouds. I want to hurl myself toward it.

"Excuse me," a woman's voice from behind Cillian draws all of our attention. "Sorry, order for David?"

"Yeah, that's me," David reaches past Cillian to accept the bag, immediately turning to bring it inside. Embarrassment heats my cheeks.

"Thank you," I say to the delivery person before she heads down the stairs.

"We have food to get to so—" David begins.

"Give us a minute," I cut him off.

David looks Cillian up and down, while I can't bring myself to look at him at all, no matter how much I want to. "Sure."

I step out onto the porch, letting the door quietly close behind me.

"So that's David," Cillian says, unimpressed.

"I . . . It's..." I shake my head, trying to find the words.

"You don't have to explain."

I finally look up at him.

God, I missed him. Seeing him made me realize just how much. This was not the bittersweet nostalgia I'd felt when

David arrived—a nostalgia that was quickly souring the longer we were in each other's presence. Instead, this felt elemental, a longing for something vital.

"Cillian—"

"It's okay." His smile doesn't touch his eyes. "I just wanted to give you this," he holds out a plain gift bag, "and let you know I intend to hold up my end of our bargain. Just let me know when."

Before I can tell him he has it all wrong, David opens the door. "You said you were hungry."

Cillian looks at David in a way I can't entirely describe. Cold, furious, and honestly a bit terrifying. David doesn't miss it either, taking a half step back.

"Enjoy your dinner," Cillian says, voice barely above a growl.

Before I can say another word, he's walking back toward his car.

⟡

BACK INSIDE, DAVID DRONES ON ABOUT OUR FOOD order. Something regarding the lack of utensils. I hardly register a word.

"What was with that guy, anyway?" He asks.

"Huh?"

"Rude. Tattoos. Knuckles all fucked up."

I noticed Cillian's knuckles when he handed me the bag. His beautiful hands were bruised and scabbed.

"Looked like a real—"

"Don't." My voice is calm but resonant. "Whatever you were going to say. Keep it to yourself."

"Forgot how touchy you get when you're hungry."

The paper from the bag crinkles as my hand flexes. I realize I haven't even looked inside.

Tears sting the back of my eyes.

Cream silk. A peacock pattern. I didn't have to touch it to know it would feel like cool water between my fingers. Didn't have to smell it to know it would smell like Cillian.

What the fuck was I doing?

"I don't want this," I say, mostly to myself.

David sets the plate I hadn't realized he'd be holding down with a thud. "Well, you should have said something before I—"

"I don't mean the fucking food!" I snap. "I don't want this." I gesture between us. "And you don't either."

"How can you say that? I flew across the country to fix this."

"No." I shake my head. "You don't want me. You don't want to fix this. You flew across the country to corner me, so you'd have the upper hand."

"Come off it."

"Just like emailing me, and sending me packages, and flowers, and calling me. You did all of it for yourself. To prove you were the one in charge."

"Toni, I think you're being a bit—"

"Unreasonable?"

"Yes!" he barks, slamming his hand on the counter.

All my internal alarms, the ones that protected me throughout my childhood and had usually served me well as an adult, begin screaming. I realize, with a touch of shame, they'd been screaming for years. I just ignored them. Buried them, dampened the sound under reassurances from friends, justifications that he was a nice guy. He never lifted a hand to me. He was the safe choice.

Now? Now, they are impossible to ignore.

"Get out," I say, void of emotion.

"What?" he hisses.

"This is done. We are done."

"Antoinette. Let's take a breath." The calm in his voice is so at odds with his body language that it's unsettling. "Throwing away three years of our lives isn't a reasonable decision."

"David, I'd trade the three years we spent together—three years you spent berating me, belittling me, trying to make me something less than what I am so you could feel like more— for this last year without you in a fucking heartbeat."

He stares at me in shock.

I walk the short distance to the living room and scoop up his duffel. He grabs my arm with enough force that I know there will be bruises tomorrow.

In this moment—with him staring down at me, nothing but vitriol and the threat of violence in his eyes—I see the kind of man he is for the first time. The pristine packaging finally cracking to expose the rot beneath.

"You don't get to throw me out." He says it like his words are law. Like they mean anything at all.

Pathetic.

"If you don't get your hand off of me, David, I'll feed you your fucking teeth." My tone is measured, but something in my expression must've reminded him that I was a force of nature, while he was nothing more than a sad little boy.

He lets go of me, recoiling like he's been burned, and rips the bag from my hands. "Don't come crawling back to me when Hurricane Toni inevitably fucks everything up."

I can't help but laugh. A loud, big, echoing laugh. The laugh he always hated. Too much. Too boisterous. Too me. Too bad for him, it was the last time he'd be lucky enough to hear it.

"Get the fuck out of my house, David. And have the life you deserve."

Slamming the door behind him feels like finally closing a chapter.

CHAPTER 33
Toni

I IMPATIENTLY WATCH FROM A CRACK IN MY FRONT curtains until David's ride finally arrives, taking him to whatever midrange hotel he'd be spending his night in.

The moment he's gone, I call Cillian.

Straight to voicemail.

Nervously, I pace around my apartment, put up the food David and I hadn't touched, anything to kill a few minutes before trying to call again.

No luck.

By the time the third call goes to voicemail, I'm already getting in my car.

Cillian's car isn't in the lot behind Two Sons, but Oliver's is. Even if Cillian wasn't here, maybe he knew where I could find him.

The place isn't too busy, which means I have a clear line of sight to where Lucy and Oliver chat over the bar.

"Hey!" Oliver says as I approach.

Lucy opens one arm, and I let her pull me into her side. "Is Cillian here?" I ask.

The look they exchange speaks volumes. "We thought he was with you," Oliver says.

I sigh and take the stool beside Lucy. "He came by." My voice sounds tired. "My ex was there and—"

"David?" Lucy asks, shocked.

"Yeah, he showed up today. On my fucking porch." I give them a quick rundown of the shit show.

"What an ass," Oliver says.

"Understatement," I agree. "And Cillian came over to ostensibly give me a robe."

"One of his robes?" Lucy asks.

"To keep?" Oliver adds. Both of them appear comically dumbfounded.

"Yes?"

"He's very protective of his robes," Lucy says. "I tried to borrow one for a costume once, and it was a whole negotiation."

"Oh." I think back to how, our first night together, he'd offered me a robe as though it was nothing. That ache returns, the absence of him in my life howling.

I clear my throat. "I think he got the wrong idea with David being there and assumed it meant he lost our bet, that I was moving."

"You didn't tell him?" Lucy asks.

"No," I grimace. "We hadn't been talking—well, he hasn't been replying to my texts—so I wasn't sure if he'd care."

"He cares." Oliver's conviction makes me squirm with embarrassment, as though I'd missed something obvious.

"Anyway, I told David to fuck off and tried to call Cillian a few times, but it went straight to voicemail."

Lucy picks up her phone and dials. "Same. Voicemail."

I rest my elbows on the bar, covering my face with my hands. "I can't believe I let him walk away," I groan. Desperation spreads from my chest throughout my body like a stain.

"I let him think I chose that piece of shit instead of telling him that I—"

Love him.

The words catch in my throat. The weight of them is too heavy for my tongue.

I'd been doing mental gymnastics for so long, trying to keep those words far from my thoughts. But I didn't have to think them, much less say them, for the feeling to be there all the same.

I love Cillian. Love him in a way that is so big it feels . . . Unreasonable.

The revelation almost makes me laugh.

"I need to find him."

Lucy nods, a knowing smile on her face. "Oliver, is he at the gym?"

"Let me check." He pulls his phone out, and I hold my breath. "I don't see him on the cameras but there's a class going on, so it's not impossible he's there somewhere."

"Alright, let's go," Lucy hops off her seat.

I stare at her offered hand. "Lucy, you don't have—"

"I know his hidey holes, can navigate without GPS, and have a spare key to his house. We'll find him faster together."

Some of the tension I'd been holding leaves me. "Thank you."

"Keep me posted," Oliver says.

"Of course," Lucy assures, ushering me out.

⬦

AFTER MORE THAN AN HOUR, WE'RE NO CLOSER TO finding him than when we started.

We checked his house, the gym, and a few random places Lucy suggested. Nothing. And his phone was still going straight to voicemail.

"We should call Michael," Lucy says.

My stomach roils at the thought, remembering how concerned he'd been when he couldn't get in touch with Cillian. The last thing I want is to cause additional stress or animosity. Even though the longer we went without being able to find him, the more my own anxiety starts shrieking.

She makes a few calls but comes up empty. "We're not far from the house, we can swing by. I doubt he's there, but just in case."

"Michael's house?" I ask, having sworn he and Camille lived in Salem.

"No, Mickey and Kitty's."

Great.

We pull up to a small two-story single-family home on a densely packed residential street. It's nothing fancy, but it is clearly well-loved. The tiny garden beside the stoop is trimmed neatly back for winter, and a Christmas tree already glows in the bay window. It's the kind of house kids draw; simple yet welcoming.

"Doesn't look like the boys are here, but we can still check in," Lucy says as we pull into the drive.

Mickey answers the door, warmth and the smell of something delicious wafting out into the evening air. "Well, this is a pleasant surprise. Two angels on my doorstep."

"Who is it, Mick?" Kitty's voice asks from inside.

He gestures us inside. "Lucy and Toni."

Kitty holds her phone up. "I just saw your call, Lu. Sorry I missed it."

"Don't worry about it," Lucy waves off her concern.

"Everything alright?" Kitty asks, looking between us.

"Yeah," Lucy says a bit too brightly. "We were hoping maybe Cillian was here or you guys had talked to him."

"He's meant to be working the bar this evening. Is he not there?" Mickey asks, alarm evident.

"He was," Lucy clarifies. "Oliver came in to cover because he . . ." She looks at me, unsure of what to say.

I sigh. "He left to come talk to me. We haven't . . . things have been tense since . . . everything."

Kitty gives me a knowing nod. "He called me yesterday. We had a good talk, and he seemed ok. Especially after you two musketeers got through to him," she directs that at Lucy.

"For what it's worth, he was fine when I saw him. But . . ." *My fuck ass ex-boyfriend was there,* isn't exactly the thing I want to cover with Cillian's parents. "Our wires got crossed, and he thinks I'm still leaving at the end of December."

"Ah." Mickey nods. "He thinks he's losing ya, so he's running."

"I just need him to know . . ." I meet Mickey's eyes, and I get the feeling he understands that I'm not referring to my zip code remaining the same.

"Where have you looked?" He gestures for us to all sit on the well-worn furniture.

As Lucy rambles off the places we've been, Michael calls her back, confirming Cillian wasn't with him, and we remain at a loss.

Just as fear threatens to swallow me whole, Kitty raises a finger, cutting off whatever Mickey was about to ask. "Have you checked the bridge?"

"Bridge?" Lucy asks, sounding alarmed.

"You know, the salt-and-pepper-shaker bridge. He goes there sometimes to—"

"Feel grounded," I finish. Kitty purses her lips to try to restrain her smile but fails. Much like her son, she absolutely lights up the room with her smile.

The bridge crossed my mind earlier, but I'd immediately dismissed it and forgotten about it. He spoke of it with a kind of reverence that implied it was a place he went to as either a last resort or when something was too big—too life-changing

—to hold. No part of me could fathom that my leaving would qualify as something important enough for him to go there.

Lucy and I pile back into her car, adding Mickey and Kitty to the list of people to update once we hopefully find Cillian.

"How long has the bridge been a thing?" she asks as we make our way through Somerville over into Cambridge.

I shrug. "He said something about his fourth life . . . live—"

"Alive day," she says, sounding distant. "First the robe, now this."

I don't know what to say to that.

Without warning, Lucy cuts across two lanes of traffic and pulls into a shopping mall parking lot.

"Jesus!" I exclaim as someone honks. "Did you just really need a Starbucks?" I ask, gesturing at the sign.

"First, I'd never choose Starbucks when there's a Dunks in the same parking lot. Give me some credit. And no." She sighs, parking the car and turning to face me.

"You're my friend, and I adore you. But that man is my family."

"I know."

She takes my hand in hers. "Good. So you'll understand why I have to say this before we finish our grand mission." We both huff a laugh at the dramatics. "Be good to him. Don't . . . don't leave him guessing. If you love him—"

"I do." I take a deep breath, as though admitting it removed a weight from my chest. A stupid laugh bursts free, and I can't help but smile. "And if I can't find him to tell him to his face within the next thirty minutes, I might snap."

Lucy beams at me. "Then let's find your man."

Mine. I like—no, I love—the idea of Cillian being mine.

283

CHAPTER 34
Cillian

THE RIVER SHIMMERS WITH LIGHTS FROM THE skyline and the bridge alike. It's beautiful in a crystalline way that I'm sure Toni would love to capture on canvas.

Except she's leaving.

It's a knife to the gut. Twisting and twisting every time I think about it, made even worse by the fact that, from the look of it, she was leaving with that jackass.

I may not know the guy, but I knew people, and he didn't deserve to be in the same area code as her, much less—

And I did?

My breath forms a cloud as I force myself to unclench my jaw.

What he deserved and what I deserved didn't matter. Toni made her choice, and all I could do was honor it.

I lost fair and square. Now I get to pay the price.

Pushing myself away from the wall, I stretch, my body stiff from being slumped over in the cold. I'd been out here for far too long.

I step onto the main sidewalk just in time to see a familiar car decide to stop in the fucking middle of Mass Ave. Horns blare and Lucy curses at them as, to my absolute horror, Toni bolts from the passenger side and across the bike lane, heading toward me.

"What the fuck are you doing?" It's the most prominent thought in my head as I rush to meet her.

"You won," she pants.

I take her by the shoulders, moving us beside one of the shakers. My mind is unable to register what she's saying, too stuck on the risky move she and Lucy had just pulled.

"The bet," she laughs. The sound instantly warms me. "You won. I tried to tell you earlier but . . ." She throws her hands up, moving further around the side of the shaker and away from the street.

I follow, half in a trance, because she can't be saying what I think she is.

"But David showed up today and begged me to talk and everything was just so fucked." Words begin flooding out of her a mile a minute, hands moving like she's conducting an orchestra. "And then you were there, and I realized I missed you so much more than I thought was even possible, and he was rude to the delivery person, and I didn't tell you that I resigned my lease on Thanksgiving because we hadn't talked, and I didn't want—"

I cup her flushed cheeks in my hands. "Breathe, Toni."

She does. Those beautiful brown eyes are wide and locked onto me. For a moment, everything is still and perfect.

"I love you," she says, with no preamble.

My body goes still. Some part of me is scared that if I move, I'll wake up from what must be a dream.

Toni covers my hands with hers, pulling them from her face but not letting them go. "That's not why I chose to stay. I . . ." She trails off, looking at the city. "I fell in love with this place, too. I want a life here. A home. One that's mine."

She takes a wobbly breath, letting go of my hands, to take

a step back. "And I want you to be a part of that. I want a life here, with you, so badly it hurts." She shakes her head, looking anywhere but at me. "But I know I am a fucking hurricane. I'm loud, and messy, and stubborn, and I can be unreasonable, and-"

"And I love all of it," I say, unable to hold back any longer.

Her attention whips back to me so fast a few curls tumble free from her clip.

I reach for her hand, blissfully happy she doesn't pull away. "I love all of you, Antoinette. Every loud, messy, stubborn, unreasonable part of you," A tear rolls down her cheek, and I gently brush it away. "You're a goddamn force of nature, and my life has been better since you blew into my bar and threatened to punch a frat boy."

Another beautiful laugh tumbles into the night air. "You're fucking wonderful."

I roll my eyes, pulling her closer. "I don't know about that."

She reaches her arms around my neck. "That's ok. I do."

When our lips meet. It feels like coming up for air, as though I'd been drowning in our weeks apart. I hold her to me, greedy for her, welcoming the world to see that this woman, this glorious woman, is mine.

The End

Epilogue

TONI

I CHECK MY PHONE FOR THE HUNDREDTH TIME IN the last hour.

Ben and his family were supposed to get in earlier today, but their flight was delayed. Instead of us all meeting at Cillian's—where, at his insistence, they'd be staying—before heading to the O'Sullivan's for Christmas Eve, they were coming straight here.

No buffer. No time to prepare—myself more than anyone else. Just straight into the crucible of family holiday chaos.

"Doll," Cillian places his hand over the screen, "relax. They'll get here."

"I know." I let him pull me back onto his chest, his chin resting on my head as he rubs a hand up and down my back. "I just need nothing else to go wrong with this trip. I just—" I sigh.

The thing I don't want to admit, even to Cillian, is that I want my older brother to approve of him, of my choice to stay, of all of it. Because, according to the little Toni in my chest—the one who always wanted a home that felt welcoming and a family that felt safe—if Ben approved, maybe we could have more Christmases together.

A gentle rap at the bedroom door draws our attention. "I don't wanna interrupt anything," Kitty says cheekily.

"Ma!" Cillian groans. "Just open the door."

She laughs, poking her head inside, an apron partially covering her over-the-top Christmas sweater. "Toni, I just wanted to double-check that the boys are good with seafood. I don't mind making them something else."

I sit up. "Kitty, I promise you, they've grown up on a steady diet of both seafood and swamp food, they're going to be thrilled." While she wasn't doing the full Seven Fishes meal, she was going all out with several dishes that had this house smelling divine.

"Alright then. How's the leg, sweetheart?" she asks Cillian.

"A little better," he assures her. The cold that rolled in yesterday was taking a toll on him, but he was determined not to let it ruin the festivities.

"You want any help?" I offer, even though she'd already turned me down several times.

"You know the answer," she sing-songs as she heads down the stairs.

"Stay out of your kitchen," Cillian and I say in unison.

I roll my eyes and laugh, falling back with him and letting my eyes wander around his childhood bedroom.

Posters from rock and metal bands I'd also loved as a teenager still hang on the walls, alongside Polaroids and disposable camera photos of Lucy, Oliver, and Cillian over the years. The bookshelf is packed with well-worn paperbacks and sheet music, as well as trophies and medals from choir and boxing competitions. A little time capsule for the boy he once was.

I love it.

My phone vibrates and I shoot upright. "They're on their way!"

Cillian chuckles. "Wanna go tell the horde downstairs?"

The O'Sullivans' home is already buzzing. Oliver would be coming by later, having his own family festivities to see to. But Lucy, Michael, and Camille are here; Cillian's uncle Bobby and his husband Rick even came up from Florida; and of course, Mickey and Kitty are milling about. In all honesty, I wasn't sure how we were going to shove four more people in here.

"Fantastic!" Mickey declares when I announce my brother's—er, my family is only about ten minutes away.

"Well, darling," Bobby—an older, leaner, and decidedly more fabulous version of Mickey—threads his arm through mine. "Let's get you a proper drink to celebrate."

Lucy leans over to whisper in my ear. "The eggnog is delicious, but it will absolutely knock you on your ass."

"Thank you," I mouth as he pulls me toward the kitchen.

Bobby, who does indeed have exceptional stories just like Cillian promised, gets me so caught up in conversation that I'm surprised when Lucy announces my family's arrival.

I suck down a far too large gulp of flammable eggnog and cough my way to the door.

Cillian laughs, patting my back. "Lucy did warn you."

"I need the strength." *Because if this is a disaster, I don't want to be sober for it.*

We step onto the porch, and the boys bolt from the rental car.

"Ant-Ant!" They shriek, rushing toward me.

My nerves flee, catching their enthusiastic hugs at the bottom of the stairs, kissing them on top of their dirty blonde heads.

"We missed you!" Asher declares.

"The roads here are worse than New Orleans," Parker says over him.

I hear Cillian laugh from behind me, and my smile grows impossibly.

"I missed y'all, too. And yeah, they're pretty bad."

"Let the woman breathe, boys," my sister-in-law says, shaking her head. They release me only for Dianne to deliver her own crushing hug. "Oh, it's so good to see you!"

"You, too."

"And you must be Cillian," she says, looking behind me.

I turn as he braces himself on the banister, a somewhat bashful smile on his face. "Guilty."

Dianne introduces herself and the boys as Ben finally makes his way over to me.

"Told ya we'd make it," he says, chuckling.

I roll my eyes, smiling, "So did Cillian."

Ben pulls me in for a hug, which may possibly be the longest one we've ever shared.

"And this—now I know it may be shocking because they look nothing alike—" Dianne says, "is your girlfriend's brother, and my loving husband, Ben."

Ben and I give her identical looks.

"Uncanny," Dianne teases.

"Good to meet you," Ben says.

"Likewise." Cillian shakes Ben's offered hand.

"Something smells great," Parker says. Asher sniffs the air as if to verify.

"We've got plenty of good food in here, boys," Mickey says from the doorway.

"Go on," Ben says. And the boys barrel inside.

"Ask before sticking your hands in something!" Dianne calls after them as we filter in. Everyone gets a good laugh at that.

Introductions are made all around while my nephews

simultaneously negotiate their way into eating several cookies before real food and pepper Mickey with questions about the instruments scattered around the house.

"Cillian, are you sure you want this chaos in your home?" Dianne asks, shaking her head at her children as they pluck at a banjo with delighted grins on their faces.

Bobby chuckles. "Technically, it's my house. And trust me, love, that place has seen far rowdier boys than those two in its time."

Camille laughs, "I must warn you, tread carefully or you will get the orgy stories."

Dianne gasps with delight, extending a hand to Bobby. "Oh, we're going to be great friends."

Which, to my absolute relief and delight, turns out to be true all around.

The rest of the night is bursting with food, family, music, and laughter.

After we've all glutted ourselves on Kitty's incredible cooking, the O'Sullivan boys entertain my nephews by showing them how to play bodhráns. Dianne is howling with laughter, enjoying a drink with the other ladies and Rick, while Ben and I hang back, soaking it all in.

Ben gestures to Cillian, patiently coaching Asher on how to hold the drumstick. "Nicer than I thought he'd be."

I huff a little laugh, my heart soaring. "What were you expecting?"

"Maybe less tattoos," he teases.

I playfully punch him in the arm. He rumbles a deep laugh, slinging an arm around my shoulder.

Cillian high-fives Asher when he gets it right.

"That's a good man," Ben says.

I can't help but compare this moment to my last Christmas. The contrast is so jarring it feels impossible.

"The best." I let my head fall onto my older brother's shoulder. "Thank you for helping me get here."

He tsks. "You're the one who made it work, Toni."

I send a wave of gratitude out to the past versions of me, even the one who chose David.

Cillian meets my eyes from across the room, smiling that pure sunshine smile.

I thank them for every unreasonable choice that got me— that got us—to him.

Inspired By

If you ever find yourself in the Boston area, check out these local spots that helped inspire *Unreasonably Yours*.

- The Burren - Somerville, MA
- The Druid - Cambridge, MA
- The Crystal Ballroom - Somerville, MA
- Saloon - Somerville, MA
- gather here - Cambridge, MA
- 1369 Coffeehouse - Cambridge, MA
- Yego Coffee - Somerville, MA
- The Isabella Stuart Gardner Museum - Boston, MA
- Trident Booksellers & Cafe - Boston, MA

Acknowledgments

Unreasonably Yours simply wouldn't exist without my people.

I don't know what cosmic glitch or divine favor landed me in a community this generous, this brilliant, this wildly ride-or-die—but I'm endlessly grateful. "Thank you" barely scratches the surface.

To my partner: thank you for every last pivoted dinner plan, every chore you quietly took on, and for believing I had it in me, even when I didn't. Your steady, behind-the-scenes support kept the wheels turning and the litter box clean.

But this book? This book belongs to my friends.

To the ones who beta read sending hilarious reaction texts and giving me pages of notes, who flagged weird turns of phrase and the times I used the wrong name for Michael's wife, who cheered on every messy draft and read chaotic, half-baked snippets—you made this possible. You saw something in this story (and in me) long before it was ready. You held space, gave notes, cracked jokes, and loved me through every single word.

I couldn't have written this without your brilliance, your patience, your encouragement—or your lovingly aggressive threats should I not finish this one. You are, hands down, the best part of my life and the reason this story ever made it to the page.

And to Boston and Somerville: thank you for being the most charming, pothole-ridden, stubbornly magical backdrop a writer could ask for. I'm so damn lucky to call you home.

About the Author

Charlotte Jean is a fat, queer, neurodiverse author with an obsession for uplifting voices and perspectives that are often left to the supportive side character, if they're included at all. Forged in the Bible Belt, she now lives in New England with her two perfect felines and nesting partner.

instagram.com/charliebrazen

goodreads.com/charlottejean

tiktok.com/@charliebrazen

threads.net/@charliebrazen

Also by Charlotte Jean

✧

The Elixir